A SUDDEN DEATH AT THE NORFOLK CAFÉ

Winona Sullivan

IVY BOOKS • NEW YORK

Ivy Books
Published by Ballantine Books
Copyright © 1993 by Winona Sullivan

Library of Congress Catalog Card Number: 92-33852

ISBN 0-8041-1213-4

This edition published by arrangement with St. Martin's Press, Inc.

Manufactured in the United States of America

First Ballantine Books Edition: April 1995

10 9 8 7 6 5 4 3

Paul was grinning when Sister Cecile returned. He had the file open on the table and his feet were propped up.

"Nice friends you have, Cecile."

"Raunchy?"

"I can't believe you haven't looked through this. It's all original stuff: letters, documents; bank slips that show big deposits; bimbos' statements of illicit liaisons with local notables. There's a list of names if you want a woman: Lilith McKay, Angie Little, Martha Bowen, Gloria Peacock, and more. It's a screw file. You could screw anyone with this stuff. I can't wait to hear the tapes."

"I'll wait," Cecile said. She actually blushed. "But maybe I should look at the papers so I know what I'm dealing with."

Paul pushed the pile of papers across the table. "Go for it." He grinned.

Sister Cecile went for it.

Dedicated to my husband, Edmund,
for always being there.

1

It was early April. Jane Hersey was sick to her stomach, eighteen, and almost finished with high school. On Tuesday she took a ten-dollar pregnancy testing kit home and watched it work. It said she was pregnant. She figured four months.

She should have known, but she was active and normally very thin and young, and time had passed without her even thinking of the consequences of playing with fire. She'd blamed the minor physical changes on eating too much. Fatter stomach, too, but what else was new? How dumb could she be, she thought, and started talking to a few friends about the problem.

The week that followed was a very bad week for Jane, but she did a lot of thinking and talking with those friends and she came up with several possibilities and settled on one. She knew Martin Moon was old, probably thirty-two, at least, but she was an idealist. At the end of the week she proposed to the would-be father.

Martin Moon turned down the proposal. Had Jane bothered to mention "pregnant," he might have done something besides laugh, but her sacred honor was at stake and she'd be damned if she would mention that. He hadn't wanted *her*, and that was it. They were at his place when all this happened, eating Reilly's Roast Beef sandwiches and drinking gin and tonics. She was drinking a plain tonic herself because of the baby. Jane was no dummy. It was easy to switch her drinks because Jane usually mixed them herself. Tonight she took advantage of that fact and gradually upped the power of Martin's usual five drinks until she was bringing him doubles. Damn it. Damn him. She had actually believed he loved her.

As was Martin's habit when he felt good, he went to his desk to do a little business. First he pulled out his red file to gloat. In the file were papers and pictures on a lot of people and a few sordid tapes stuffed in separate folders. Martin Moon was an extortionist.

At eleven thirty he slumped over the file and began to snore. It was a disgusting scene, Jane thought as she carefully removed the file. She was going to get even with the bastard for not loving her, and in a big way.

Instead of taking a cab to her home as she usually did, Jane took a taxi from Martin's home in Brookline to the Convent of Our Lady of Good Counsel in Dorchester, Massachusetts. The convent was on Adams Street, a long way from the red brick and stucco Jane had grown up with. The cabby was used to odd trips late at night. This fare was red-haired and tall and looked like his niece. Childless himself, he had always wanted a kid like that. She should be home in bed.

The girl was nervous. He could see her in the rearview mirror fussing with her hair like girls always did, but she kept looking back. Her head turned once, then again, then a third time when they made the rotation from Columbia Road, right after the big Ford sedan got behind them. He just made out her "Oh, God," as she ducked down. Then she popped up again. She couldn't help looking back. Then she shifted on the seat, sideways, so she wouldn't have to turn her head like that and he could see how she was biting her fingernails and looking everywhere.

The cabby's name was Jacob Zuber and he was getting nervous too. Something was going on here. He didn't like it. It was weird. Maybe he should gun it? Take evasive action? Another car pulled in behind him; this time it was a big old Caddy like the kids drive in Area Four. He heard a soft "Shit," and the girl ducked down again.

2

"What's going on?" he finally asked. "You got trouble?"

"My boyfriend's going to kill me, like I just split on him tonight." She had sat up to blurt out her answer, pushing her fluff of red hair back so she could see.

"Oh, yeah?" He didn't quite believe the part about being killed.

"I ask him something, and he just laughs. So I took something of his and split. Serves him right." She sounded scared and a little crazy. The enormity of what she had done was making itself felt. She held something up into his line of vision. A huge red envelope. "See? I'll show him. He laughed at me." Now she sounded as if she was going to cry. Suddenly the big Caddy behind them made a roaring sound and cruised by. She ducked again. "Bunch of damn kids," she murmured softly from below the top of the seat.

"I see," Jake Zuber said, one eye on the rearview mirror, one eye ahead. Maybe she wasn't just talking about being killed. This was Boston. The old Caddy was gone and there wasn't much else out this time of night, but the going was rough. He was an experienced cabby and slowed down. Boston's legendary spring potholes were dead ahead, black pits in the headlights' glare. There was no one behind them now. He was sure.

"You know the nuns?" She asked it cautiously. "Sister Martha Przyblyska? She was my grammar school principal."

"Nice people, sure. You're going to the nuns." Jake's wife had been Edith O'Shea before she had become Edith Zuber. He knew all about nuns and for the most part he liked them, but he kind of missed the old habits. He pulled up at the dark convent door with a squeal. He had made good time.

"He won't kill me here," Jane said under her breath, looking at the solid oak door set in crumbly brownstone. She fished into her purse and pulled out the fare. She paid him through the open window and walked up the two steps to the convent and knocked.

Jake sat in the cab and kept an eye out, tapping his fingers on the wheel. It took three minutes for a nun, wearing something long and black, to appear. The door opened and Jane vanished into the gloom. Safe. Jacob Zuber made a U-turn. Nobody would kill her with the good sisters to guard her. Kill her? He looked up and down the dark street again, but there was nothing there out of the ordinary. No hoods in sight. He gunned the old cab and drove home. Fast. These days one never knew.

Within the convent there was soft scurrying at Jane's arrival. Lights flashed on and off and quiet words sounded along narrow corridors. Eventually Jane Hersey found herself tucked into a single bed in a barren room. She slept restlessly for what was left of the night and well into the next day, tossing and turning on the edge of consciousness, finally falling into a dreamless slumber for only a few brief hours long after the convent was stirring. The heavy Boston clouds rolled in, pushed by an early sea breeze, dimming the morning sun as she finally slept.

It was ten o'clock when Sister Raphael peered out of the front parlor window to check for machine gunners in the same manner Jacob Zuber had checked the night before. The old nun had been the one to let Jane in late at night and to hear the fear in her voice when she had asked for sanctuary.

"He's going to kill me. I've got to hide," Jane had said; by this time she had lost her cool entirely. Sister Raphael had believed right away, being a woman of deep faith. Raphael had just finished a Jack Higgins thriller.

Raphael had made her own check of Adams Street after Jane had been tucked in. But Adams Street was still empty of suspicious characters. It was as dismal and inhospitable as ever.

It was just as dismal now when Sister Raphael looked out again, intent on discovering at least something to report to Sister Cecile. But nothing seemed out of the ordinary until Abe Hersey, Jane's father, arrived, and Sister Raphael missed his approach entirely. He came to the convent door moments after the small nun had left her post by the window; the buzzer called her back and she almost threw the door open. Abe entered slowly. He didn't like religion, didn't like convent doors, didn't like nuns. They reminded him of his deceased wife.

Sister Raphael stared up.

"Can I help you?" she whispered.

"Mr. Hersey," he rasped. "I'm here to see Sister Cecile at ten."

Sister Raphael nodded, her old heart thumping. "Follow me."

Sister Cecile had telephoned Jane's father early that morning after an even earlier discussion with Sister Raphael about what to do with a teenager who claimed she was fleeing from sure death because of some file she had stolen from a man who wouldn't marry her. Jane was either seeking attention or death; Cecile wasn't sure which. Cecile had left a cryptic message designed to lure Mr. Hersey to the convent without telling him exactly why. Sister Cecile was good with words, and she had a knack for investigating. In fact, she was a private investigator licensed by the state of Massachusetts. Sister Cecile's private-investigator certificate was on the wall, and she looked up at it for reassurance. It hung between a copy of the Sistine Madonna and a gold-framed photograph of her mother.

She heard Raphael's knock on her door. "Come in."

Abe Hersey walked in and Raphael vanished. Abe stood exchanging looks with the seated nun. She was pretty, but not too pretty; in her thirties, curly auburn hair, and a partial habit. She had a plain gold band on her wedding-ring finger, signifying that she was a bride of Christ. Abe shuddered at the thought. Sister Cecile saw the little twitch in his shoulders and began speaking immediately.

"I'm so glad you could come, Mr. Hersey. Please have a seat." Her speech was Connecticut prep school.

"Yes, thank you." He reached into his suit pocket for a pack of cigarettes.

"Do you mind if I smoke?" He hoped she minded; he

5

wanted to annoy her. He really disliked all this holy shit and he had better things to do today than discover why this nun had lured him here with hints of life and death. He took the biggest leather chair in her office and lit up before she even answered.

"Please. Enjoy yourself." She pulled out a blue glass ashtray that had old ashes in it and spun it across the desktop to him. He didn't exhale until the ashtray stopped within inches of the edge.

"Now, Sister . . . what was the dire matter you called about?"

"Your daughter," Sister Cecile began. "Mr. Hersey, she has a problem."

There was a moment of silence.

"Jane?" Jane attended Boston Latin High School. She had gone to some kind of victory event at the school the afternoon before, then off to celebrate with her girlfriends. Jane was always with her girlfriends. She was a bright young thing but plain, like her mother had been. Since her mother's death six years ago she spent most of her time at girlfriends' houses. A lot of overnights.

"A problem?"

"Jane is . . . she is . . . having a baby."

Abe Hersey blinked. Sister Cecile could almost hear the mechanisms of his mind grind. His mouth turned up on one side. He lit another cigarette and let the smoke stream out slowly.

He coughed. Suddenly he was furious. "That no good . . . I gave her everything—taxi fare, clothes. God. I even got her Celtics tickets! You have any idea what that cost me?" He got up and sat down. His outer shell was loosening and there was a bead of sweat forming on his upper lip. Everybody got pregnant, he told himself. Everybody. Who cared. "How the hell do *you* get into this?" he asked the nun. He looked around the office wildly, hoping for some explanation, and his eyes rested briefly on Sister Cecile's certificate on the wall. "Who's the bastard did this to her?"

"A man," Cecile nodded. "Of course she did come here

6

and ask for sanctuary. Jane wants to have the child, put him or her up for adoption, then join the order."

"All the time she said she was at her girlfriends'? Sanctuary? Sanctuary from what? Nonsense. She's part of my image! I need her. But not pregnant." He was trying to think, but nothing was happening.

"She's apparently four months along, and her image is definitely changing. Jane says she *will* have this child. She did mention you were running for Congress."

Abe put his hands to his head. "All right. She can have her baby," he said. He was beginning to think again.

"She will," Sister Cecile agreed.

"She's a child! I have jurisdiction. You would dispose of the baby, and then actually let her join the order!"

Sister Cecile waited.

"You must have a home for people like that," he continued. "Hide them away until they can return to polite society." His mouth twisted maliciously at strings of medieval possibilities.

Sister Cecile giggled.

"This is serious," he said. He didn't like this nun.

"We have the Good Shepherd program. Jane will be fine if you don't care to be involved. As for her entering the Order of Our Lady of Good Counsel," Sister Cecile said, "if Jane has her child and still wishes to dedicate her life to Our Lord, her earlier indiscretion won't be held against her. And there are hundreds of couples waiting to adopt babies. On the other hand, we do have a long postulancy. There is a great deal at stake." Sister Cecile paused.

"I knew it would mean money."

"Giving oneself to God," Cecile said quietly. "She must have a full understanding of what it means to profess final vows."

"I suppose you expect her to bring some equivalent of a dowry. That's why you want her."

"We don't want her, particularly." Cecile decided to change the subject. "When are elections?"

7

Abe moved to a standing pose by the window. He was a good-looking man, tall, with a full head of hair and a craggy face that was contorted at the moment. He was thinking about murder as it relates to one's teenager. But he was still thinking, nevertheless, and his eyes kept straying to the private-investigator certificate.

"All right, keep her! I'll give you all the money you want! My kid! Hell of a nerve. She should know better, doing this to me right now. Some damn horny teenage kid with pimples knocking up my kid."

"You should know more about this pregnancy."

Abe knew enough. Damn Jane. She picked the worst times. Always used to hang around those nuns. It just proved the nuns had made a mess of things after all. But he would do good by her. Yes. He stood up a little taller at that thought. He *was* her father.

"At first she thought she should marry her Martin," Cecile continued. "He wouldn't marry her, Jane said, and then Sister Martha had already suggested she wait a bit. You see, Jane went to see Sister Martha at her old grammar school for advice right after she found out she was pregnant. Girl talk, you know? Martha was not in favor of a quick marriage to Martin. So many of these things end in divorce."

"Martin, you said?" Abe questioned. He felt a tingle in his gut that began to grow.

"Jane felt you wouldn't have approved of her marrying Martin Moon either. Martin is so much older and she could be looking for security or approval. Then there's the desire to enter the convent. Motives become so confused when a baby is coming, especially in the early stages."

"Moon, Martin Moon." Abe muttered. His eyes grew redder. "I'll sue the bastard. He bleeds me, knocks up my kid! I'll take him to court for child abuse . . . rape. My God, I can get that man on statutory rape."

"Jane was eighteen in October. She began seeing Mr. Moon in November, so I'm afraid that won't work. She tells me it wasn't rape. She's very definite on that point."

"No. Yes. I've got to think. I need some advice. . . ." Abe Hersey rose. Martin Moon. Eighteen? Impossible. The man was a bastard. He was a crook, for God's sake. A killer, from what he'd heard. "Listen. What's that thing on the wall?"

"My license. I'm a registered private investigator in the state of Massachusetts. I offer discreet services. I do investigative work."

"You're a nun."

Sister Cecile felt an irritating moment of boredom that she had to explain herself again. "Nuns do very unusual things these days. We make pottery, we die in San Salvador, we're CEOs of major hospitals, Sister Angelica runs a television station. Our order is self-supporting, and with all my prelaw courses at Barnard I was naturally drawn to this field." Of course there was more to it than that, but she never told people about her first case when she had found one of the neighborhood children involved in murder. She had discovered the real culprit and it hadn't been easy. It was then she had realized that there were things to do in this area and she had gotten her private-detective license. A whole new world of opportunity had opened up before Cecile, and her career was born.

"I can hire you? Confidential, like?"

"Like," she agreed. "Two hundred fifty dollars a day plus expenses."

"Right." He nodded. "Keep her away from Moon. He's a real bastard. I'll pay. He's got this information, too; stuff I don't want out for general knowledge. We gotta deal with that. I gotta talk to Moon. You do that kind of thing? She needs protection. I mean, serious protection. You don't know Moon." He stopped talking for a minute and frowned, his eyebrows almost touching in the middle, and when he spoke again his voice was even more raspy. "Look. He's got something on me. He has a letter I wrote when I was at some school I messed up at, you know what I mean? I need the letter, see. If you deal with this bastard

9

about Jane, maybe you could make some kind of deal? What do you think?"

Cecile raised her eyebrows. "Is he a dangerous man, do you think?"

Abe frowned and lit up a third cigarette. The room was becoming hazy, like a saloon in an old movie. His second cigarette was still burning. "Maybe. Sure. See, he might think he owns her or something. She's going to need a lot of protection—I mean *real* protection—from this guy. He's bad news. He is dangerous, damn it. You gotta protect her!" He stopped, motionless, surprised at his own vehemence. "And get my letter back."

"I understand. Like a bodyguard. You want to hire me as a bodyguard, and if the chance arises, get this letter back. Jane may want to see him herself at some point. Although she . . . well, she might not. She said she was afraid of what he might do. She took . . ." Cecile stopped in mid-sentence. Maybe she shouldn't tell about the file yet. "She left in a hurry," she completed, "she took a cab."

"She came here to get away? That means she didn't want that bastard, Moon. You hide her, protect her. Get the letter. I'll pay. Damn Martin Moon. My baby. Got that? Keep her outta sight."

"I'll only charge for the days I actually work on this," Sister Cecile said evenly. She *wouldn't* tell Mr. Hersey about the file Jane had mentioned. Not until she had read it, anyway. Maybe the letter was actually in it. "I'll place her somewhere he'll never find her and I'll take care of everything. Then send you a bill." She pulled out a pen and some paper and began taking down the facts. Name, address, telephone. Where to send the bill. Not much, she thought, but Jane could add to things. "If you want to keep in touch with her, do it through me. I'll forward her mail. We can sort things out once you think there's no danger." She passed Abe Hersey her card.

"Fair," Abe Hersey nodded, stuffing the card in his suit pocket. He looked strangely pleased. "Keep her under wraps. Can I see her?"

10

"She said she wouldn't see anyone. I gave her my word."

Abe licked a piece of tobacco off his upper lip and stubbed out his cigarette in a cloud of smoke. "Right. I guess. Hard to face people yet. Hard to believe. And me, a grandfather. Whaddya know. Didn't think I was that old." He grinned suddenly, and then sighed. "Well, in that case I'll be off. Everything seems to be under control. Get that letter for me."

His first anger had passed. Cecile couldn't pinpoint what was going on in the man's head. His daughter was temporarily safe and he was relieved, she could see that, but there was more going on than just his daughter. This letter he wanted. She wasn't quite sure which was foremost in his mind, the letter or his daughter. "Right." Cecile pressed the buzzer that would summon Sister Raphael to lead him out. She stood up. "It was certainly nice meeting you, Mr. Hersey. I *will* be in touch."

Sister Raphael came running back to Cecile's office after she had escorted Abel Hersey to the door. "Well?" she asked.

Sister Cecile didn't look up from dusting cigarette ashes off her desk. "I'm going to be a bodyguard, and locate an important document," she said, then lifted her head so Raphael could see her seraphic expression. "I have a job!"

Dinner in the convent was the only meal at which meat was served. It was often chicken done in the French style, with lots of sauce. The order was of French origin, Notre Dame de Bon Conseil. Sister Germaine, the cook, was the daughter of a five-star French chef. Tonight they had coq au vin, simmered gently with unconsecrated altar wine and shallots from the herb garden.

Jane Hersey was there and Sister Cecile sat down beside her. Jane was still wearing her school clothes—lilac polo shirt, tight jeans, white Reeboks with fluorescent laces. She stared nervously at her folded hands while Sister Francis recited a lengthy grace. Jane began speaking when the nun stopped and silverware began to clatter. Her head was bowed and obscured by dangling hair. "You saw my father?"

"He was disturbed," Cecile said.

Red hair began to bob up and down frantically.

"Yes. Isn't he awful! He probably goes, 'She's gotta get an abortion.' Right? I should get an abortion, I bet he said that."

"No. He didn't say that."

"I don't believe it."

"It was Martin Moon that disturbed him."

Jane looked up. The look in her dark-blue eyes was pained and somehow very adult. "I've had enough of Martin Moon. He knows my father, you know. That's how I met him. I thought he loved me."

The coq au vin arrived. Sister Cecile took the platter quickly and began murmuring about food. She didn't want to hear the story of Jane's love affair. Yet. "Help yourself, Jane." She set the dish between them and removed a drumstick and thigh portion for herself, spooned over mushrooms and gravy and began to arrange it on her plate before cutting off a bite. Jane began scooping from the other side.

"It's a myth that sisters eat only pasta," Cecile murmured. "Chicken and carrots. Sometimes peas."

The bowl of carrots followed the chicken, then a salad, and shortly after the potatoes came along. The sisters were all talking, but hesitantly; they seemed more interested in listening to Sister Cecile and Jane, but Jane was speaking too quietly for the curious nuns to hear much.

Sister Louise listened carefully. She was on Jane's right, and Sister Mary O'Malley was on Sister Cecile's left. Across the table, Sister Helen strained her ears, her mouth full; she only heard about the carrots.

"Martin and your father are friends?" Cecile asked.

"Not exactly. Daddy really hates him, I think. There was something going on, like I always got the feeling Martin had something on Daddy, but he would hang around sometimes. And now I know," Jane said. "A real book."

12

Sister Louise decided they were talking about school.

"A book?" Cecile asked, and Sister Mary O'Malley decided they were discussing contemporary fiction.

"Well, you know that file I took? I told that nun last night I got something. It's like, stuff on people. Bad stuff. And Daddy's thing."

"Oh!" Sister Cecile repressed the grin she felt welling up inside. The case was half over already."

"It's upstairs. I took it when I left." Jane's face was sullen. "I looked through it this morning. It's full of pictures of sex. And there's some tapes, and other stuff."

"Jane, maybe you shouldn't have read it all."

All seven sisters looked.

Jane continued, defiant. "I didn't *read* it all. I skimmed it. And now he'll *really* miss me." She dropped her head and a strand of red hair just missed the chicken gravy. "He must have hated me all along."

"This file wasn't yours," Sister Cecile sighed. "You really shouldn't have. I mean, it's got to be serious trouble for you."

"I read it. I mean, shit, Sister Cecile." Jane's eyes were wide. "It was totally, I mean really, dope. I mean, I know a lot of shit, I mean," she giggled, "stuff, you know? You wouldn't believe ..." She stopped abruptly, realizing her voice had become louder and everyone was staring. Her chicken was half eaten; it looked naked. Jane pushed the plate a fraction of an inch to the side and began to work on the salad.

Cecile concentrated on a large mushroom. "I expect Martin will be looking for his papers."

"I guess."

"Anxiously?"

"I think he'll be angry."

Cecile nodded. "Does he know where you are?"

"No. Daddy does, doesn't he?"

"Actually, Jane, I never came right out and said you were here. He said we should take care of you. Hide you. He

13

probably assumes you're here. He's paying to keep you out of sight because he's afraid."

"Sounds like Daddy looking out for Daddy. He wouldn't know I have Martin's file." Her hand shook on the salt shaker. "It isn't me he cares about."

"Maybe. Maybe not. He seemed to care. Would Martin go to extremes to get the file?"

Jane grinned. "He can be . . . extreme."

"And the people he has information on?"

"I could retire on that stuff."

"Well, we'll retire to my office, Jane. We'll let the sisters clean up tonight. We have serious business." She looked at her empty plate. Tonight she would skip dessert.

Moments later, in the privacy of her office, Cecile began questioning. "Martin doesn't know you're pregnant?"

"No."

"And he doesn't know you have the file?"

"He must now. He doesn't care about me. He goes, 'Marry? Get off it, Janie. Get off it. You gotta be nuts.' Never did . . . He's not in love with me. I really knew that all along, but I was kind of hoping he *did* love me. God, I thought he would hit me when I asked him to marry me." Jane sounded casual but she lit a cigarette and held it exactly as her father had. Her hand shook. Hereditary, Sister Cecile thought and looked at the glass ashtray, still holding Abe Hersey's half-smoked cigarettes. A perfectly good Camel, she noted, and resisted the temptation.

"Why? I mean, I would think if you had even considered the possibility that he didn't love you, that after a while, uh, you might want to, uh . . ." the nun began, then stopped.

Jane laughed. It was a startlingly womanly sound, and Cecile felt a déjà vu as though it were she herself laughing in another world.

"Maybe he did once in a while. Maybe I loved him. Whatever. He made me feel good most of the time. Not your idea of good. You're a nun, Sister Cecile, and you probably don't know. I used to feel there was nobody; no mother, no father, no me. That was the thing. No me. Then

14

there was this big, warm man in my life making me feel like I exist. I knew he was rotten, believe me, but he said, like, he loves me. *Me.* At first I thought it was me. And now I know all about him and why Daddy was nice to him. Sometimes I wondered why he liked me." She shrugged. "I don't know. He'd fall asleep. A couple of drinks and he'd be out for the night. Five drinks exactly." She laughed, remembering last night and how easy it had been. "Sometimes he'd stay awake and look through all this stuff he had on people, but I never paid too much attention except I knew it was bad stuff. That's why I took it, because it was really important to him. He'd laugh about what he had in that file. He was mean, you know. He didn't need the money he screwed out of people. He just enjoyed doing it. He hurt Daddy. Sometimes he hurt me. That really stinks. It really stinks."

"So he doesn't know about the baby, and he does know you have his papers." The nun stood up and wandered around the office. "Will your father tell him about the baby?"

Jane shrugged. "It doesn't matter. It has nothing to do with either of them."

"That's pure fiction," Cecile said. "It matters. Baby, father, love. Those are things this man should know."

"If he knew it wouldn't matter. He'll only want the file. He'd do anything to get it. It doesn't matter what I feel. That's why I took the file."

"Would he come here?"

"If he knows I'm here. He'd kill me to get it back. I know he's had people beat up, like, I've seen it. He gets mad, sometimes he hits. It turns him on. See, Martin knows about Sister Martha and the convent because I talked about her a lot. It kind of got him, you know? Like, there I was talking about nuns. It gave me a kick."

"I'm sure." Sister Cecile's patrician features became impassive as her mind worked. "I want that file," she said, "and I want you to bring everything you brought with you downstairs after vespers. Be right here at eight thirty tonight." She looked down at her watch. "That's in a little more than an hour. You may go now."

Jane didn't even question why. She just left, looking relieved.

Sister Cecile sat. She shook her head and reached for the ashtray, emptied it of temptation and replaced it in her drawer. She made a quick phone call. Then she went into the small chapel to pray.

2

THE chapel had stained-glass windows, almost dark now because it was evening. The small room was filled with the murmuring of vespers and the scent of yesterday's candles. It was a good place to pray. Sister Cecile wandered out in a cloud of nuns and went to her office, where Jane was waiting in the same chair her father had chosen earlier that day. Jane was hugging an oversized schoolbag.

Cecile sat down behind her desk, and Jane began to speak quickly while she unzipped her bag and pulled out the large red carry-all file. "I brought down the file." She put it on Sister Cecile's desk and lit a cigarette. "I'm quitting after this pack."

"You wouldn't happen to have a passport, would you?" Cecile asked.

"Sure. I got one when I went to Cancún over spring break. I figured maybe I'd need it for something, a foreign country and all. It's here. I keep everything here. Why?" She patted her shrunken schoolbag. "*He* was there," she added.

"Daddy didn't know?"

Jane laughed quietly. She was feeling immortal again, like most teenagers.

"All right, Jane. A passport." Cecile tried very hard, pushed her thoughts aside and got down to business. She took the file and placed it in the center of her desk. "I spoke to a friend of mine after dinner tonight, and he knows about Martin Moon. He said, well, he suggested that you may have bitten off a pretty heavy piece of sausage."

Red eyebrows rose. Jane began to turn red all over, then she realized the poor nun had no idea how her words sounded.

"Martin Moon could be dangerous," Sister Cecile said finally. "I mean, he *is* dangerous."

"Yes," Jane agreed.

"So perhaps you should go somewhere far away until the dust settles. Or until you know what to do."

"I do know what to do. I want to have the baby and join the order." Jane looked a little less sure of herself on that matter than she had the night before.

"That's certainly positive."

"What else can I do?"

"Oh." Sister Cecile ran a finger under the edge of her veil. "Of course we have some problems to surmount first. I'm glad you have a passport."

Jane nodded.

"We'll head out to see my friend Paul tonight. I'm sure Martin will be looking for you when he can't reach you at home, and your father will or won't tell him you came here. That file you took along," Sister Cecile added, "promises trouble. We really have to do something with it."

"Want to read it?" Jane asked.

"Later. I'll take your word that it's trouble for the moment, because if we want to see Paul, we'd better leave here right away. I don't like riding the subways after nine, and we're already pushing it."

"Sure."

"The Red Line is close. Do you have any cash, Jane?"

"No, I hadn't planned on splitting last night. It just sort of happened."

"Of course. Perhaps I can manage something for you. Speed is important, I believe, if this file is what you say. Mr. Moon is bound to be sending out the troops. I suppose he'll check your house first, and when he discovers you aren't home it's just possible he will come here, even if your father doesn't mention us. Especially if you talked about Sister Martha as much as you say. This is the main

18

residency for the order in Boston, and we're in the telephone book. Of course Sister Martha lives in town. I'll have to tell Sister Raphael to be in touch with her," Cecile rang her buzzer. Sister Raphael was on hall duty tonight, and she needed to give the old nun last-minute instructions before they left.

"Cecile dear." Raphael burst into the office as though she had been hovering an inch from the door. "There's a long, black car outside. Did you call for a limo?"

"A limo, Raphael?"

"Heaven help me, there are two men in the front seat, another one in the back. I went out to water the window box, and I took a very good look."

"A limo," Sister Cecile said dryly. She turned to Jane. "Does that sound like Martin? A long, black car?"

Jane's face had turned to chalk. She nodded.

"You ran out on the man. He's come for his woman, or his file." Cecile felt herself tensing inside. She forced herself to relax and think. She was responsible for this child. She turned to the older nun. "Sister Raphael, do you suppose you could find me a habit someone's kicked?" The two nuns laughed. They loved old habit jokes, no matter how feeble or in what awful circumstance. It took the edge off the near-hysteria they were both feeling.

"Yes," Sister Raphael gasped finally. "Jane, why don't you come along with me. We'll outfit you."

When Jane reappeared with Sister Raphael, Sister Cecile was pleased. Jane's hair was hidden beneath a veil and her dress covered her knees with baggy, black material. Jane was no longer slim but appeared to have gained twenty pounds. She was wearing wire-frame glasses through which she couldn't see, and her makeup had been scrubbed off.

"You look as though you're entering the third trimester already," Cecile said.

"What's that?" Jane returned.

"Oh, pregnancy is full of trimesters. You've gotten wider is all. You look grand. Let's go. But we'll walk slowly . . .

dignified. I'll put the file in my black bag. I see Raphael got you a black bag, too. Ready?"

"Yes," Jane nodded. She felt awkward. The habit was scratchy and smelled of mothballs. "I can't see."

"We'll go arm in arm. Nuns do that, particularly in Europe. Do you speak French?" Cecile nodded to Sister Raphael, well satisfied with the way she looked.

"Six years' worth of French."

"We'll speak French then, Jane. These men will be listening, I'm sure, and we have to walk right by them. Make your voice higher or lower. We take a right from the door and go directly to the subway. No hesitation! We must look as though we know exactly what we're doing."

"What if it's Martin?" Jane was feeling panic.

"He won't know you, believe me. Don't look at the car as we pass, that's all. Not a glance. Maybe you could pray?"

"In French?"

"Je vous salue, Marie, pleine de grâce . . ."

They left. Jane was letter-perfect looking down at the sidewalk before them; the heavy black nun bag that Raphael had exchanged for her schoolbag was hanging from one elbow. Sister Cecile cast a glance at the car, a long black thing filling one full parking space and extending onto the crosswalk catercorner from the convent. Raphael had been accurate: three men were inside. The driver wore a uniform. The man in the front right seat was an obvious thug. His heavy hand dangled from the car window ledge, and through the open rear window she could see the broad, pale features of what must be Martin Moon himself, his eyes sliding back and forth over Adams Street. Cecile had seen that face before. Somewhere. Mob indictments? She felt slightly sick and took a big breath. Martin must know his file was missing. He must have followed the lead looking for Sister Martha.

"Le Seigneur est mon berger," Cecile said loudly.

"Je ne manque de rien," Jane completed in a low voice, and they were past. The men didn't stir.

"Just keep it up, Jane, you're doing fine," Cecile whispered. She was shaking inside.

"Passerais-je un ravin de ténèbres, je ne crains aucun mal," Jane said in normal tones. Then she laughed, "Was I scared! Are they still here? Can I look back?"

"Walk, just walk. Did you see Martin in the back seat? I think it was him; a pale sort of man?"

Jane's shoulders gave a convulsive jump. "I can't see anything!"

"And a chauffeur and a heavy man in the front. Muscle. I believe that would be Martin's muscle."

"Sister Cecile, you know the strangest words for a nun. Can I take these glasses off? I can't see."

"We're almost to the T. Keep them on. We don't know if they're still watching us. You're being terribly brave, Jane."

"I don't feel brave. I mean, you can do anything if there's nothing . . ."

The subway station loomed ahead, high rusty metal. It was aboveground, and the stairs were well covered with graffiti. Sister Cecile knew it by heart; Jane didn't see it. She could barely see the steps beneath her feet.

Cecile reached into her black purse for two tokens and handed one to Jane. "Take the glasses off before you fall in front of the train." They passed through the turnstile.

The Red Line had new cars, new the year before, and most of the slippery plastic seats were still intact. In fact, the train pulled up incredibly smoothly and the doors opened with a shushing sound. Fields Corner. Jane could see the sign now, but not for long.

Sister Cecile hurried her onto the train and they sat. Jane's gabardine skirt was slippery on the seat, and she righted herself carefully, placing the black bag on her lap.

"Where to?" she asked.

"My friend lives on Beacon Hill. He'll know what to

do." Cecile wasn't sure what to say about Paul, so she said nothing.

The train started up, lurching violently. It was uncrowded: three black youths smoked at one end, five white youths smoked at the other end, several women wearing sneakers carried small bags that probably contained shoes, a bald man, a bearded man ... the usual. And two nuns talking softly and piously.

Savin Hill, Columbia, Andrew. They passed Dorchester, swaying monotonously to the rush and clatter.

They got off at Charles Street Station, by the Salt and Pepper Bridge that shook cars from Cambridge into Boston. Cecile grabbed Jane's arm and dragged her down the stairs and through traffic as though she were a piece of baggage. There was only one way to cross the messy streets here, and that was with a touch of insanity.

"My God, Sister, you almost got us killed!"

"Pedestrians have the right of way, Jane. Besides, there's no 'walk' light here and we're in a hurry. Those men looked dangerous to me. I don't believe we were spotted, but one can't always be sure."

"Oh." Jane had not replaced the glasses, so at least she could see. Her pillow had slipped to the side, and she gave it a leeward shove. "Where are we going? Are you sure it will be safe?"

"You'll stay with Paul tonight. You'll be safe there—for now, anyway," Cecile said.

"Paul who?"

"Paul Dorys. He's a lawyer, and eminently respected in legal circles. He has a spare room—several, in fact. So don't think you'll be putting him out."

They were walking along Charles Street at a good clip, passing gas lamps and quaint, expensive shops selling imported pasta and simulated antiques.

"*Who* is he, not what." Jane was persistent. Cecile thought Jane was beginning to act like a nun because she was wearing a habit. "I just want to know who," Jane repeated.

22

"He's an old friend of mine. He's done some legal work for me. Your father probably knows of him. Paul is discreet. You're going to like him."

" 'Sdope," Jane muttered, falling back on indecipherable teenage words. She was gulping for breath as they charged up Revere Street. It was steep and lined with brownstone town houses surrounded by wrought-iron fences and dry-looking hedges. When they finally reached Paul's, Jane was puffing audibly and wondering what this mad nun did to stay in shape.

Sister Cecile wasn't even out of breath. In fact, she appeared jubilant as she pushed the bell beside Paul's heavy front door.

A buzzer sounded and after a few moments' wait the knob turned and Paul appeared. "Ladies," he said, and smiled, moving back so they could enter easily. There was a pause for introductions and Jane began to relax as she took in the man in the hallway. He was of medium height and had gray hair worn in a 1950s-style crew cut; his eyes were blue. He wasn't as old as his hair was gray, Jane thought. Then she looked around. The interior was dark and pleasant, cool after the evening heat. The rug, a red Oriental, was mush under her feet, and there was a huge Chinese urn in one corner. She could fit inside it, Jane thought, and wondered if anybody ever had.

"In the library," Paul said, and Cecile led the way through the door on the right. It was another welcoming space lined with hundreds and hundreds of books. The desk was set in a recess, leaving the center of the room for a round table that reflected a brass ceiling lamp off its polished mahogany surface.

"Pick a chair," Paul said and removed the papers from the round table while they got comfortably seated. He joined them. "I like your nun suit," he remarked, grinning at Jane.

"Sister Cecile thought . . ." Jane began, "well, there was someone watching when we left."

"Someone?" Paul asked. He looked at Cecile and she

shrugged. She would tell him about that later. He nodded and turned back to Jane. "Now, Cecile tells me you're in an interesting condition," he said. "What do you plan to do?"

"Me?" Jane looked flustered, and her hand ran over the black bag in her lap. Cecile took one look at her and unpinned the black veil that was strangling Jane's hair.

"You," Paul said. "Tell me your ideas?" He was looking carefully at the pale young woman before him. She looked half dead with fatigue. Leave it to Cecile, he thought. She'd been making his life interesting for years.

"I thought, well, weren't you going to do something?"

"Like what?"

"Uh." Jane looked at Cecile for help, but Cecile's eyes were on a wall map that had been pulled down over some books. She was in Libya.

"I asked for sanctuary," Jane said firmly. "The Church gives sanctuary to people who might be killed. I read about it. Besides," she paused, not wanting to admit she had nowhere else to go. "Because . . . Sister Martha said to."

"Because you managed to put yourself into a mess," Paul murmured. "And in jeopardy."

"Double jeopardy," Cecile mumbled. She was in Egypt now and humming under her breath. Of course she had told Paul about Jane's file and the baby already. She had spoken to him on the telephone right after Hersey had left that morning. Paul already knew that Cecile had been hired as a bodyguard. Paul was just fishing. And Jane needed some help, poor child. She didn't look well.

Cecile pulled out her bag and withdrew the bulky red file. She tossed it on the table to add to Jane's story. Its presence helped and Jane began to speak again. "Maybe I could stay at the convent? I was thinking that when I came." She looked at Cecile, then down at the red file.

Sister Cecile mouthed a tiny no. "I'm afraid not. We like our convent intact. It wouldn't be wise."

"You say you have some money from my father?" Jane said.

Sister Cecile nodded. "Sort of. He agrees you should be

hidden but he didn't suggest anywhere in particular. I told him you would be safe. I'd see to it. That's what we're here to work out."

"About the file," Jane tried again. "They'd both worry about that more than about me. They wouldn't care about the baby. Even if Martin knows, neither of them would care." Jane's head drooped. It was true that she had slept little the night before, restlessly tossing in a twilight of not-quite sleeplessness, and her freckles seemed to stand out against her white face. It was nine thirty at night and she was exhausted. Sister Cecile caught Paul's eye over Jane's fallen head.

"I think Jane should go to bed," Cecile said. "Should I take her to the spare room? We can continue to work on this without her."

Paul nodded. "I threw in some night things for her—Christmas presents, never been worn."

Sister Cecile smiled and she and Jane vanished. The young woman was a wax creature in an outmoded nun's habit.

Paul was grinning when Cecile returned. He had the file open on the table and his feet were propped up.

"Nice friends you have, Cecile."

"Raunchy?"

"I can't believe you haven't looked through this. It's all original stuff: letters, documents; bank slips that show big deposits, possibly from embezzlement; bimbos' statements of illicit liaisons with local notables. There's a list of names if you want a woman: Lilith McKay, Angie Little, Martha Bowen, Gloria Peacock, and more. It's a screw file. You could screw anyone with this stuff. I can't wait to hear the tapes."

"I'll wait," Cecile said. She actually blushed. "But maybe I should look at the papers so I know what I'm dealing with."

Paul pushed the pile of papers across the table. "Go for it," he grinned.

Cecile went for it.

It was just as Paul said. There were original photographs and negatives of familiar and not-so-familiar faces accepting envelopes from unknown people. There were pictures of people making love that Cecile flipped through very quickly, trying not to look too hard. Each picture was dated with names and times written on the back. There were two letters from a woman who declared she had been the lover of two Boston politicians at the same time. There was a letter from a man who claimed to have been another male politician's lover. There were copies of bank statements from the Cayman Islands Banque Extérieur with very large deposits circled in red ink. There was a letter addressed to an unknown female and signed by Jane's father detailing how he had gotten a young lady pregnant while in college and had subsequently arranged for a quasi-legal adoption. "Interesting. Jane has a half-brother or -sister somewhere. I wonder if she realizes that," Cecile mused. She set that letter aside and continued.

She ran through a list of women's names with notes detailing prices and places these women would go for business. There were more indecipherable bank statements and at the end there were photographs of various women making love to Martin Moon, along with another packet of negatives. One of the pictures was an almost unrecognizable snapshot of Jane herself with Martin. Sister Cecile closed her eyes. "Terrible." Then she shoveled everything but Mr. Hersey's letter back at Paul, who had been watching her from the other side of the table.

"Bad man," Cecile said, and put Mr. Hersey's letter in her purse.

"I should turn the entire mess over to the district attorney, but we just had a falling-out last week. Besides, where would that leave Jane?"

"I knew your impeccable moral sense would enter into this," Cecile said. "But that poor baby. Totally exhausted. And she could be in such danger."

Paul cleared his throat. "Poor baby?" He patted the closed file. "Did she realize she was in there too?"

Cecile shook her head. "Somehow I don't think she does. We'll have to remove that picture. She mentioned . . . well, that it was a learning experience. She didn't mention that she was in it. I have a feeling she didn't recognize herself."

"How the hell Moon got this collection together is beyond me," Paul said. "Most of it is just scummy stuff, not big crimes but serious embarrassments. There are a few indictable possibilities, but he must have just gotten off on tormenting people. Jane's father wouldn't stand a chance in the election if his letter came out. It makes him look like a prize jerk."

"Everybody screws up," Cecile said. "He did a foolish thing a long time ago. It's not half as bad as I expected from the way he was acting. Just an embarrassment, really. And of course now Jane is actually expecting her own baby. I suppose that could really wipe him out politically. No wonder Mr. Hersey went away talking to himself."

"Well, there's Moon too. He's from a fine family, lost a lot of money a few years back. Martin's kind of the black sheep, from what I hear. If he's using this stuff the way it looks, your 'poor baby' is in deep shit." Paul picked up the file and stroked it. "Every one of these documents is an original. His game is going to be over. But I think he might really want this all back." His eyes were half closed and he was frowning. Lawyers, even atheist lawyers, had moral dilemmas too. "Why you?" he asked and put the file down. "Did you know Jane from somewhere?"

Paul settled back. It was her turn and he loved to watch Cecile speak, the way her eyes widened at certain words, the way her hands moved, her mouth . . .

"Jane told me that a week ago she went to her old grammar school principal, Sister Martha, for advice. Jane's mother's been dead for quite a few years and Jane became very close to Sister Martha back then, and of course Jane needed a mother, of sorts. Sister Martha is just a wonderful woman. So Martha suggested she come to the convent, knowing I have curious connections. Well, I mean, maybe I could place her in a nice family?"

She stopped to rearrange her words, then continued. "I gave Sister Martha a call last night to check with her after Jane told me her story. Sister Martha was surprised by the turn of events, but not too surprised. Jane didn't tell Martin Moon she was pregnant, you see. She just asked him to marry her and of course he laughed at her. That's what precipitated all this. Jane is angry, hurt, pregnant; she wanted to get even with him for laughing and for not caring about her as an individual."

Cecile stopped abruptly and turned into her own thoughts. Paul could see an emotion much deeper than her words warranted crossing Cecile's face. But then, Cecile's mother had died young too, her brother had left, her father had always been inaccessible. Paul remembered her at Jane's age.

Cecile pulled herself up from a slouch and returned to her story. "Martin Moon isn't going to let that file go without a fight. He was in front of the convent when we were going out. Martin and some heavies, sitting outside in a limo. Unfortunately Jane told Martin about her closeness to the nuns. It gave her a kick, she said. She always talked to him about us. Martin must have figured she might hike to the convent. Jane talked too much. Luckily Sister Raphael spotted the car and of course then we put Jane in that absurd outfit." Cecile's eyes came back to the red file that Paul had refilled and set back on the table.

"Now what, Paul?"

Paul tapped the file for a full minute before speaking. "From what I know of Martin Moon, he wouldn't hesitate to hire a killer to get this file back. He's had people beat up, and there's a rumor about a young woman found dead. No proof. He definitely appears to have something to do with that list of prostitutes in here. That would be an easy indictment, not to mention charges of extortion if we wanted to go that far. There are indications of racketeering, and there's always income-tax evasion. Besides, there are

28

other people who would kill to get this collection. If word got out that this file was going public, Martin himself might be in danger. He's really going to want this back." Paul pushed the file away. "She needs to get out of town."

"I'm doing fund-raising for the retirement community," Cecile mused. "I was planning to travel this month. How about Kentucky?"

"Too close."

"Paris? She has a passport with her."

"Better," Paul said. "When can you go?"

"Now. I'm the boss, don't forget. The Reverend Mother Sulpicia has been wanting us to get together and discuss plans for development for some time. She's at the Mother-house in Paris. I could do that, take Jane and introduce her. I'm afraid Jane requires a bit of explanation even to those French nuns, but it could work out very nicely for Jane. She even speaks some French. Yes. That would do." Cecile looked at Paul expectantly. "Pick us up some tickets?"

Paul got up and went to his desk and began flipping his Rolodex. He pushed the telephone buttons and began to wait for someone to pick up the other end. "Passports?" he asked Cecile, then began to speak to someone on the line about reservations on Air France. Aristocrat, he thought, watching Cecile nod an answer to his question. Her manner was still imposing, humbling everyone around her. No one had ever told her that; they just reacted to it by doing things for her automatically. As he was now.

"Reservations are confirmed for tomorrow evening at eight." He scribbled down the flight information and passed it to Cecile, then hung up the telephone. "And you'll need some cash. Still have that credit card?"

Paul's eyes twinkled. The credit card was Sister Cecile's bane; an evil creature through which she had access to her expired father's millions. Her father had effectively disinherited her upon her entry into the religious life. A professional atheist, he had had high hopes for his children. In his will, he had specified that the money left to Cecile could never be used by her for religion of any sort. But with the credit card, expenditures could all be corroborated as having no connection to her vocation. It had been Paul's legal solution to a peculiar dilemma. And she could charge things related to her detective work and even deduct them as business expenses.

"Yes. I still have that credit card," she said. "I'm tempted to charge a new retirement home for the Sisters, but I suppose the bank would frown?"

"The bank would frown."

"So send me a big bill for helping Jane and doing something with this file. That's a legal charge. I can pay it with the card and you can donate to the retirement home. And Abe Hersey is paying for me to be Jane's bodyguard and to find the letter. I put that under 'discreet services.' You know all my private-investigator fees go to the convent here, and any extra goes to the retirement home. Those sisters need that home now. So many are over sixty-five and still teaching because there's nowhere else to go. My silly father . . ."

Mr. Buddenbrooks had wanted his child to marry and have children. Specifically, he had wanted his daughter to marry Paul Dorys. Had that unlikely event come about, they would have been a very rich couple. Paul had a lucrative law practice, but Sister Cecile had a vocation. And their lives went on . . . and on and on. The money sat in a bank account drawing interest except for what Cecile could charge to several credit cards. There was no way she could loose that money on her order. The items were checked monthly by a disinterested banker chosen through the courts; if the items passed, the bills were paid.

"Daddy meant well," Cecile said and rose to go. "I pray for him."

"I'm sure he appreciates that. I'll call you a cab," Paul said. "My treat."

3

MARTIN Moon had a habit of dropping his voice at the end of a question. When he was upset his voice sank even more, leaving the listener to wonder if there had been a question at all. When Martin sat back in the Eames chair in his office on Beacon Street, up near the British Consulate, his "Well?" fell to the Aubusson rug.

Tom Dempsey squirmed. He knew what was expected. An answer. He didn't have one, in spite of a late-night search in full uniform. Full uniform meant black. He always wore black for night break-ins. The black turtleneck was hot and itchy because it was a warm office, and the black pants clung, but it was important to dress right. He was still in uniform. "Jane's gone. She ain't living in that house now."

"You mean she wasn't last night."

"Weren't nobody there except her fucking old man, and he didn't catch on I was there until I left. I sprung the alarm system when I was off, man. Thought I'd give him something to wake up to." Tom giggled.

Martin turned away and looked out over Boston Common. Dempsey could barely speak English, Martin thought. But Dempsey was reliable, if only because Martin held information that could put Dempsey in jail. Of course that information was in the red file.

"Damn." Martin stood up and began to pace. "I want her, Tom. I want her badly." His fists clenched. When he had discovered that Jane had hijacked his file he had come very close to murdering Jane. Of course he couldn't find her, but if he had, he would have. He didn't understand why she had done it.

Martin stopped by his desk, pulled open a drawer and removed a pile of twenty-dollar bills. He counted out a stack. "This is on account," he said and dropped the money in Tom's lap. "Ten times this when you bring her in. Understand?"

Tom nodded several times. "I'll get her, I'll get her fast. Where's she hang?"

Martin sat down and began to think, trying to be reasonable. "She's an odd girl, different . . . smart. Four years ago she went to a Catholic grammar school in Hyde Park—St. George's. She used to talk about it a lot. That order has the convent in Dorchester where we stopped last night. But they were tight. Some old bag of a nun said they had no guests there. You check with the principal at St. George's, a Sister Martha. Jane liked her. Used to talk about her like she was her damned mother. Play it cool. You're a nice Irish kid. Nuns ought to be crazy about you."

Tom Dempsey flinched visibly, but Martin didn't notice. Tom had been subjected to nuns in his youth. Nuns didn't care much for Tom Dempsey. He tried another tack. "Drugs?" Tom asked hopefully. "Wasn't your girl into something?" All kids did drugs, at least all kids Tom knew.

"No, no drugs. Jane was surprisingly mature in some ways." Her only vice had been Moon, and Moon didn't consider himself a vice. She had been a good lay, and fun. He couldn't understand this sudden madness that had possessed her. "Check out the convent again; rattle those nuns. I mean it, Dempsey. Get results."

"Okay. Sure. No problem." Tom had a crawly feeling down his back. Results. Right. If he didn't get results, no telling what Moon would do. Moon was one crazy dude. Dempsey had seen Moon punch a guy up once, real bad. And that wasn't all. Dempsey left quickly, stuffing the pile of twenties into his right front pocket as he went. He went through the receptionist's room just as the telephone rang. He nodded to Mrs. Parks behind her mammoth desk, and vanished out the door like a sneak thief. Mrs. Parks watched the door close behind him. She didn't care much for that man. Then she picked up the telephone before it rang a second time. "Yes? Yes, hold one moment, please."

"Abe Hersey on line one," she said to the intercom and clicked off when she saw that the call had been taken.

"Moon?" Jane's father's rasping voice was familiar to Moon. Abe always took it for granted he was known before he announced his name.

Son of a bitch, Martin thought. Jane's old man. Martin held back a chortle. "Abe, what can I do for you?"

"You been seeing my Jane," Abe said.

"Sure. Nice kid, Abe, real nice," Martin said.

"You been talking to my Jane lately?"

"Sure. We do lots of talking." Martin laughed at that one. He smoothed the mahogany surface of his desk as though it were Jane's body. She had incredible skin, the kind of creamy smooth skin that came with redheads. He'd like to strangle her.

"You know where she's at?" Abe persisted.

"Me?" Martin said. "Why? Have you lost her?" When Abe didn't respond, Martin continued. "No, I don't know where she's at, Abe. Do you?"

"No, I don't know," Jane's father said. He breathed a sigh of relief because Moon didn't know Jane had split to the convent.

"So?" Martin asked.

"I gotta see you, Martin," Abe said. "I got business with you. Important. Your wire's tapped, isn't it?"

"Maybe," Martin said. Abe sounded strange. Confident. He never sounded confident. "So you want to see me?"

Abe nodded to the telephone. "How about we meet at the Grill in Brighton. Have some lunch maybe. How about noon?"

Martin never met people in bars, but he wanted Jane and he wanted his file. Abe might have a lead.

"All right, Abe. Noon at the Grill. Be there."

Meanwhile Tom Dempsey had located St. George's

Grammar School in Hyde Park in the telephone book. He had gone directly to a small pharmacy in downtown Boston and planted himself in a telephone booth. He stared at the number and reached for some change, then stopped. What he was after was worth a hell of a lot more than a few nickels. He had to have a plan. He rubbed the coins in his pocket two times for luck and stepped out of the booth.

He would go home and think about this. Getting information out of a nun was no easy task. He knew nuns.

The Grill in Brighton was on Washington Street, in a district cluttered by tracks and trolley wires and traffic. Parking was impossible. It took Martin ten minutes to find a space for the Mercedes on Elko Street. Then he had to walk half a block to reach Washington Street and then up Washington, taking his life in his hands crossing the street. The Grill was just the kind of place Abe would pick—red and gold decor and grease. The bartender wore a red jacket with gold fringe.

Tacky, Martin thought. He couldn't see Abe.

"Marty!" Abe's voice was loud and startled Martin. Abe was in the last booth, clutching a draft beer. There was an empty shot glass on the table and an ashtray that contained three smoldering cigarettes.

Martin walked to the rear reluctantly and sat down facing Abe. His senses wounded by the red Formica tabletop and the red Formica waitress. Martin ordered a draft, Abe ordered another round for himself while a television over the bar blared the twelve o'clock news.

"What is it, Abe?" Martin asked.

"It's Jane . . . Jane . . ." Abe grinned foolishly. He couldn't say it.

"Jane." Martin said it softly.

Abe gulped. "She's having a baby." He grinned again. "Your baby."

The beer had arrived, and Martin had picked his up. He set it down. "My baby."

"Your baby." Abe was triumphant. He could see by Martin's face that Martin hadn't known. It was his triumph, and for the first time in their relationship, Abe felt he had the upper hand.

"What you gonna do, Martin?"

Martin sat and stared at his beer. It was a shock. Jane and a baby. Things began to fall into place very slowly as he looked at the bubbles in his glass. Jane having a baby. What an interesting idea. The little party girl having a kid. He'd kill her when he saw her.

"My daughter," Abe confirmed, "but it's your baby. You going to make an honest woman out of my daughter?"

Abe Hersey sat up straight with those words, and Martin got the image Abe Hersey was trying to get across: the father standing by the door with the shotgun.

Martin gave a chuckle. It was high-pitched and out of character. He pulled a long drink and ended up gasping into his glass. "You want me to marry your daughter, Abe? Make an honest woman out of her? Get off it. I've got better things to do."

"Sure," Abe said thoughtfully. This could be the end of Martin's blackmailing him. "How about if you give me that letter you've got on me. Make some promises to keep your mouth shut. I'll take care of Jane. Deal?"

"Where is she?"

Abe shrugged. "Not sure. She has some nun friends. Maybe she went there. She'll be back."

Martin kept a straight face. He knew better than to ask more. Tom would find her. "Sure. She can go to that place out in Marlboro, she wants to have the kid. Send me the bill," he said.

"I know that place." Abe tapped his fingers nervously on the table. "So, give me the paper you got on me. Fair's fair."

"Sure, Abe. You get me Jane, I'll get you the letter. Damn daughter of yours, Abe. You see her, tell her I got business with her. She's got something of mine. She gives it to me, everything's cool. *Capisce?* Otherwise, no deal."

35

Abe frowned. He wasn't sure of what he was hearing. Moon couldn't be talking about the baby. What the hell had Jane done?

"I want to see her," Martin repeated. The smile came hard. "So you tell her that . . . No worries. Come to Papa." He withdrew his wallet and counted out an immaculate collection of one-dollar bills and laid them on the table. Green against red. "For the drinks."

Martin left in a hurry. He wanted to wreck Abe Hersey and his political campaign. It would be so easy. What a jerk. But Abe was the key to Jane and the file. And if that file got out, Moon knew he'd be walking a very thin line. The girls listed in the file had their own pimps and none of those sweethearts would want him messing with their ladies. And there were other problems he didn't want even to think about. Like sure death at the hands of at least one of the creeps he was squeezing.

Abe sat at the table for almost five minutes after Martin Moon had left, running his fingers over the crisp new bills. Martin must have gone to the bank or maybe someone had paid him off today. A few other people did, Abe had heard, but not Abe Hersey anymore. Not as soon as he got in touch with Jane. Abe found himself humming along with a TV commercial. He could arrange a talk between Jane and Moon, maybe with himself right there too, and Moon would give him that damn letter back. He was going to be free. Somehow. Jane would do it. Where was Jane, anyway? He had to call those nuns. He had almost forgotten his daughter was having a baby.

Students were reassembling in the school yard after lunch recess when Tom Dempsey arrived at St. George's Grammar School in Hyde Park. Girls in plaid skirts were straggling into order, boys were milling around nastily, dressed in white shirts, dark ties, and plain-colored pants. Sedate bunch, Tom thought, until he saw a rock fly and hit a chubby girl. He saw who did it: a boy with short-cropped blond hair and a two-inch-long "tail" down the back of his neck. Tom looked scornful. Nuns wouldn't have allowed such a thing in his day. Discipline was all shot to hell.

Tom felt prickles running up his back as he walked into the building. He sniffed. Parochial-school smell: chalk and dead flowers, urine, and parochial disinfectant. A neat woman approached him cautiously. She wore a gray skirt, pink blouse, and a cross. She smiled, showing silver dental work. "Can I help you?"

"Uh, Jane, my cousin, went here. Jane, Jane Hersey. Do you know her?" Tom blushed and fumbled, part act and part real. He had gone to a school like this. "My cousin . . ." He looked at his frayed blue suit sleeves, rubbing a finger over the cuff. He needed a goddamned new suit. He mentally repeated frantic profanity in his mind to keep his equilibrium.

Sister Elizabeth stepped back for a good look. She didn't trust young men, and never had. She knew Jane all right. Jane had been there on Monday. Today was Thursday. "I would suggest you see Sister Martha, our principal. Second floor, first door on the right." She nodded the way to the stairs, then slipped into a classroom. A bell rang and students began heaving by in waves.

The closed door of the principal's office had a small white card with green lettering: Martha Przyblyska, O.L.G.C.

Tom knocked. He held a primordial scream in his stomach with difficulty. Sister Martha, he repeated to himself, is a person, not a monster, a regular person. But she loomed monstrous in his subconscious along with the memory of himself caught filching money from the mission box. He'd spent the money on candy. Twenty years ago the five dollars had bought caramel squirrels and baseball-card bubble gum. And Heath bars. Twenty Heath bars. The Heath bars had made it all worthwhile. His chest swelled a little with the memory, and he was ready when the door was opened by a small boy on his way out.

* * *

37

Sister Martha was standing behind her desk, so that her face was right in his line of vision: straight gray eyebrows, a tag of gray hair from under the heavy veil. She was an anachronism, a nun in full habit. Huge habit. Over two hundred pounds and only five feet tall, swathed in black.

Tom Dempsey paled. She would see right through him.

"Yes?" She smiled, her blue eyes riveted on his tie.

His neck itched. Fucking tie must be crooked. Never could get ties on right. "I'm Tom Hersey, trying to find out about my cousin." It came out backward, scratchy. He cleared his throat. "Jane Hersey. She comes here sometimes. We ... uh, Mom's been talking to her sister, uh, Jane's mom, and they don't know where she's off to. We thought you might know."

Perspiration made his underpants stick at the back and he twitched. He'd killed men. Killed them! And he couldn't talk to a fat nun.

"You're a Hersey? And your mom talked to her sister. Did your mother marry your uncle?" Sister Martha smiled, a jolly elf smile. Jane's mother had been dead for years.

"Dempsey. I get embarrassed sometimes."

That, at least, was the truth.

"Jane was here Monday. She was thrilled to be graduating from high school." Sister Martha decided she didn't trust this Dempsey but she was polite. "She's a dear girl. I was so proud."

"Where is she? That's what I gotta know."

"Where?" Sister turned and pushed a button on a large clock set into a box on her desk. A bell clanged loudly. "Afternoon classes begin now. Mustn't change the schedule." She turned back to Tom. "Mr. Dempsey, I couldn't say. She could be anywhere. Obviously she is somewhere, but I wouldn't want to speculate aloud. Teenagers being the way they are and all. Sometimes I think all teenagers are absolutely nowhere."

The walls were closing in. Sister Martha was the Queen of Hearts and he was the rabbit. Martha wasn't finished yet.

"But, then, Jane was always liberally endowed with

38

common sense; so I'm sure she will choose the right path. Ultimately." Sister Martha stopped talking and looked pleased, hiding the acumen that a few select souls knew she possessed. Tom Whatever-His-Name was bad. No doubt he was a gangster connected with that man whom poor Jane had latched on to.

Sister Martha decided on some deception, but not a lie. She never lied. "I mentioned an order in Marlboro to Jane. They're very good at that sort of thing."

"She didn't go home," Tom said. Marlboro meant nothing to him. "I want to know where she is." He forced his mouth into what was supposed to be a smile. "I know you ain't tellin' me, Sister. You know. I know you know. You gotta tell me."

"Where did you go to school, young man?"

"St. Anthony's," he mumbled. "You gotta tell me."

"Yes. I thought so." She nodded. "No, I can't tell you a thing about the young lady." She glanced at the big metal clock mounted on her desk. "In three minutes I must begin the fifth-grade religion class. You do understand." She rose—enormous, and done with the interview. She had a class to teach.

Tom felt himself carried up and around on a wave of nun air. He was almost physically washed before her out of the office, like a bit of flotsam caught in the surge. His face was red, his mind confused. He didn't feel anger until he was outside the school yard, where the hot morning sun melted into his antique blue suit. There the anger rose like a bad smell, filling every pore with hatred. He spat on the sidewalk for relief and said "fucking asshole" three times.

Sister Martha watched him from the window of the fifth-grade classroom. She waited until he had turned down Cotton Street and was out of sight. "Children, you are to answer the first five questions on page 154 in *Christ Is Our Neighbor*. There will be no collusion. I will be in my office for a few moments."

She moved fast for her size and a minute later was dialing the convent in Dorchester. Sister Raphael answered.

"Raphael, this is Martha. They've started. Just what I was afraid of. Young hoodlum looking for our Jane."

"She's gone. Jane left with Cecile last night," Sister Raphael said. "She was wearing Sister Mary Eulalia's old habit."

"I didn't like this man," Sister Martha said. "He was wearing a gun."

"Did you see it?" Sister Raphael asked.

"He had a lump there on his side."

Sister Raphael nodded, forgetting she couldn't be seen. "Cecile will handle it. Don't worry. She took Jane to Paul's last night."

"Paul's?" Sister Martha frowned. She had never liked her friend's long association with that man. It had gone on for years and Sister Martha had never understood it. She sighed audibly.

Sister Raphael understood. "Don't worry about Paul. They knew each other back then, you know."

"I know." Sister Martha had never been slim and beautiful, and her understanding of the male sex was derived from her observance of boys progressing from kindergarten through the eighth grade. She knew a lot.

"That's exactly what worries me." Her eyes were focused on a pigeon outside her window. The bird looked for peanuts on her ledge each noon, and today Martha had forgotten to put them out. "All right, Raphael. I'll leave it in the Lord's hands. Tell Cecile this Tom Dempsey was here looking for Jane."

She rang off quickly and opened her right-hand drawer. The box labeled "paper clips" was filled with peanuts. She took out a handful and opened the big window quietly. "Two for pidge, two for Martha."

4

RAYMOND McVEY was thirty-two years old and had trafficked with lawyers for the past fifteen years. There was one lawyer in particular. His mother had called her old friend, Paul Dorys, countless times to get Ray out of the slammer. Public drunkenness, minor drug dealing, assault and battery, car theft, forgery, and ultimately manslaughter. Ray had gone up from one game to the next; but he loved his mother sometimes and he would always return home when released from Billerica or Westboro or from an occasional night sobering up at the Cambridge police station. His last real stretch had been for the manslaughter charge. A real bummer. He had been drunk and couldn't even remember what had happened.

Ray's last memorable good deed had been to rob the Salvation Army boxes in Watertown in order to give the clothes to some poor neighbors. Deep down, Ray had a heart of gold. When he heard about the Public Works truck running over his mother's flower beds, that heart began to beat loudly for righteousness and justice. He decided to seek revenge. For Mom.

"What's his name, Ma, what's his name?"

"Now, Raymond, what do you care? I've already called Paul about it. Paul will fix it. He's taking them to court this week."

"Him? Ma, he don't do nothin'. I just spent three years away. You think he couldn't've got me out?"

"He did his best, Raymond. If you could only stay out of trouble, get a job . . ."

41

Lyuba McVey sighed. She had trouble breathing some-times. Emphysema. Her son was such an aggravation, it didn't help. His presence made her feel as if her chest was closing right up.

"What's his name, Ma?" Ray jumped around the small room. The windows were dirty and sunlight filtered through in hazy patches. "What's his name?"

"Marshall, Mr. Marshall." She never could deny Raymond anything for long. That had always been the trou-ble.

Ray McVey nodded. "Marshall, Marshall, Marshall. I think I can remember that. Marshall, Ma?"

"That's right, Raymond. It's Marshall. He drives a trash truck."

Raymond got a knife and put it in his sneaker top. He got two six-packs and ten dollars' worth of uppers and sat out on the back step of his house for a picnic. He knew the Public Works department got off at three o'clock, and by three he had finished off all the beer and just enough pills to give himself courage. What he planned to do was going to take a lot of courage.

His voice didn't sound quite right when he arrived at the DPW on Cambridge Street, but the first man out of the yard, Mr. Dillworth, understood what Ray McVey wanted.

"Where's Marshall? You know somebody named Mar-shall here?" Ray asked. Raymond McVey had marched the three blocks from home with sweat rolling down his back. He was defending his mother's flowers and he spoke with a sense of mission.

Dillworth figured Ray McVey was one of the local boys who bought drugs from Howie Marshall. "Sure. Marshall's the big guy, in a yellow shirt today. He drives number 235."

"He comin' out soon?" Ray asked. He was leaning against a telephone pole for support and didn't think he could stand up much longer without another drink.

"Howie will be along," Dillworth affirmed, his eyes wandering over Ray McVey. Ray was ugly. He weighed close to three hundred pounds and had a white scar across his cheek where battery acid had splashed when he had tried to whack a car battery into shape. Dillworth managed a smile and left. He didn't care much for Howie Marshall's buyers.

Ray waited. Six, seven men came by, none in a yellow shirt. Finally a big man that fit the description walked across the yard. Ray could feel his heart pumping.

The man drew near.

"Marshall?" Ray asked.

"Sure. For you, baby, I'm Marshall."

"I got business for you. We gotta talk. How about we go down the Norfolk Café; I'll buy you a drink. You ever been there?" Ray's tongue was thick and his nose ran. He wiped his nose on his arm. He had no intention of having a drink with this bastard, but Ray was clever. He had a plan he'd worked out while sitting on his porch step. He'd lure this creep to a place where nobody could see, and he'd kill him!

Howie was used to people like Ray. Ray wanted to buy drugs. He sold them. "Let's go," Howie said. "Get this over with."

They walked silently. It was three blocks and the sun cooked the sidewalks, melting the bubble gum and raising a smell from the gutters. Ray could make it without a drink, he told himself, and put one foot ahead of another heavily. He had worn his new red sneakers for courage and because the high-tops could conceal the knife better than his worn white Nikes could, but the new shoes were padded leather and hot. He was nervous too. He had decided to kill Howie Marshall because Howie had driven his Public Works truck over his mother's flowers. Killing the bastard would make anyone scared. He was being really smart about this and it was the most he could do for his mother. He'd have a real drink later.

"You drive a trash truck?" Ray asked finally. They were by the driveway that went to a parking lot behind the café.

"Yeah."

"Let's talk in the parking lot," Ray said. "Right back here."

43

Howie was agreeable. Druggies like privacy for buys. He knew that but he didn't know what was coming, and he followed Ray into the lot, vacant except for two cars and an abandoned Volkswagen bus, stripped. The fence that Howie had driven through was still down and the flattened garden beyond, Ray's mother's garden, was still littered with crushed rose bushes.

"You done that?" Ray asked and gestured to the downed fence. He began fumbling in his boot for the knife, trying to make it look as if he had an itch. "I mean, run over that stuff?"

Howie laughed. "Sure as hell did. Rolled right over it."

"You friggin' asshole!" Ray roared at the top of his lungs and produced the six-inch blade, holding it up for the fatal plunge. Ray's eyes were wild, and so was his coordination. It didn't take much for Howie to deflect the blade and, with a kick that was pure accident, Howie sent the weapon flying off wildly toward the fence.

"Son of a bitch," Howie muttered, backing off fast. Ray was a good ten feet away from him now, sweating profusely and gurgling, "I'm gonna get youse" over and over.

"Sure," Howie said. "Sure." He was safe from this crazy bastard now. The knife was gone, and he had a gun, picked up from a buyer who didn't have the cash. And this crazy guy here thought he was gonna get his? No shit. No druggie ever better try. Howie was mad. Not that he had ever planned to use the gun, but it sure felt good and he practiced with it empty every Saturday morning when the "Bonanza" reruns were on TV. He'd scare this creep good. The gun came out of his belt fast, just like Hoss did it. Without thinking that Ray was now unarmed and sniveling, he blasted him with one shot, so fast Ray barely had time to squawk. Ray hit the ground hard, blood pouring out of his chest. It had been a lucky shot and Howie stood with his mouth open, stunned. He didn't even know why the fat creep had wanted to kill him. Drugs, he thought. Drugs.

It took Howie five minutes to get the body into the dumpster parked behind the café. No cars pulled in. No kids came by. No eyes looked out from the surrounding houses. Ray had been right about privacy in the parking lot, and Howie Marshall had committed the perfect crime. He even remembered to wipe the gun clean of prints, very, very carefully. He looked at it. No one would ever know, he thought, and stuffed it back into his pocket. He'd toss it in the Charles River later.

Howie wiped his shaking hands on his pants and walked down the drive, around the corner, and into the Norfolk Café. He ordered the first of eight drafts and allowed the third inning of the Red Sox doubleheader to wash over him. "Goddamn," he said. "Goddamn."

Sister Cecile traveled for her order at frequent intervals. She spoke French like a native, made passable hash of Italian and German, and could mumble in several other tongues. A school in Switzerland had done that for her. Her education had been the chief factor in her position in the order, and she made good use of it. Hiding a pregnant teenager in Paris was only another use of her talents.

Cecile was preparing for Jane's escape. She packed a large bag with some clothes that she had picked up at St. John's Thrift Shop on her way back from morning Mass, and then she looked for Sister Raphael.

Raphael was old and smart. She was the one person in the Order of Our Lady of Good Counsel in whom Cecile confided, the one person who had an understanding of almost everything.

Sister Cecile found her old friend immersed in an investment report and beckoned her into the office.

Raphael was bubbling over. "Martha called from St. George's. She said some hoodlum was there looking for Jane."

Cecile nodded. "That means Martin Moon will be back again. He didn't see us leave last night, at least. But you're going to have to deal with this for me, Raphael. Nobody else here knows anything about the situation. Don't tell them a word. Then nobody will have to lie."

Sister Raphael nodded. "They won't even ask me. I'm too old. They think I'm dumb."

Cecile agreed. "Exactly. Now I believe that Martin doesn't know why Jane did what she did, and he will be desperate to get her back."

"What did she do?" Sister Raphael asked. "I do have a need to know, Cecile." Blue eyes looked out stubbornly.

"She stole a file from Martin, a file that contains incriminating evidence that could be used against some very important people. Scuzzy stuff."

Sister Raphael sat up straight in the brown leather chair. Sunlight played on the black sleeve of her sweater and her heart began to quicken. "I see. It's dangerous."

Cecile paced the floor. Her desk was a mess and would probably get worse if Raphael took over, but the aging nun was a genius with figures. And the bills would all get paid on time for a change.

"I don't think there's any danger. Besides, we're leaving tonight. I was planning a trip to the Generalate in Paris soon. Mère Sulpicia and I have a great many things to discuss about the order. Paris will be safe for Jane. I don't know how long a reach this Martin Moon has, but I don't believe it's international in scope."

Sister Raphael nodded. "Everyone knows about your fund-raising tour," she said. "They'll think you went to Kentucky. I'll tell everyone here you went fund-raising, but I just won't mention where. I won't mention Paris."

"Good. Let them think I'm doing it in Kentucky as planned. It will necessitate that I make a few parish visits in Paris just to keep us honest, but that's acceptable. The French are very generous."

Sister Raphael looked skeptical. She had heard about the French.

"Don't worry about the convent. I can handle it." Raphael had exercised important responsibility in the order in her day, and she enjoyed the weight of it again. It was exciting to be really useful. Her old hands shook as she realigned a pile of canceled checks that were strewn on the

46

desk. "If Mr. Moon comes back, I'll pin him down for a donation. You'll see."

"I'm sure you will, Raphael. Be blunt. We're taking care of his baby. Although I suppose you can't come right out and say that without giving things away. He's not to be told where Jane is or even that we saw her. Just tell him the need is great."

Cecile felt a twinge of conscience. How far should they go in looking for donations? "Raphael, you do know about Jane's condition, but be discreet. I'm not at all sure if Martin does, although Jane's father may tell him."

Raphael looked bemused. "The baby's father doesn't know? No wonder . . ."

Cecile smiled and looked around her office. She always missed it when she traveled, and she would miss Raphael too. The older nun was somewhere in between friend and mother to Cecile, though she hoped that this mess brewing wouldn't strain their relationship. Cecile watched quietly as the different aspects of the situation coalesced in Raphael's mind. She seemed to be enjoying the complexities.

"And then there's my client, Jane's father," Cecile added. "You could call him. Tell him only that Jane is well cared for and that everything is fine. He was obnoxious but he has worries, and of course he *is* paying us. I suppose you could submit a bill for three days. But you're so good with money, Raphael, maybe you could talk about the stock market with him, and investments. Tax laws are changing; so you might remind him that what is a deduction this year might not be next. Tell him about the old nuns."

"Wonderful. I'll enjoy myself, Cecile. And when I get the money, well, I was talking to our broker yesterday, and he's got this new stock . . . Now, Cecile, you know I've done well with our investments, and I could double this money in weeks if things go as my broker feels."

Cecile sighed. They might be the only order in America to have a stockbroker. Sister Raphael played stocks like horses and usually came out ahead. "Put half in mutual funds. Promise me?"

Sister Raphael looked disappointed, but the cloud lifted swiftly. She still would have money to play with if things went well. She thought carefully of the rule of obedience. "Yes, Sister," she said meekly and her thoughts turned to the prospects of Jane's having a baby. Her gnarled fingers itched to begin work on a tiny sweater. Pink or blue? "I wonder what she will have," Raphael said aloud.

"Have?" Cecile was suddenly hungry. It was mid-afternoon and she hadn't eaten since last night.

"Boy or girl," Raphael explained. "I was thinking of making a tiny sweater."

"Um." Cecile rose to leave. "A boy," she said firmly. "With all the men involved in this silly business, it couldn't be otherwise."

Raphael smiled serenely as Sister Cecile left for the kitchen. She had some lovely pink angora tucked away in mothballs in her closet. It would make a cunning sweater for a little baby girl.

Pan Am Flight 310 left for Paris at eight o'clock that evening carrying Jane Hersey and Sister Cecile. They had arrived at the airport at six thirty in disguise, wearing identical yellow raincoats and blond wigs. Red lipstick and heavy mascara made them look like women on their way to a good time. Paul had said his farewells earlier at his apartment, since both he and Cecile had decided his presence might give them away. Jane was horrified at her own appearance and scandalized by Cecile's, but settling into the lush plane seat, she finally saw the humor of it. After the flight leveled off, a flight attendant came along with complimentary cocktails, and Cecile stayed in character. "Straight Scotch, honey, and a seltzer for my little friend."

The dark young man in the steward uniform looked twice. Cecile was attractive in an incongruous way and Jane, as a blonde with war paint, resembled a refugee from Boston's Combat Zone. He smiled and nodded and began dumping ice into two plastic tumblers.

The two women accepted their drinks and settled in for

the long ride, Cecile sinking into a familiar déjà vu of trips to Europe, Jane exhausted and thrilled by the turn of her life.

The plane's engines droned. At last Jane drifted into comfortable sleep. She was safe at last, mysteriously hijacked by an irregular private detective nun dressed like a hooker who hadn't even bothered to tell Jane what would come next.

Sister Cecile looked pleased as she sipped her Scotch. Jane was snoring lightly, her heavily made-up face innocent in repose. Sister Cecile would sleep too, but first, from her oversized flight bag, she pulled out a small black book. With a plastic tumbler of Scotch in one hand and the book opened in the other, the nun began to read silently and reverently, "The just have cried out, and the Lord has answered them and rescued them from all their distress."

By nine thirty the following morning, Martin Moon had heard from Tom Dempsey that the order of Our Lady of Good Counsel knew where Jane was. By ten, Martin had Sister Raphael on the telephone.

"Our provincial head?" Sister was saying. Her elderly voice quivered nicely. "She's out of town on a fund-raising tour. Your name, sir?"

Martin hesitated, then gave his name. Sister Raphael smiled, running a finger over the pink angora in her lap. "If you're interested in giving a personal donation for the retired sisters, we'd appreciate it if you would mail a check. The need is urgent."

"I'll come by and hand it to you in person," Martin said.

He arrived at one thirty. When he left an hour later he had written a check for five thousand dollars to aid the retired sisters and had discovered that the provincial head was on a fund-raising tour, somewhere. He had already found out her name was Sister Cecile. Martin had written the check with half a mind on the possibility that money meant they would owe him. The other half had been on Jane and, surprisingly, his first anger had melted. He still wanted to get her, but not to kill her. He had better things he could do with Jane. Round two, he had thought. I'm finding out about the order that has hidden Jane somewhere.

Unconsciously, he had focused on a bit of pink fluff the nun had on her desk. What he didn't know was that the fluff was the beginning of a sweater for his new baby.

At three o'clock that afternoon, Sister Raphael deposited Martin Moon's check into the convent's account at the Dorchester branch of the Suffolk County National Bank. By three thirty, Sister Raphael had gotten through to her stockbroker and had put in an order for three hundred shares of a computer stock.

Martin called Tom Dempsey only minutes after returning to his office. "I've got a name, Dempsey," Martin growled into the telephone. "I have the name of the nun and the lawyer that handles her money. You get to the lawyer, you'll get the nun." Rage was brewing again, rage not so much against Jane but against the fact that he didn't know where she was, and with his baby. The idea that Jane was carrying his baby was beginning to do strange things to him.

"I never knew a nun with money." Dempsey was still smarting from his encounter with Sister Martha, but he knew his nuns. Poverty. They loved it.

"This nun has bread. She's different. Lawyer's name is Dorys, Paul Dorys." New fury kept his own tone even and emotionless. "He's in Boston, big office on Beacon Street, 11 Beacon Street. Get this, Dempsey; I want Jane. I want her personally."

"You don't want her wasted?" Tom was surprised. Moon was going soft maybe.

"She did something with something of mine. She'll tell me. I'll take care of her myself." He wasn't sure now if he was speaking of the file or the baby. Either way, he wanted Jane.

Sure he would, Tom thought. He was already leafing through the yellow pages under "Attorneys." Dorys, it was

50

there. "You sure this lawyer's going to know?" Tom asked. It was too simple.

"Bet on it."

Martin hung up. He could tell Dempsey thought he was going soft. Damn Irish creep. Tom Dempsey was trustworthy, though, and he did what he was told. Five years ago, Martin had lent him big bucks for his sick mother, and from then on Tom had been like putty—any favor was okay. Tom had never killed a man for Martin, but he had for someone else. Martin knew that for a fact. It kept the putty soft. It was all in the red file.

Paul Dorys made five complete photocopies of the red file. He took the original file and four of the copies to his bank on State Street and placed them in his safe-deposit box. The fifth copy he kept in the red-white-and-blue envelope from Copy Cop on Boylston Street, where he had had the work done. That envelope went into his briefcase along with the material he needed for an afternoon at court.

He lunched at a small diner on State Street—pastrami on rye, pickle, and cole slaw. It was a poor substitute for the meals he had eaten in New York, when he was at Columbia Law School. There he'd learned about the real thing. Those had been the years when Cecile had been plain Cecile Buddenbrooks and a student at Barnard, when he had thought they would marry and Cecile had known otherwise. Growing up in the cook's cottage of her parents' estate in Connecticut hadn't prepared Paul for the shock of her vocation, but he had stood by her then against her father. He ate the sandwich in her honor.

By now he had made a habit of standing by her: he'd contested her father's will, which had stipulated that nothing could be used from the estate for her religious order or for any church-related use. He had gotten court approval for the document that allowed her to spend the money as she did, through a collection of credit cards where the expenditures could be validated as "non-religious." Paul had set up secular charities in Europe and several states in the

U.S.A. to enable Cecile to travel; as long as she spent some time on the charities, the travel counted as non-religious. Cecile hated it all but knew her order depended on her to be the human link between continents. And now there was Jane. Cecile had plans for Jane in Paris, plans she had discussed at length with Paul while Jane slept. Thank God for the Buddenbrooks money, he thought.

Paul was working on a Middlesex County case across the river at the Cambridge District Court and was scheduled to confer with Judge Arnolds at two. Paul and the opposing lawyer were trying for an out-of-court settlement; but it was a city lawyer he was dealing with, and certain requirements had to be met. His client, Lyuba McVey, was suing the City of Cambridge Public Works Department for destroying a flower bed with one of their trucks.

Paul walked over to the courthouse from Boston to have a pre-trial conference. He was feeling good as the city attorney laid out his client's position for the judge. "Ridiculous," Paul retorted. "Lyuba McVey wants punitive damages. She worked for two months on that flower border."

"The cost of the original flowers was determined at eighteen dollars and seventy-two cents. The city has agreed to award Mrs. McVey another twenty for her labor." The city lawyer was named Harkenson. He was tall and very young, and his father worked for the board of assessors.

"Bullshit!" Paul slapped the wood-patterned plastic table. "My client is sixty-eight years old. She put her soul into those flowers. She prepared the soil with her own hands, using compost she'd prepared two years ago." Paul was keeping a straight face with difficulty. "I suggest an award of five hundred dollars and that the Department send over a man to replant the flower bed. The truck not only mashed the root systems; it leaked garbage onto the plantings. It's a disgrace!"

The judge sat impassive. He was black and smart. Fourteen years on the bench had turned him cynical but exceedingly fair. "Where does your client live, Mr. Dorys?"

52

"Elm Street, your honor. The garden is adjacent to a parking lot behind the Norfolk Café. The fence had been previously damaged by a drunk driver. The city truck backed through the hole where the fence had fallen. Ostensibly he was turning around. I question what he was doing in the lot to begin with."

"I believe that lot was built to accommodate cars from a residence for moderate-income and handicapped persons on Norfolk Street," Judge Arnolds remarked.

"But used exclusively by patrons of the Norfolk Café," Paul added. "Do you have a statement as to what the member of the Public Works department was doing there with a city truck?"

"No, Mr. Dorys," the other lawyer responded. "However, the fence was to be replaced by the housing authority. Mr. Marshall, the driver, claims he thought it was a driveway."

"Had Mr. Marshall been drinking?" Judge Arnolds asked.

The city lawyer looked uncomfortable. "I didn't ask, but he couldn't have been. He was on city time."

"I see," Paul said. He looked bored; his eyes rested on the blue carpet of the conference room. The new Middlesex County Courthouse was done in shades of brown and royal blue and was a vast improvement over the fallen plaster walls of the old Bullfinch Courthouse across the street. The old courthouse was being renovated and turned into multimillion-dollar cubicles for private enterprise. Money. That was Cambridge. Without looking up, Paul said, "I suggest the city award my client the full amount. If not, I will be forced to investigate the matter further. We would ask for a jury trial."

"I hear that as blackmail," Mr. Harkenson sputtered. "My client will be demoted if the ruling goes against him." He looked at the judge, who was sitting with half-closed eyes and a half-smile. He was enjoying this.

"Judge Arnolds?" Paul raised one eyebrow. "Should I look into Mr. Marshall's reason for being in the parking lot? Is it germane?"

Tight white curls began to nod slowly, and the lawyer for the city of Cambridge saw that he had lost. "We'll settle," he said, before the judge could answer. "The town will pay. Five hundred dollars and a replanted yard. I'll do the paperwork immediately."

The judge agreed. It was a proper settlement.

"I believe you've made an intelligent decision," Paul said. "I'd like to be able to present Mrs. McVey with a check next week and have the work done as well. It's already April and she tells me everyone else has cold frames going already."

"That sounds reasonable." Judge Arnolds spoke with finality. "Plantings and money by planting time." He scribbled the outcome on a sheet of paper. "I'll have the paperwork on this rushed along. Thank you, gentlemen." He rose, majestic in black, and walked out. Paul and Mr. Harkenson stood until the door closed behind him, then resumed sitting to do their own paperwork.

"Damn all," Harkenson muttered. "The city isn't going to like this. The Public Works? You know them? Union. They'll have my ass for this. So the guy has a drink for lunch and hit-and-runs the old lady's flowers. Marshall's demoted to trash picker and I start looking behind me every time I walk down the street."

"They're dealing drugs in the DPW, aren't they?" Paul asked. He knew they were. He had the file copy in his briefcase. Jane's father hadn't been the only politician in the file. Cambridge names were there too.

Harkenson looked shocked. "If there's any drugs, I'm sure it's on a strictly private basis. I doubt there's much substance abuse among city employees." Harkenson was playing it safe. Drugs were around.

"No big-timers?"

Harkenson's expression passed for innocent. "To tell you the truth, I've only been on the payroll for six months. And I'm afraid this settlement won't sit well somewhere. Marshall is one of the union boys, and they'll have to set him down for this. God, I can't believe it."

Paul felt sorry for him. "It might change things for you?"

"Well, working for the city is steady pay, but there's good work and bad. This was supposed to be a little thing. The judge was supposed to think the old lady was nuts and let it pass for the cost of the flowers. The minute you get punitive damages awarded, you face the fact that someone was negligent. Cambridge doesn't like that."

"Marshall did it." Paul's eyes were steady. "Ever meet him?"

"No."

"I think you might. If there's any trouble, do me a favor." Paul waited for a response, and Harkenson edged half off his chair.

"What's that?"

"Send Mr. Marshall to see me."

"Trouble?" The young lawyer grimaced. "Got a card?"

Paul pulled out his wallet from his suit-coat pocket and withdrew a card. He slid it to the other man.

Harkenson picked it up and looked at it. "Criminal attorney," Harkenson mused. "What do you get for representing the old lady? State Street law firms get big bucks."

"Mrs. McVey worked for years as a cook. Friend of the family, so to speak."

Harkenson laughed deprecatingly. "Sure."

Paul shrugged and tapped his pile of papers into an orderly heap. "I'd like to deliver the check in person. Where can I pick it up?"

Harkenson didn't notice Paul's eyes. If he had, he wouldn't have been so glib. "City office. I need nearly the full week to get all the authorizations. You know what it's like getting money from the city. I'll leave it with my secretary at City Hall, room 87." He stroked Paul's card before adding it to his papers. "I may be in touch. God knows I might need help if the union thinks I did something wrong. And I'll refer Marshall to you if he questions it."

"And get those flowers ordered. She had some perennials too: hollyhocks, coreopsis, shasta daisies. Give her a call. I'll see her myself when I bring her the check."

"Flowers. You know these Public Works guys?" The young lawyer looked ill.

"It's in black and white. The list of damages is right there in your hands."

Mr. Harkenson looked at his hands, long and delicate like those of a tall woman. They clutched his legal work. "Fine. I'll take care of everything." It was time to leave. He rose, smiling tensely, and extended his hand. Paul took it and shook hard; he didn't smile.

Tom Dempsey was running scared. When he left Jane's old school he had shucked his suit jacket and gone directly to the convent on Adams Street. By the time he got there he stank. He had worn the wool jacket for three hours; that and the stiff white shirt and sticky underwear had all combined to cause unprecedented deodorant failure on an unseasonably warm April day. Sister Mary O'Malley, in fact, didn't want to invite him in, so she didn't. One whiff was enough. "May I help you?"

"I need to find the kid, my cousin Jane. She been here?"

Sister Mary was hesitant to answer because Cecile did such odd things, but the girl *had* been there, and she was now safely gone, so it wouldn't matter. In fact, she would be doing the convent a favor, she thought. And Sister Mary wanted to get rid of this smelly young man in a hurry. "Well, she's gone now. Who knows where. I believe that lawyer friend had something to do with it. Mr. Dorys. He's in Boston."

"Oh, yeah? I heard of him. Well, great. Where's the kid now?"

Sister Mary frowned. "Oh, off on her own, probably," she improvised. "That's all I can say."

Tom Dempsey felt a surge of elation even as the door slammed shut, and Sister Mary had been quick enough to see it. "Oh, dear," she said out loud. "I shouldn't have." And she determined never to say a word about the smelly young man's visit. After all, she hadn't said much of anything.

It was still hot. The late afternoon sun was soaking into the pavement on Thorndike Street when Paul came out of the court house. The sky was pale, pollution-blue. He had a date at eight, which left three hours to kill. Leslie Urqueheart. At forty-two, Paul was still in love with Sister Cecile, but that didn't stop him from enjoying life. Leslie was a serious career person, and they experienced each other without any strings attached. Leslie was three years younger than he and plump. They had been getting together a lot lately. He walked fast to Cambridge Street.

"Dorys?"

Paul heard his name, mispronounced. He didn't like the tone of voice; so he kept walking toward Lechmere Station.

"Hey, man, that's you. Dorys. I know it is."

Paul stopped abruptly and the speaker smashed into him hard from behind. Paul stepped forward a foot, turned and looked back.

"You him?" The man was medium-sized, with black curly hair and a typical weightlifter's physique, all chest. He wore an open-neck knit shirt with a small bird on it. Dempsey had gone home and changed his clothes before his next encounter, but he still smelled.

"Sure."

"I need some info." Tom Dempsey puffed up another two inches. "I wanna know where the kid is. Where'd you put her?"

"I've got no kid."

"The Hersey kid."

Paul looked at the man. They were the same height. Paul kept in shape and wasn't much older, ten years older? Paul laughed and walked on, still grinning, still heading for the subway. He felt the punch, not too hard, on his right shoulder. Paul turned, still grinning; he loved a fight. One quick one to the jaw and the younger man swayed back, surprised. Cambridge Street just after five was always crowded, and the police were seconds away. It wasn't the place for a good fight.

"Get off it, punk," Paul said, continuing to grin. "We got too much company for what you have in mind." The briefcase with the Copy Cop envelope was tucked under his left arm. He made a gesture with his right, something only a fighter would understand. Paul was still impeccable in his expensive dove-gray suit when the officer came up. "Little misunderstanding, officer," Paul said. "Man here, I stepped on his toe. Hot day, hot temper. No harm done."

The officer eyed Tom Dempsey skeptically. "That so?"

"No problem, officer."

Paul waved cheerily and walked away. It took him five minutes to get to Lechmere Station, another four to get on the train. It was jammed, but Paul got off at the next stop, just across the Charles River. He was almost home. By tomorrow he would hear from that weightlifter again. He could count on it. Martin Moon wasn't being subtle sending a creep like that. What a fool.

5

ORLY was an airport cliché. Too windy outside, too cold inside, too much plastic. Voices, one language after another, and security, like a hidden nightmare, just visible on the edges. Sister Cecile's gold cross set off the metal detector. The alarm was painful, especially after three Scotches over the Atlantic.

"I only take off my cross at airports," she told Jane after the noise stopped, and she deftly flipped it over her head and handed it to the guard. She walked through the halo of protection a second time, silently. *"Merci,"* she smiled and retrieved the cross.

Passport control was curious about the two blond wigs in Jane's carryall. *"Pour la nuit,"* Jane said and was surprised when the words actually worked.

They took their time going to collect the baggage; gaggles of children wandered by and Jane listened. "All those little kids speak it," she muttered. "It took me six years, and I still can't do it right."

"You will," Sister Cecile said. "In six months you'll be a native."

"Will *she* speak it?" Jane looked at her stomach. Still somewhat flat, but queasy.

"Let's have a coffee somewhere and talk about that, Jane. I've got a car waiting for us, and we can head downtown and sit somewhere."

There wasn't much in the way of luggage. Jane would need an entirely new wardrobe. She would have soon anyway, maternity-style.

"Downtown," Jane repeated. "I'm in Paris." She was talking to herself. Her red hair stuck to her pale face, and the bright-red lipstick was worn to a respectable glow. She was a vibrant youngster, tall and slim, with more than the beginnings of womanhood. She had a dignity and self-knowledge beyond her years and a joy of living that Sister Cecile hoped would never leave her. But she was not cut out for the convent. What she needed was a nice young man.

"Avis next," Cecile said. "I asked Paul to order a little car, a Fiat. He probably put in an order for a Porsche." She picked up the bag and forged ahead in the direction of the car-rental office. Jane followed, blue eyes wide, trying vainly to see Paris in its airport. Then she watched Sister Cecile with her credit card, filling in forms, speaking in rapid French and finally leading Jane to the car—a low white Porsche.

Sister Cecile tossed the bag into the trunk. "He did it again," Cecile muttered. "Hop in."

Cecile drove fast. Jane found herself gripping the seat, and her question, stuck somewhere inside her during the first five high-speed miles, finally emerged when they slowed for heavier traffic near Paris.

"Are you really a nun?"

Cecile downshifted into third. The engine groaned softly, cutting in behind a slim tour bus filled with sunglasses and cameras. An ambulance went tooting by. "Yes, I really am. I have this credit card . . ."

Cecile hated explanations, but she had to tell Jane something about where all the clothes were going to come from. "Jane, I have quite a lot of money of my own, and I can charge unlimited things but only in certain categories, like anything of a nonreligious nature or not designated for the order. I use it for traveling, like this. And anything I buy for you is all right. And this car, it's all charged to the card."

"Don't you take vows?"

"Poverty, chastity, obedience. Mother Sulpicia, our Generalate, insists I make use of this card in any way I can.

I do it out of obedience. It does help the order indirectly because it pays for my travel. And I find secular charities. We stock a number of soup kitchens. Anything I can work out. But Paul . . ." She accelerated into the fast lane and passed a red Citroën. The speedometer read 100 kilometers per hour. "He always orders Porsches. He's got a thing about them." Cecile played with the gas pedal, in and out, around a slow truck loaded with bottles. Jane knew Sister Cecile was enjoying herself. She also realized Cecile was an exceptional driver. Jane had moved with a fast set in high school, and Martin had driven fast. Martin. Damn Martin. Jane forced her thoughts back to her predicament and it occurred to her for the first time that she may have brought it all on herself.

"You drive like you grew up behind the wheel," Jane said.

Sister Cecile smiled and looked straight ahead. "Yes."

Paris was closing in. They were coming from the south. Orly was eleven miles out into the country, but it wasn't country; it was French suburbia. Poplars in rows flashed by. Lots of traffic. Cecile couldn't resist another burst of speed and passed them all. "I'll fill you in," she said, "because you'll be here for a while, until the dust settles."

"What was I supposed to do? Be a good little girl and have an abortion? Kill the baby? Forget it happened?" Jane's words came out in a sudden screech of nerves and jet lag. "And then what? I could never face Martin. He hates me. My father doesn't love me! I had to do something, I really did! They were both so wrapped up in their tiny worlds: Martin squeezing every dishonest politician in town, Daddy running for office as though he were important. Do you wonder?"

The explosion subsided in an equally sudden burst of quiet. Cecile finally responded.

"Your father was insecure. He does love you. And he's not the first politician to have personal problems. It's time to tell me about Martin. How did you meet him?"

Jane wiggled in the bucket seat uneasily. Now that she

61

had spoken she felt better, but everything else was the same.

"He came to see Daddy one night about a year ago. To pester him about that letter, I suppose. Daddy wasn't home yet; so we sat and talked. I thought he liked me. I guess he did."

"Apparently he did. He's an older man. How old?"

"Oh, maybe thirty, thirty-two. He works downtown somewhere, in an office, I guess. He's got a secretary, Mrs. Parks, that I could call up when I wanted to reach him. He's listed in the phone book under 'Investment Advisories' or something. He gambles. I mean, he spends a lot of time at Rockingham now, that racetrack. He likes the Red Sox. People were always giving him money. Now I know why. I saw him hit some dude once, whack, whack, in the face. The guy started crying. Martin *does* have a lousy temper. It was awful. I was really embarrassed." Jane put her hand on her stomach and looked slightly sick. It could have been from Cecile's driving, or more likely the thought of Martin Moon.

"Extortion."

"He's crazy about money and he loves to control people."

"Apparently. Some people like power. He never hurt you, did he?"

"Well." Jane stopped. "I guess maybe I deserved it once in a while. It was nothing."

"No, it's never nothing. Believe me, nobody *ever* deserves to be hurt." Sister Cecile was suddenly furious at the thought of Jane's being hurt and thinking it was her own fault. The car took a wild swipe to the left, veered back to the right and straightened out.

"Shit," Jane choked, clutching the door handle.

"Sorry." Sister Cecile ground down on her teeth. "What else?"

Jane looked worried. "He might want me back."

Cecile already had figured that. She took a deep breath and forced her words to come out softly. "You're safe here, believe me. All you have to do is ride out your time and we'll work everything out."

Jane relaxed back against the seat, almost convinced. "I know," she said. "I know." Remembering the time Martin Moon had knocked her to the floor didn't upset her anymore. It was history and was never going to happen again. But she had seen the nun's distress and was determined not to tell Sister Cecile any more details of her life with Martin.

"Anyway, we're in Paris," Sister Cecile said, "the City of Light, and it's still early, I think." She blinked at her watch. "Six hours later here. Our flight left at eight, we were in the airport at four, our time. It took two hours to get through customs and collect the car . . . and my watch says six, which means twelve, I think. Is that right, Jane?"

"Right," Jane said.

Sister Cecile felt gratified by the quick response. Jane was back to normal. She wasn't sure *she* was, though, but she kept trying. "Lunchtime. It would be a little overwhelming to hit Notre Dame de Bon Conseil just yet. We should fortify ourselves first, don't you think?"

"Absolutely," Jane said. She had been calculating time herself. She looked down at her watch again. It was noon here, but she was functioning at a 6:00 A.M. level and had already been up for two hours. She had gotten up at four o'clock in the morning; no wonder her eyes felt sticky. "I'm not too hungry, though. I don't eat breakfast."

Cecile ignored that and pressed the horn down hard. Traffic in Paris was the same as in Boston except the cars were smaller, the streets were narrower, and the horns were like a hundred sheep bleating. Jane's head started to pound. She could just hear Sister Cecile's words floating above the din. "Breakfast is over. We've got to get by the time change fast, and the best way is to pretend we've been on their time all along. That means we eat a decent lunch. Otherwise we'll never manage dinner. You can take a nap once we arrive."

The nun turned abruptly onto another street, this time a

large one lined with trees and divided down the middle by an endless garden with statues at intervals.

"Comm. Ave.," Jane said, fighting for normalcy.

"Commonwealth Avenue in Boston was modeled after this particular street. L'Enfant designed Washington, D.C., after Paris, star-shaped and very confusing. Boston one-upped that by already having the major streets in place before city planning came into vogue."

"You're a tour guide," Jane murmured. "You have that voice."

"When I was seventeen I spent a summer here being the voice on a Cook's Tour bus. Sorry." She pulled off onto a tiny side street.

"*Rue du* something," Jane said, trying to read the poorly placed sign.

Minutes later the Porsche was jammed into a tiny space between two motorcycles and a huge truck. "Hop out, dear. We can walk to Le Camion from here. They have fabulous *jambon de Parme*."

Le Camion was a diner with sausages. Sausages were strung everywhere, alternating with cheeses, like Christmas lights. They were real. Jane had grown up eating in diners with perfectly scratched tables covered with a solid inch of polyurethane to preserve the antiquity and with walls strung with plastic sausages. Things were different at Le Camion. The table they sat at here was not round, not square, but somewhere in between and polished by a century of grease. Bread was brought by a waitress dressed in slim black pants with legs cut off at the calves and a knit top that fit. "*Oui?*" she said. She seemed to have no hips. Jane was to learn soon enough that many French girls gave that impression.

"You order," she whispered to Sister Cecile, and Cecile did so in her astonishing French.

"What was all that?" Jane asked when the waitress left.

"Basic ham and eggs for you. With cheese sprinkled around. And something resembling coffee." Sister Cecile pulled at the long loaf of bread and passed some on to Jane.

Suddenly Jane was starving. She had finished off half the loaf of bread by the time her omelette arrived, hot with melting Gruyère and tiny strips of ham. The coffee looked strange, white with scum; but it tasted more than adequate. Jane ate frantically, oblivious to Cecile, oblivious to France itself. When at last she stopped and sat back, her dark-blue eyes had lost their glazed look.

"Now," said Sister Cecile. Her own food had vanished discreetly.

"Now?"

"We talk."

"Talk." Jane looked guilty. She had an inkling that life was not always first-class airplane rides and omelettes, and she braced herself.

"You're safe here, Jane. Now, you told me you wanted to join the order and give up the child for adoption once he's born."

"She," Jane corrected. "Did I say all that?"

"Yes." Cecile decided to be merciful. "There was some anxiety involved. And some panic. But now you have time to think clearly. I want you to think over your plans, discover your motives. Look at the man you involved yourself with and see if you can find some truth somewhere. And, just in case you're worried about what you left behind, I did make sure your father got that letter of his. The one in the red file. I gave Paul instructions to return it just before we left. It's all taken care of and that part of the case is closed. We only have Martin to deal with."

"Good." Jane poked at the flotsam left in her coffee, then licked her finger cautiously. "About Martin. I thought I loved him," she said quietly.

"Until you decided he was bad?"

"Ummm."

"Or until you got pregnant and he wouldn't marry you?"

"That too."

"And your father was bad too?" Cecile probed.

"He was! You read the letter he wrote. He got some kid in trouble, wrecked her life."

"Like you? Your life is still very much intact." Cecile saw another clue of real distress in the tears that began to form in Jane's eyes. It was about time. "They're bad, you're bad, everybody's bad."

"It's true," Jane gulped.

Outside a heavy truck squealed by, rocking the building. They were still in Paris.

"And you want to be with good people like nuns and be good?" Cecile asked.

Jane nodded. Her nose turned red.

"You must remember we are all sinners. ALL." Sister Cecile had mastered the art of speaking in capital letters, and she smiled into Jane's skeptical stare. "Even ME," Cecile said.

"I really don't see how it's possible," Jane said.

"It's possible." Cecile looked at a sausage that was swinging very, very slowly above a huge jar of pickles. She wasn't supposed to scandalize children. The Lord had said that very firmly. "We all fight temptations every day." She was careful. Jane was not going to hear of Cecile's great sins, and she was clearly disappointed. Cecile could feel it. The waitress appeared again, eyeing the empty plates.

"L'addition, s'il vous plaît," Cecile said to the waitress. She spoke again to Jane. "I have a job for you in town. You can stay at the convent and work in our small hotel. It will give you time to yourself. The work will be enough to fill your days, and you'll have free time to see the city. And to think. How does that sound?"

Cecile's lecture on sin had stopped abruptly, and Jane felt she had been taken from one cliff edge to another. "Fine," she said. What else could she say? And a job would fill the time. It seemed she had a lot of time.

The convent of Notre Dame de Bon Conseil was set back behind a high red brick wall. Cecile dismounted from the Porsche to swing back the iron gate. Trees from an earlier century shaded the brick terrace where she finally parked and she sat back to take a deep breath of convent air. "It's not the same as out there," Cecile said. "The air here is definitely older. I guess because it was all built so long ago. . . ." Yet there was a breeze when Jane stepped out. It had to come from across the wall where Paris shimmered in the afternoon sun; a cool Parisian breeze. Birds sang and flowers grew along the wall where the sun scattered drops of filtered light.

The convent was the former home of a duke guillotined back when it was fashionable to guillotine dukes. The coat of arms, carved in stone, still showed. Only in the last thirty years had chemicals in the air eaten into the noble crest of two lions and the angel carrying a flaming sword. Pollution did exist here after all, Jane told herself. The thought offered a small degree of solace that she hadn't left everything behind.

An old sister in a full habit walked slowly up the path from behind the massive house. She was smiling broadly. *"Soeur Bernadette!"* Sister Cecile was more excited than Jane had ever seen her, and she watched as Cecile planted a kiss on each old cheek.

Jane began to speak slowly but in clear, unmistakable French. It had begun.

The good sisters had run a home for unwed mothers in Paris for half a century. Embarrassed children of nobility and bourgeoisie alike had found a safe haven here, hidden until they could return from their "visit with dear cousins in the country." Then abortions became popular and pregnancies became less an embarrassment than a burden of love. "Love children" were in, convents were out. Too many babies were no longer carried to term. The home for unwed mothers was out of business.

In 1968 Mother Sulpicia, hard-pressed for money to keep her good works afloat, talked seriously with a young investment counselor, her brother Frédéric. Freddy had pointed out that to be cost-effective, they needed more customers. "Run a hotel," he advised her in a string of French clichés.

67

"You have the building. Take out a loan, buy new sheets and dressers, and you're making money."

Now the Auberge de Notre Dame was well established, with a high-class clientele. The rooms were spacious and decorated with antiques donated by the patrons of the original building. Gratitude was a living thing. The food rated five stars and was prepared by Pierre Renoird, who had forsaken the pressure of a famous restaurant in the same arrondissement.

The Auberge faced Rue D'Argent but had a covered walkway winding between backyards that connected it with the convent. It had been essential for the nuns to have clear passage in winter to the home for their girls. Now the vine-covered corridor was used only by the several sisters still employed at the Auberge.

Sister Eugénie, with a degree in finance from the Sorbonne, was business manager. Sister Louise headed housekeeping. Postulants spent several hours each day with a variety of tasks. After some discussion it was decided to offer Jane a job as chambermaid. It was low visibility, and the bending and stooping would be good exercise for someone in her condition. As she grew more unwieldy, something less strenuous would be found.

"Does that suit you, Jane?" Mother Sulpicia had Jane before her in her office. Jane was not the first girl in such a condition in recent times. Even in the nineties there were others—an infrequent dribble of pregnant young women.

"*Oui, Mère Sulpicia,*" Jane said.

"I have arranged for our doctor to see you on Tuesday. You will receive room and board here at the convent, and the cost will be deducted from your salary. Sister Cecile suggested you might like to take classes at the Sorbonne this summer. We can adjust your schedule around your classes without any trouble, and you should have a full life. You will be working with several girls your own age, and you may do as you please during your free time. Mondays and Thursdays are off. Mass is in the chapel on those days at six thirty A.M. Other days it is across the way at St.

Damian's. Here is the key to the convent. Please inform Sister Madeleine if you will be later than midnight. She gets nervous."

"Oui, Mère Sulpicia," Jane said again. It was all in French, and Jane was cross-eyed with the effort of following the words. But she thought she had understood it all, and the convent key was in her hand. It was brass and ornate.

"You will begin work in five days. That should allow you ample time to become oriented." Mother Sulpicia rose in dismissal. She was computerizing records today and was behind schedule.

Jane stood and did something resembling a bow. *"Merci, Mère Sulpicia,"* she said. She had read a book about convent life once.

Mother Sulpicia laughed and strode out. She was fifty-seven and wore a gray business suit and a touch of pink lipstick. Her hair was iron-gray and waved nicely. Girls, she thought, will be girls.

6

MR. Harkenson was given the task of informing the union head of the Cambridge Public Works department that the matter of Howard Marshall and Lyuba McVey's flower garden had been settled. He finally called the union boss on April twelfth.

"She will receive damages of five hundred dollars from the city. I'll have her lawyer pick up the check within the week. But the area has to be replanted. Uh, her lawyer mentioned some perennials." Harkenson, the city lawyer, looked at his notes. "Shasta daisies, coreopsis, hollyhocks? That's your department."

Bill Harkenson held the receiver away from his ear for a full minute waiting for the union official's blast to subside. He smiled and returned the receiver to his other ear. Words were still pouring out. "I told him," the union man bellowed, "I told him he'd . . ."

Harkenson interrupted. "Now, I'm sure it was a mistake on Mr. Marshall's part; but even mistakes need recompense."

"I don't like disciplining my men for small matters, Mr. Harkenson, but I play by the rules. Mr. Marshall is not going to like this, believe me."

"I'm sorry about that, sir."

"How long have you had this job, Mr. Harkenson?"

"Uh, I don't see how that affects the case. The fact is, those flowers must be replanted. You must respond to justice. The opposing attorney made reference to the matter of why Mr. Marshall was in that particular place at that partic-

70

ular time. He even suggested that Mr. Marshall might have been having a drink in the café. Of course, I said this was impossible because it was on department time." Mr. Harkenson coughed discreetly.

"I see." There was silence.

Mr. Harkenson continued carefully. "The judge felt that the matter was equitably settled. I will have the papers sent over today about the settlement, but I felt you would like to know immediately. The plantings must be put in at the proper time, by court order. I'm sure that will pose no difficulty with the city union."

Another long silence.

"Mrs. McVey's attorney asked me about drugs in the department," the young lawyer continued. He was playing for his own defense now. He had no desire to change jobs just yet. "Apparently there has been a rumor about certain people in the field, uh, department, dealing with drugs, sir. Now, I told him I couldn't imagine such a thing, although what individuals do in their spare time is another matter entirely." Harkenson smiled into the receiver.

"Yes, well, I appreciate your giving me a call on this." The union man was suddenly more reasonable. "I'll take care of the matter."

"Wonderful. 'Bye now."

Bill Harkenson walked out of the office. He felt good at his power, but the union wasn't happy and that could mean future trouble. This just might be a nice time to take the two-week vacation he had coming after six months on the job. He had been thinking of skiing next winter. If he went now, there would be no vacation time then. Or maybe he should just quietly disappear for a while within the department itself.

"I'm going down to records, Esther," he told the secretary. There was always research on those housing permits. He could spend an entire month in the archives. Now, that was an idea!

Howard Marshall was duly informed by his union chief that his coveted position as driver had been awarded to

Darrel Smiley and that Howard would be on pickup. That meant trailing behind the big orange trash masher and tossing the trash in.

Howie's reaction to the demotion was silence, but there was a look in his eye that the union official didn't like at all. Mad Howie, they called him. An hour later Mad Howie himself was trailing behind the Works truck instead of driving it. He had put on considerable weight in the two years spent behind the wheel, and his muscles had lost some of their tone; but he managed, cursing and yelling and feeling sorry for himself. He would show these people, whoever they were, that got him demoted. He'd make more money than they'd ever dreamed of. He threw up a black plastic trash bag and it exploded in midair, dropping last week's leftover Spanish rice on Appleton Street. He laughed.

"Motherfuckers," he roared. "Motherfuckers!" He thought about the man he had shot behind the Norfolk Café, and it didn't feel half bad. It was nothin' but manslaughter, he told himself. Nothin'. He was a tough bastard; that proved it. If he had known the connection between his new job and poor dead Ray McVey, he just might have exploded too.

Paul Dorys had spent several days tying up loose ends. He had hand-delivered Mr. Hersey's original letter from Martin Moon's file. Paul's law partner would be taking his work load for a few weeks, and the paralegal had been given instructions. Cecile was gone, safely out of the country with that little redhead, and Lyuba McVey's case was settled. Everything was quiet and Paul was about to embark on a much-needed vacation to Mexico. Except for Lyuba's check, and that he really wanted to deliver himself. Paul had already contacted Harkenson about the money for Lyuba and was waiting on the Cambridge attorney's call. Paul had been a little concerned that the driver of the intransigent trash truck might cause trouble for Lyuba. It would bear watching.

Paul locked his office safe and gave his secretary her last

instructions. "I'll be out of town, Bessie. Call my answering machine and leave a message if there's an emergency. I'll check it now and then."

Bessie Bowen nodded. She had watched Paul reading Martin's collection of oddities earlier that week and had wondered about it. She was new in the office, a temp sec while Paul's ordinary secretary was taking a three-month maternity leave.

Paul walked home from his office with light steps. He felt great. Leslie was coming for dinner tonight, the weather was warm, and the Red Sox were winning. He ducked into Pasta Pronto on Charles Street and picked up a container of hot spaghetti and meatballs for their meal. He had wine at home, and Leslie had promised to bring some bread. He started to sing "O Sole Mio." It would be a good night.

Tom Dempsey fell into step beside him. "Dorys, we got things to settle."

"Sure we do." Paul nodded and grinned. He recognized the creep he'd met up with in Cambridge.

"Walk home, hot stuff. We've got business."

Paul looked at his bag of spaghetti sauce. "I don't have office hours there," he said politely. "Maybe later?"

"This gun says we walk." Tom was close beside him, and the gun in his jacket pocket glinted briefly. Paul saw it and nodded.

"Don't you trust those big fists of yours?" Paul asked pleasantly.

"Shut up and walk. You know that nun. I want that nun. I want that kid."

"I see," Paul said. He walked a little faster, throwing Tom off-stride. "Let's go."

"Right." Tom fingered the gun.

"Could you wait a minute?" Paul stopped abruptly and began to open the bag that held the hot food. "I think my spaghetti sauce is spilling."

Tom stopped, twisting the gun inside his pocket to point it at Paul, who had moved in front of him. What he wouldn't give to shoot the sucker.

73

Paul removed the round paper container from the bag and dropped the bag. "Hot," he murmured and opened the carton of sauce. He dipped a finger in and licked it. "Good stuff. Ever been there? Pasta Pronto."

He dropped his briefcase onto Tom's foot. "Pardon me," Paul apologized and flipped the open carton into Tom Dempsey's face.

"You slime." Paul said, too softly. Tom was covered with tomatoes; meatballs rolled down his chest. Then Tom's gun went off. A bullet ripped through Paul's jacket cuff. Scalded by hot sauce, Tom began roaring, "Fuckin' asshole," dropping his gun as he wiped frantically to clear his eyes of sauce. Meatballs were everywhere. Paul lifted a knee to plunge into Tom's stomach. Tom was swinging his fists by then, wildly, his eyes still blinded. He got in a punch to Paul's jaw, mashing him with tomato sauce. Paul turned, feinting a left, then smashed a quick right to Dempsey's head. Spaghetti sauce was flying, and the crowd that was gathering half a block down Revere Street where it met Charles Street thought it was blood. Nobody dared come close but somebody called the cops. It wasn't long before the wail of sirens could be heard.

Tom's gun had been kicked aside by the time a police officer arrived with his service automatic out. Paul had Tom on the sidewalk, his knees on the heavy man's elbows.

Paul was laughing. He saw the officer out of the corner of his eye. "Officer O'Reilly, this man accosted me. He must have been starving. He jumped me for my meatballs. Crazy fool jumped me for my meatballs!"

Paul got up from his stunned opponent. "I'd say take him down to the station and see what he was doing with that Saturday-night special over there." Paul eyed the spaghetti-sauced gun distastefully. "Cheap gun. Could blow up in his hand."

"Mr. Dorys, you're pressing charges?" Officer O'Reilly had Tom up and was slipping the cuffs on. It wasn't easy. Tom's wrists were slippery with tomato sauce.

"Officer, he's in enough trouble having this gun. I'd say

74

what this poor man needs is a good meal down at the station house. Having spaghetti tonight, aren't you?"

"Might be, might be." Officer O'Reilly read out the rights just as the Metropolitan police car arrived.

"Bloody murder," the second policeman muttered. "I don't want this sucker in my car. Call the wagon."

Paul nodded. "Good thinking. I'll be off. Officer O'Reilly, if you need me, I'll be around."

His briefcase was near where it had hit the ground. Paul retrieved it and looked inside. There was no sauce on his papers, just the few briefs he was planning to look at tonight. He wasn't carrying the file copy anymore. In fact he had it at home and was planning on burning it. After a very thorough reading he had decided it was too hot to keep with him. The originals and the copies in the bank were more than enough. He closed the case and started a slow jog up the hill, waving to the policemen.

Cecile would have enjoyed that, he thought.

Two hours later, showered and shining, Paul opened the door to Leslie. Leslie had brought fresh Italian bread and a large bottle of chianti, and she was wearing an ankle-length red skirt and loose white top. With long, black hair falling to her shoulders, she looked beautiful. Paul kissed her on the lips. She smelled of lilies. "Pesto sauce on the spaghetti tonight," he said, relieving her of the bread and wine. "Sound good?"

"Parfait," Leslie said, sniffing delicately. "Funny, I could have sworn I smelled tomato sauce somewhere."

7

RAY McVEY's body was found by a street person who lived on the edges of Boston Harbor. The tramp knew about the trash barge that docked there and he couldn't miss the bright red sneaker showing among the trash bags. Hopping onto the barge was a trick he had perfected years ago, and he did it again. He pulled at the shoe, size ten, cursed that it was stuck, then gagged at his discovery. But when Leonard Barker, formerly of the Pine Street Inn, went down to the precinct house to report the body, he was wearing new red Reeboks.

By evening the police determined that the trash with the body had most likely come from a dumpster situated behind the Norfolk Café in Cambridge. The subject's identity had been made immediately from visual recognition by one of the officers in charge. Definitely Raymond McVey of Cambridge. Fingerprints on record confirmed this.

Lyuba McVey was informed of her son's demise and was rushed immediately to Cambridge City Hospital with severe breathing problems. The Cambridge police were informed and shook their collective heads at the murder. Ray had provoked the ire of half a dozen minority groups in town. Haitians, Portuguese, Greeks, Italians, Vietnamese. Not to mention half the police department itself. Anybody would have killed him given half a chance. Detective Limper was assigned to the case in Cambridge.

"A plum," he said bitterly, when handed the assignment. "A plum." He had known Ray McVey.

He began by checking bars. Ray had regular habits, and

it should be easy to find who had sold him a beer last. Strangely enough, nobody had, but a salesman in Miglani's Liquor Store on Hampshire Street remembered selling two six packs to a man of Ray's description. Fat, facial scars, red sneakers.

Detective Limper called the station house. "What kind of shoes was McVey wearing when they found the body?"

"None. He was in his socks. Tramp that reported the body was wearing new red sneaks. Like, maybe they came off the stiff. Desk officer made a note."

"That's it. Ray for sure."

A neighbor on Elm Street told Limper that Lyuba McVey was in Cambridge City Hospital. There, in a ward with three other women, Detective Limper found that Ray had indeed been wearing new red Reeboks on the day he had vanished.

"And what was on his mind last, Mrs. McVey?"

"My flowers," Lyuba wheezed. "My lovely coreopsis." Tears streaked down the old woman's face. "He was a dear boy, a wonderful son, always thinking of me."

"Flowers," Detective Limper said and dismissed the whole idea. He knew Ray McVey better than that. "And who was he hanging with?"

Lyuba looked dazed. Her old skin was the color of limestone, dented and pocked by age. "Nobody. I don't know. He was going straight, Ray was going straight. He was looking out for his mother. He was such a good boy." She ended with a blubber. Distraught with grief, she hadn't even realized herself that she had as good as named the murderer. She began to wheeze loudly and Limper backed out, convinced Lyuba knew nothing.

There were no nurses in sight. A cleaning woman was aiming a huge floor buffer at him, and he smiled at the cleaning woman, who said something to him in Portuguese.

It was going to be a long, slow case.

Paul was packed for his vacation and waiting to clean up his last problem when he finally heard from Bill Harkenson. He had stopped by the office to see if there had been any important calls, and he was there when the call came in.

"Cambridge City Attorney's office," Bessie told Paul. Paul was standing two feet away leafing through the mail.

"I'll take it," he nodded. Paul went into the inner office and picked up the phone with a litigious grunt. Meanwhile Bessie started looking through the mail, curiously.

"I've got the McVey check here. You wanted it personally?" It was Bill Harkenson.

"Yes."

"And the new plantings will be done in May."

"Any problems?"

"Mrs. McVey was out, apparently. I'll call her again later. My notes here say they ordered half a dozen coreopsis, couldn't find any hollyhocks but can get tea roses, and some ageriatum. The Public Works department wasn't happy with the settlement."

"Any problem for you?" Paul was legitimately concerned. Howard Marshall was a real heavy. Paul had reread the red file, and Marshall's Cambridge drug supplier was a city official who wouldn't like to see his gofer moved down.

"No, not a word. I was concerned at first, Mr. Dorys, but I mentioned what you had said about drinking during hours and the possibility of drugs. The Department of Public Works offered complete cooperation."

"Smart." But not too. "Bill, I'd go light on that. Stir muddy waters, you don't know what's down there."

"Is there something I should know?" Bill Harkenson was nervous. He had the sensation he was feeling his way blindly through the morass of politics and nepotism of Cambridge.

"The waters are muddy," Paul repeated. "I'll be by later today to pick up the check."

Bill Harkenson hung up with a very restrained "damn." Paul Dorys knew something that he, Bill, should know, and he hadn't the foggiest notion of how to find out for himself.

78

Harkenson was in the file room when Paul arrived for the check. It was a simple matter to get it, sign a receipt, and head back to Elm Street for a triumphant presentation of the money to Lyuba McVey. She would love it. Traffic was light on Broadway, and by two thirty Paul had pulled up his car in a parking place near the McVey residence.

Lyuba came to the door almost instantly. She looked ill. "Paul!" she gasped. "Tea? Whiskey? I'm so upset! I just got out of the hospital this morning. I couldn't breathe! My life is at an end ... my joy ... my son. My son is gone!" She backed in to give Paul room to enter and spilled her whiskey on his suit jacket.

"Where is he this time?" Paul was not sympathetic. It was cheap whiskey.

"Dead. He's dead." Her voice turned to a hush. "My baby. My boy." She was already at the coffee table where her bottle waited. Her old hands shook, but she managed.

"Get a glass," she said. "I'll pour you one."

Paul did as he was told. He went to the kitchen and returned with a glass, almost clean, and allowed her to splash whiskey around it. He took a hesitant sip and set it down. He was truly shocked about Ray. "Lulu, I'm sorry. Poor kid. What happened? You take it easy. Sit down. Sit." Lyuba was moving restlessly, her hands quivering over tops of furniture as though searching for her son. The drink was pressed against her bosom, precariously held by her forearm. She sat.

"God help him, Paul. They found his body in Boston on a barge. He was shot. They think he was tossed in a dumpster here in town, and the dumpster was taken to the harbor. The café dumpster. The damn Norfolk Café dumpster." Her words were low and moaning. "I cried a lot for that boy, every day of my life it seems like. For thirty years I cried for him, and I ain't crying no more. But he had a good streak in him, Paulie. You know he did."

"He was your son, Lulu, he must have." Paul made a mental reservation. He had brought Ray out of detox at the

Cambridge Hospital too many times to hunt for the man's good points.

"I know who killed Ray, Paul. It was that man he was going to see. Ray asked me all about him before he went out the last time. I told the police what was on his mind then, I told them about my flowers, so they'll get that killer. It's only a matter of time. I'll let them do it, but they better hurry. The police will find out, won't they, Paul?"

"Absolutely. They always get their man." Paul reached for the check in his pocket, relieved that the police had it all in hand. He was free to leave town. "When is the funeral?"

"Tomorrow. The wake's at Brown's, the funeral at Saint Mary's at nine. Can you be there, Paulie?" Tears dripped down her face.

"I'll be there." Paul shook his head sadly for the old woman. "And I've got the check for you, for the flowers."

Lyuba's hand was out before he finished his words. The money would go a little way toward making her feel better about Ray.

Paul was prattling, which he rarely did, but he felt just a touch of guilt for his lack of sorrow for the deceased. He had a soft spot for Lulu. "The town's going to put in some flowers for you. At planting time, they said. Can I see the flower bed?"

"Yes. Thank you, God. Something has come out from all this. The man called me about that. Terrible, terrible . . ." She stuffed the check into her dress front. "Roses, flowers, new flowers, like they knew there was gonna be a funeral coming. Flowers for my boy."

Paul followed her out the back door as she was speaking, discreetly dumping his drink down the kitchen drain as he passed. He went behind her into the backyard while her words rose and fell like an unhurried stream, slow and dense with age. Paul missed the meaning of what she was saying entirely. An hour later he was back in his apartment on Revere Street, opening a Sam Adams and thinking about

Mexico. He'd be leaving directly from Ray's funeral, to-morrow.

Sister Cecile was enjoying Paris, and after quite an effort she was satisfied that Jane would manage in her new environment. She had taken Jane shopping for maternity clothes at *Au Printemps,* and then on to other stores. It had been fun, outfitting in Paris. They had dined out, seen two shows (to acclimate Jane to Parisian culture, Cecile had explained), and climbed the Eiffel Tower. Jane was blooming under the attention. Their last trek was to the Louvre. When they returned to the convent later that day, there was a telegram from Paul, and Cecile stuffed it in her pocket to read later when she caught her breath. Mère Sulpicia had left a note for her to stop by for a chat. That seemed more important at the moment. She told Jane she would catch up with her later.

She met Mère Sulpicia in her office and immediately was put to work.

"Maybe I should have married Paul and been a mother," Sister Cecile confided to Mère Sulpicia. They were sorting computer printouts into stacks for mailing. Sulpicia had bought into another hotel and had decided some promotional activity was in order. The newly acquired Hôtel du Lac, in Grasse, needed serious renovations.

"We've been through this before." Sulpicia pulled out her postage meter. "Paul isn't a Catholic. He's Jewish. It would have been a difficult marriage."

"He should have been a Catholic." Cecile snipped excess paper off a crooked printout.

"You would still have entered the order."

"I know."

"So you're doing it again, Cecile."

"What?"

"You still have trouble letting go, don't you?"

"All that money. Daddy's money."

"You would have given it away if you'd received it, Cecile. Even when you were little you used to give away

81

everything in that big apartment in Nice. Every beggar in France used to head down when the word was out that Cecile Buddenbrooks was back."

"Once I gave away a Chinese vase to a traveling peddler," Sister Cecile reminisced. "My mother had to call her friend in Marseilles, who had a similar one, before Daddy found out!"

"You gave all your clothes to Marie La Farge, except for one old dress. What a trial! I had to explain to your father. He almost took you out of the school. Remember?"

Cecile nodded. "Good thing Swiss schooling has snob value. I had to convince Daddy I was getting a superior education to let me stay. That was when I made the deal with him to go to Barnard. Four years of secularism. He was sure that would cure me, especially with Paul still in New York. He thought we would marry. He just didn't understand the concept of having a religious vocation."

"Um . . ." Sulpicia riffled through more papers, pressed some computer keys, and waited for another printout.

"Paul thought we would marry. He still proposes now and then." Cecile stared out the window.

"He still loves you." It was a statement. The older nun was worried. Cecile hadn't been on this track in years.

"Yes. But he dates other women."

"Good."

The printout was complete and Mère Sulpicia pulled it out. It was a list of creditors.

"I would never leave the order," Cecile said after a long silence. The ghosts fled, but words came out softly. "But I love Paul, and I'll always love Paul."

Sulpicia smiled. "When temptations cease, you'll know you're dead."

Then Cecile spoke normally.

"I tried to tell Jane that none of us are immune," she mused. "She didn't believe me. I'm actually quite sure that she doesn't have a vocation, but the Lord knows better than I. Have you discussed it with her?" Sister Cecile had given up all pretense of working. Her hands were busy with the scissors, cutting graceful pictures in the air while she spoke. Mère Sulpicia watched, still bemused by Sister Cecile's dignity, which held true to form in the most remarkable situations.

"We haven't spoken about it yet," Sulpicia declared. "Of course God does choose the strangest people for his work. She needs some time to understand our life. No doubt she'll change her mind. She appears to enjoy being a chambermaid, but it's only been a short time. Marie is on with her. Marie is the same age and avoiding a difficult situation at home—two of a kind, as I see it. Marie is from a rather fine family, but the father drinks and the mother can't cope and Marie was running around with a bad crowd. Drugs, you know. She's doing well now and has a boyfriend. Nothing serious so far, but time will tell. She and Jane will be taking summer courses together at the Sorbonne as you suggested."

"You have been busy." Cecile snipped, annoyed that Mère Sulpicia had done so much already. Jane was her charge, after all.

"You're miffed, Cecile."

"I'll get over it." Cecile put the scissors down. "You're right as usual, and I'll feel grateful eventually."

"You'll be back in Boston next week."

"Yes." Cecile nodded. "I'm speaking at Sainte Germaine du Bois tomorrow about the retirement home. It's always been a generous parish, and the home being in America might appeal to them. So many French still regard America as barbarian, and they feel they're helping support a community on the edge of civilization."

"How true," Sulpicia murmured. Even Sister Cecile had been wild not too many years ago. Part barbarian.

"I have return reservations for May third. I'll be way ahead of time for our Independence Day. Ours came first, you know."

"Really no comparison with Bastille Day. We were never owned by another country."

Cecile allowed one eyebrow to rise. "There have been

moments. I recall some recent history when the Germans sat in this very room. Didn't your predecessor say something about the rum in the basement?"

"Well, the resistance was in a section of the Auberge then. You know that, dear."

Cecile rose. It was time to go, and she wanted to read the cable from Paul before vespers.

"Thank you, Mère Sulpicia," she said as a matter of form, and she backed out. Her earthly boss nodded and breathed a sigh of relief as the door closed. Rum in the basement—how had Cecile ever found out about that?

Sister Cecile went to the chapel and slid into a back pew. She knelt and said a quiet prayer, conscious of the flickering red light on the side altar and the presence of her Lord. Then she read the cable: "S. Cecile. Raphael has big check from Abe. Martin on warpath. Watch out. Love. P."

Dinner came and went, and not one of the good French sisters questioned Sister Cecile's absence. She was so often somewhere else. Night fell. No one knew that she wasn't in her bed until 11:00 P.M. when Soeur Léonie came to Cecile's room with a second cable marked "Urgent" and found the bed empty. Sister Léonie left the cable there on Cecile's bed and tiptoed out without question. Earlier she had seen the door to the chapel open, had seen the small figure in the back pew, and had guessed that Sister Cecile was still there.

Not until some time after breakfast did Sister Cecile discover the paper in her room, resting on her unused pillow. She opened it almost unconsciously. "Cecile," it read, "Sister Mary Aida dead. Funeral at St. Gregory's Tues., 11 A.M. Please come. Raphael."

Aida was dead? Cecile felt cold. "Please come." That meant dire urgency. Cecile packed rapidly. There was nothing to pack, really, except the spare toothbrush she had picked up before leaving and the peculiar outfit she had arrived in. She had bought another dark skirt and white blouse while shopping with Jane, and today she was wearing that. The blouse could have been rinsed out, but there was no time.

Cecile knocked gently on Jane's door and found only rubble: clothes strewn with teenage abandon, several copies of the fashion mag *Elle* on the half-made bed, and cosmetics in wild disarray on the dresser. This was the child who was a chambermaid! Cecile smiled and wrote a note on the back of the menu from Méditerranée, where they had dined together two nights earlier.

"Good luck. I'll be in touch," she wrote.

That should do, Cecile thought, and she signed her name in her small, orderly script and placed the menu on top of the scattered cosmetics. Then she went to tell Mère Sulpicia.

The only seat available on the next connecting flight between Paris and Boston was in the first-class section. Not at all hungry, Sister Cecile was presented with a lunch of truffles and foie gras and braised duck. She forced herself to eat and drink the champagne. There were blanched asparagus tips in hollandaise sauce and a salad with slivers of radishes and a light dressing. She skipped dessert to contemplate the endless blue Atlantic below and the dancing clouds, cream puffs in the sun. It was May first and she was returning a few days earlier than planned. Jane was settled in, Sister Aida was dead. It was hard to take it all in. Finally she slept.

8

THE funeral was packed. It was a sad assemblage in shades of gray and black and blue, solemn and decorous and, for the most part, old. Sister Mary Aida had been seventy-three years old and very sick. Her death had been expected. But not like this. Everyone had contemplated a long and peaceful passing in a comfortable hospital setting. Everyone's face registered shock. Sister Raphael, a contemporary of the deceased, looked deathly pale. Her wrinkles were quivering and the look in her blue eyes registered urgency as she glanced to the rear of the church each time there was a sound from the old swinging door. She was looking for Cecile.

The Mass of the Resurrection had already started when Sister Cecile finally crept in and slipped into a back pew. The first reading was about to begin and she still didn't know what had happened. She had arrived to an empty convent and, after a quick change, had raced to the church, barely in time. She had already decided against going to the actual interment in Brighton and was trembling from fatigue from the long flight and the hurried jog to church. And she was understandably anxious. Besides the usual contingents, the funeral Mass had attracted several Boston policemen. What could have happened?

Groups of religious from all over the diocese came piling out of the church after Sister Aida received the Church's final blessing. Raphael quickly found Sister Cecile.

"Cecile, I've got to talk to you," Raphael whispered loudly. Nuns and priests were milling outside the church, finding cars and limousines for the drive to the cemetery. Cecile moved close to Raphael so they couldn't be overheard.

"Can you make it back to the convent now, Raphael? Can you walk?" Cecile asked.

"I can walk." Sister Raphael allowed one of those looks to appear on her face. The look, Cecile told herself, of an old woman who can still, contrary to popular opinion, move mountains and walk miles. "Can you make it yourself?" Sister Raphael began to walk briskly, not waiting for Cecile. The convent on Adams Street was six blocks away.

Cecile caught up. "Tell me, Raphael. What happened?" She took her old friend by the arm, not sure who would be holding up whom. Sister Raphael began speaking fast.

"I'm glad you understood. Sister died fending off those villains. It was terrible, Cecile, terrible."

Tears dropped softly, and Sister Raphael slowed down to cry better. Cecile could feel Raphael shaking. "She was dying of cancer. Did you know that, Cecile? She had just months to live, weeks to suffer. Stomach cancer, and she had asked me not to allow them to give her painkillers. She wanted to suffer for sinners. They say she died instantly."

"Exactly how did she die? Who was there? What happened?" Cecile felt a growing sense of panic.

Sister Raphael sighed deeply and produced a large white hanky from up her sleeve. She blew her nose. "Well, you see, it was heart failure. Those men came to the convent. Threatened her, I'm sure, and she just collapsed."

"What men? What were the police doing at the funeral?"

"Well, here's what happened." Raphael had regained some control of herself. The fresh spring breeze and the walk were working wonders. She gasped for air and began to speak. "I was the only one who saw them. Poor Aida had taken over answering the telephone in the mornings. She wanted to help, and it was something she could still do. So, of course when these men came to the door, she was there and answered it, and we'll just never know everything they said. I was in your office working on the bills and had the door open. I could hear voices. I swear one of them said, 'Where is she?' And then I think I heard someone saying, 'The kid. Where's the kid?' And there were more words I couldn't make out. Then I heard Aida's little voice. I couldn't understand a thing she said, so I got up from your desk. I thought I'd better go see. I definitely heard one man say, 'Shit, she's passed out.' That was it, exactly. 'Shit.' I heard a thud and the men must have left because the front door slammed. I came rushing in and there she was right down on the parlor rug, white as a ghost. She died on the parlor floor! I told the police absolutely everything just like that," Raphael sobbed.

"Oh, dear Lord," Cecile said, giving Raphael a big hug right where they stood on the corner of Potosi Street. "How terrible for her. How terrible for you."

They stood in silence, lost in their sorrow over Aida's death. Then, very slowly, they finished the walk home.

It wasn't until later, after a light lunch, when emotions had settled into a soft acceptance of God's will, that Sister Cecile approached Sister Raphael again. She found Raphael alone in the nuns' lounge reading investment reports. "Is there anything else?" she asked.

"I'm sure it was Martin Moon's friends," Raphael said. "But I have no proof. Of course I called Father to give the last rites, and the police, but it wasn't murder, according to them. The autopsy showed heart failure, and Dr. Flannery said that was perfectly normal in a person with Aida's problems. It could have happened for no reason at all, Doctor said. The merest exertion could have brought it on. They sent some officers to the funeral because I was worried and I'm afraid Sister Louise said something about that girl who came, causing all the trouble. They had to be the hoodlums connected with that man you told me about. They *were* looking for Jane."

"You're right." Sister Cecile felt terrible. A person she had loved was dead. Moon's evil cronies were still around and they would be back. She couldn't allow them to come to her convent. One death was enough. It was all her fault and she came very close to crying and began to sniffle. She turned to leave, but there was one more thing that bothered her.

"Did you really say 'Shit' to the police?"

"I only reported what was said," Raphael affirmed with dignity. "Exactly as I heard it."

"Exactly," Cecile said, and blew her nose. She was going to call Martin Moon.

Martin had an office on Harwich Street, near Copley Place. He was listed as a financial adviser, although he had no visible clients. When someone called for financial advice, his secretary would say that Mr. Moon was booked solid and wasn't taking on any new accounts. Most days Mrs. Parks filed her nails, read the *Boston Globe,* and had a nice lunch with her friend who owned the boutique on Newbury Street. Several times a week she was called upon to field visitors coming to see Martin about discreet matters. Often she took calls from Martin's real estate tenants. The telephone call from a Sister Cecile fit no circumstance she had yet dealt with, and she was grateful Mr. Moon was in today to take the call. "There's a Sister Cecile on line two," she said into the intercom.

Martin had been studying a racing form. "I'll take it," he said and felt his stomach stir. He hadn't been to Mass since he was fourteen, and that had been for his mother's funeral. Modern nuns were a vast unknown.

"Yes?" He had a frog in his throat.

"Mr. Moon? I'm calling about Jane Hersey. I'd like to meet and discuss her. I believe we have a mutual interest in the woman."

Martin had never thought of Jane as a woman, and he wondered if they were thinking of the same person. Jane had been a girl. Great body. Suddenly she was a woman. His woman. Shit. This was it! "What can you tell me?"

"If we could meet?" Sister Cecile asked.

"Certainly. This afternoon?" That was too quick, Martin

89

told himself. He shouldn't appear anxious. He strangled his telephone and grinned.

"Five thirty," she said. "There's a small restaurant on Hanover Street called Mandolina's. I'll be there." Sister Cecile twisted a curl, waiting for his reply. Joey Angiulo had dined in Mandolina's every day for years and had always raved about the calamari. Maybe it was time to break old habits and try something new. She could order some calamari while she was there.

"Mandolina's," Martin repeated. "I'll be there."

"Fine, thank you." Sister Cecile hung up, knowing she had scored one. The hour was early, and the restaurant would be empty. Any stranger would be suspect. She dialed another number. *"Pronto,"* she said, "Giuliano?"

"Sì?" The guttural voice was familiar, and Cecile broke into rapid, ungrammatical Italian. There would be no surprises when she dined at Mandolina's. And no calamari. It wasn't on the menu tonight.

Martin Moon was less sanguine. He had a client coming with a late payoff at four thirty. Mrs. Parks would have to deal with that, and that was too bad. He'd intended to put the screws on this guy for more money. Maybe get one of his buddies to lay a few punches, maybe do it himself just for fun. But simple pleasures could wait.

He stood up and paced the floor, forgetting to admire the new green sculpted rug that had been installed Tuesday. Then he sat down and forced himself to concentrate on the racing form. No damn nun was going to disturb his day. Not a chance. Not even the red file was worth losing a day at the races. An hour later he went into the outer office where Mrs. Parks was reading a copy of *Glamour* magazine. She didn't even look up at his approach.

"Any mail?" he asked gruffly. Mrs. Parks winced at his tone, then began her daily report.

"Something from Pratt and Lambert, a bill from the rug company, and a payment was dropped off from the Cambridge account." She spoke in a clipped voice. She pushed out an envelope filled with cash.

He scooped up the payment. That would be the politician in Cambridge who imported drugs from somewhere in south Texas by way of New York. A Department of Public Works man in Cambridge was his distributor, Howie something. Martin Moon returned to his office with a frown, his hands full of the newly received bills to count. He didn't like this one, didn't usually get into drugs, but it was too good an opportunity to score and he was greedy. Jane had never been into drugs. He wouldn't have touched her if she had. Damn her anyway. Why had she gone and got knocked up and taken the damn file, just when things were smooth? He clenched his fist around the money and stuffed it into his pocket, uncounted. Jane was a festering thorn in his mind. He'd get her.

He decided to take a walk over to the South End, drop off the cash in his bank and get some exercise. He straightened up his desk, checked out his hair in the marble bathroom in the rear of his office, then headed for the door. "Mrs. Parks, there will be someone by at four thirty; you'll have to take care of it. I'll be out the rest of the day. Close up at five."

"Certainly, Mr. Moon."

Martin glanced at his watch as the elevator dropped. Three o'clock. He should have lunch too, but he was meeting that nun in a few hours. Five thirty was too early to eat, but maybe nuns ate early. Or did they eat at all? Nuns probably ate early, he told himself. First the bank, then he'd stop for a sandwich at Ugies on Tremont Street, check out the art show at the Mills Gallery and look for something to hang on his office walls. By then it would be time to go to Hanover Street. Mandolina's. Gangster hangout.

When the client came to Martin's office at four thirty, Mrs. Parks was reading *Better Homes and Gardens*. "Oh, yes," she said coolly to the short pale man with the manila envelope clutched in his hand. "Mr. Moon had an emergency and left early. I'll take care of that." She took the envelope, opened it, counted out five hundred dollars in twenty-dollar bills, and made a careful but cryptic note in a large blue ledger. "Mr. Brown, is that correct?"

Mr. Brown nodded.

"I'll credit it to your account," she said.

The man backed out and, when the door had snapped shut, Mrs. Parks glided into the rear office to slip the envelope into something that resembled a night-deposit box. Mr. Moon would find it later. She sighed and returned to her desk, tipped her chair back, and picked up where she had left off in "Good Eating for Good Health" on page 47.

Death. Martin Moon was responsible for Aida's death. Maybe it hadn't been murder in the eyes of the police, but she knew better. The words raged quietly through Sister Cecile's mind. She was totally exhausted from the flight from France, but instead of a nap she changed into some coveralls, went out the back door of the convent on Adams Street, and began to dig in the garden.

The asparagus was up and almost gone by already. The trenches needed weeding and fertilizing, to be made ready for another year of tender stalks. Behind the asparagus the earth needed to be dug and turned for lettuce, tomatoes, squash, all the things that would soon grace the convent table. Romaine would be good this year, Cecile thought as she turned the heavy earth. It must have rained recently. Sister Germaine would take care of planting. End of May in this climate, or sooner if one took a chance on the weather. But Sister Aida was dead.

Sister Cecile cried among the weeds and the raw, damp earth.

By four o'clock Sister Cecile had showered and dressed in a white blouse and cool blue skirt. Her gold cross was in place, and her hair curled damply about her face. The veil, perched on auburn waves, stood out almost straight. She would stop by the chapel before leaving, she thought, and headed downstairs to the main corridor.

She was interrupted by Sister Raphael. "Cecile, the police are here. It's about that girl who stopped by. They think it's a clue to Aida's death because Sister Louise said something to them about it." Sister Raphael's eyes were wide and innocent, and her mouth twitched. "Can I come with you? They're in the office."

Sister Cecile nodded.

"Officers." She strode into the room, Raphael in her wake. The two men rose and looked, then began to fumble. Cecile impressed the hell out of them with her single word. They didn't even notice Sister Raphael behind her. Cecile sat at the desk, and the policemen resumed their seats. "How can I help you?" she asked.

"I'm Officer Pine. This is Detective Gomes. We want to know about the girl who was here. We think she was behind these men who came to your convent. Just tying up loose ends, after what some of the other nuns said."

"You do consider Sister Mary Aida's death accidental," Cecile said carefully.

"Of course." Officer Pine stopped; his prepared speech had run out and he turned red. His hand reached for a cigarette in his breast pocket, then pulled away when he remembered where he was. Maybe this wasn't a police matter at all.

"Yes, I remember the girl," Cecile repeated and looked thoughtful as though she were trying to recall the incident. "I believe that was a referral from one of the grammar schools in the diocese, poor thing. She arrived very late one night." She sighed. "These days teenagers have a multitude of reasons for leaving home at midnight. She knew we were here and came looking for a bed. Of course we let her in. She stayed through the next day until things cooled off. At least I hope they cooled off. And of course she left that evening. You wouldn't believe how often this kind of thing happens."

She looked at the detective, who was staring at her, wondering. He had heard about this particular nun. His chief had, in fact, warned him about a Sister Cecile who had been mixed up in odd things. It was a scandal that she held an investigator's license. Yet there had been talk . . .

Sister nodded in his direction, not missing his expression. She directed her next comment at him. "I would certainly help you if I could."

Detective Gomes drilled his fingers on the narrow arm of the chair. "I believe that," he said. "Do you have the girl's name? Her address?"

Cecile was aware of the time. She would have to take a cab now to keep her appointment with Martin Moon, and with that thought she suddenly decided to play it straight. "Jane Hersey, that was her name. A sweet child. She mentioned that she attended Boston Latin and was planning to go to Boston College in the fall but was terribly concerned that she wouldn't be able to, the way things looked. I didn't really press her on that. Schooling is touchy. It involves so much money . . . and parental approval."

There. That was enough information to choke a horse, but Cecile had serious doubts that it would lead the policemen anywhere. Abe Hersey was not about to spill the beans on Jane. Not now. "That's all I can tell you, officers." She glanced down at her watch.

The detective's pencil scribbled and he nodded finally. "Well, I guess that's fine. And what happened with the old nun—you don't think there's any connection?"

"Heavens, I wasn't even in the country when that happened. I couldn't really say." She rose. "Please feel free to come back for any reason," she added.

"We will." Officer Pine wore the bemused grin that Sister Cecile's smile caused on most men. It wasn't that she was beautiful. Or was she?

The two men left. Sister Raphael escorted them away, murmuring polite things behind them as they went out wondering about truth and beauty and other profound questions. The heavy door clicked shut behind them, and Sister Raphael scurried back to Cecile's office.

"You told them too much, Cecile. They'll get to Jane

from that. Her father will tell them everything. You shouldn't have, Cecile. I thought you knew better!"

Sister Cecile had already ordered a taxi and she was pulling some money from her petty-cash drawer. "Raphael, all I gave them was a name. They'll talk to Abe Hersey, and he won't say a word, believe me. For one thing, he doesn't know where Jane is. He did hire me to protect her from Moon, and who knows where Moon might have connections. Abe won't say a thing that might hurt his chances to win this next election; from what I hear, he's a shoo-in otherwise. The last thing he wants is the death of Sister Mary Aida connected to his daughter. He'll probably give them some tall tale about her visiting an aunt in Missouri for the summer. Or perhaps a trip to Paris." Sister Cecile chuckled. "From what I could see of Abe Hersey, he isn't a bad man. He's really quite ordinary. He spoke to Paul, who returned his letter, and Abe was really pleased, but to his credit, Paul informed me that Abe appeared even more pleased to hear that his daughter was doing well. And don't worry about the police. Of course I won't lie for Jane, but I'm not obligated to say more than I already have. If they choose to believe one thing or another from what I say, who am I to feel guilty?"

"The day you feel guilty . . ." Sister Raphael turned pink.

"Raphael, I have an incredible conscience."

"Incredible," the old nun said. "And just where are you going now?"

"Out to dinner." Cecile spoke quickly. "I've got to run."

"It's something dangerous, isn't it?" Raphael positioned herself by the door, and Cecile knew she didn't stand a chance of getting by without hearing some kind of advice.

"You must be careful, dear."

"Of course."

"Please, Cecile. One dead is enough."

"I have backup, Raphael. Don't worry."

Backup, Sister Raphael thought wryly as she watched her friend depart. Cecile's type of backup was enough to make her *really* worry.

9

GIULIANO had prepared a special table for Sister Cecile. He had been in love with her briefly, when they were both sixteen, from June to the end of that August. He had worked as a busboy at a restaurant on Cape Cod and Cecile had summered there with her family. They had gone out every Wednesday night that summer. Wednesday had been his night off, and she had taught him how to night-sail the family yacht. One late Wednesday night, after moonlight kissing had reached new heights, she confided to him her desire to become a nun. And that was it.

He could live with that. Another man, no. He would have killed another man, even then.

In June, two years later, he married Maria Marzotti, and five months later their first child, Angela, was born. Cecile was godmother and never forgot gifts for any occasion. At Christmas she remembered the other four children as well. He was looking forward to seeing her. Unlike Maria, Cecile had not put on weight and always looked slim and serene and eternally beautiful. Cecile Buddenbrooks had become a living saint in Giuliano's dark, soulful eyes; and in his business he had a great need of saints. Cecile trod on snakes; she always had, and she was doing it again. He had heard of Martin Moon, and when Martin walked into the restaurant foyer, Giuliano was there.

"Mr. Moon? Sister Cecile called and said to reserve a table. She'll be along. Maria here will find you a table." Giuliano showed perfect white rows of lupine teeth and slipped away, leaving Moon facing Maria.

Martin knew of Giuliano too, and he shuddered as he watched the slender man walk rapidly to the back of the restaurant and vanish. Nobody crossed Giuliano. Then he turned to follow Maria to a rear table covered with a white-lace-print oilcloth and set with a vase of artificial red roses. It was an attractive arrangement, better than some of the other tables with plastic tulips. The restaurant was classy Italian; gondolas slid along stucco walls, tables were round, and the floor was tile. The waitresses were young, dark-haired, and pretty. Maria, who normally worked at the cash register, was still attractive, in spite of the extra thirty pounds, and still imposing. No one passed Maria with an unpaid check. She left Moon with a smiling waitress.

"I'll have a martini, sniff of vermouth," Martin said to his waitress. She scribbled on her pad and vanished.

Martin sat and contemplated the plastic roses. He didn't know that the flowers hid a microphone routed to a back room. Giuliano had a tape recorder and earphones set up and turned on. He could see through a peep hole in the gondola.

Martin was halfway through the martini when Sister Cecile arrived. It was Maria again who escorted her to the table, by prearrangement with Giuliano, who was still in the back room ready to listen. The rear wall, through the glistening design of the gondola painted there, gave a perfect view of Martin's face. When Cecile sat, Giuliano could see her profile. He took in a quick breath as her face lifted and her lips smiled. Damn, he thought. What a waste. Then he tuned in and settled back, his hand stroking a gun at his side.

"I'm Sister Cecile. You probably know why I asked to meet you?"

Martin was nervous. The nun appeared complacent. He wondered if she had read the file. "Jane," he said.

"Yes, Mr. Moon, Jane. She's a lovely young woman."

"I always thought so," Martin said, pushing his words out carefully. "I expect you know where she is."

Cecile stared at his pasty face. He wasn't that ugly; he

97

was a big man with a padded look. He probably carried a gun under that oversized cotton sports coat. She glanced down at his hands. They were thick, with big fingers. They had touched Jane. Everywhere.

She forced herself to stop thinking that way. That wasn't the issue. "Your hoodlums disturbed one of our elderly nuns and she died of heart failure as a direct result of their presence. Are you aware of that?" She spoke flatly. She had played a lot of poker when she was young. He would never know she was shaking inside.

"No."

"They came. She died. I hold you responsible."

He shrugged. "It isn't my fault. I didn't know anyone died."

"You did send those men, didn't you? You're a murderer, Martin Moon." Cecile wasn't too sure that he was, but it was probably true, one way or another.

Giuliano grimaced in the back room. Cecile wasn't being cool now and anything could happen. Of course Moon was a murderer. Everyone knew about that whore, Louisa, they'd found in some alley. Just no one would say. Giuliano's fist wrapped around the gun.

"No!" Martin sat back. "No," he said again more quietly. "Believe me, I had nothing to do with this." Of course it was Dempsey. Moon almost smiled at the thought. Dempsey was doing all right after that little fiasco. Tom had been in lockup covered with spaghetti sauce last week when Martin got the telephone call from his lawyer about the damn Mick without the gun permit. Martin had posted bail, and Tom Dempsey had gone off mad as hell. Dempsey scared the shit out of some nun? That was just like him. He could have scared anybody to death in the mood he was in.

Martin got control of himself. He wanted the damn file and he needed to deal. "I might know who. I could look into it."

"You must stop it. I don't want my convent under siege by scoundrels. It can't happen again." She felt sick with urgency but it didn't show.

The waitress had reappeared and asked Cecile if she would like a drink.

"Yes, please. White wine, and a refill for my friend." Martin's martini was down to the olive. "And a menu, please."

Martin was nonplussed. How could this nun with her glowing Madonna face and her gold cross sit and order drinks and discuss the death of her fellow sister—and ask for a menu! She continued to speak softly, as though it were only about the weather. He never guessed the effort it took her to say, "You should have the *coniglio al agrodolce*. It's a Sicilian specialty you won't come across often."

"Fine," Martin nodded, and before he could open the menu the waitress had thrust in front of him, Cecile began to address the waitress in her peculiar Italian. He heard a repeat of the food she had just suggested and much more. The girl removed the menu again and vanished.

"I'll be having the *stufato di anguilla*. I didn't order it for you. Some people get squeamish about eels," Cecile said. "But I ordered you some *cipollata*. That's a treat. Onion casserole."

"Thanks."

"And *trunzo* for both of us. That's Italian soul food." Martin nodded as though he understood, and he didn't dare ask. Giuliano was grinning by now behind his peephole. His gun hand had relaxed. Cecile was doing just fine.

Martin finally began to assert himself. The second martini helped. He took a quick drink. "I like spaghetti. You couldn't manage a little of that, could you?"

"That's the side dish." She looked thoughtful. "Jane likes spaghetti too, doesn't she?"

"Jane," he said, and Cecile looked for a touch of softness in his eyes. She couldn't find any.

"Where is she?" He asked it suddenly. "She took something of mine." He made it sound casual.

"She has a job, working somewhere. She's very happy, I believe, looking forward to the child."

99

"You know about the thing she took? I need to get in touch with her."

Sister Cecile laughed. She had been studying Martin since she arrived. A very unpleasant man, but she could see why Jane had been attracted. A big teddy bear of a man, but mean underneath. Very mean. And Jane was right. He didn't care about her at all, just the file. It was too bad.

"You have a going business, Mr. Moon."

"Where's the file?"

"Safe."

"Have you let anyone know?"

"Know what?"

"There's valuable information in it. It might be dangerous for her to have it." Martin stopped as the waitress plopped down a basket of bread, and beside it little butter patties in a bowlful of ice. He picked up his knife and dug into one of the butter pats, then smeared it on a piece of bread. The sandwich at Ugies earlier had been greasy, and most of it had ended in the trash. He was starving, and he needed time to think. He munched on the bread, dropping crumbs.

"Don't worry. She doesn't have it." A salad arrived for each of them, and Cecile began to stab lettuce and methodically eat it. She watched Martin carefully. He attacked the salad next, viciously. "Hungry?" Sister Cecile asked.

"Um." He finished chewing. "I want the file back," he said. "It's my property, and it was stolen from me by, by . . . Jane. You have it now. Stolen property. I don't see how you can keep it in good conscience."

"You must think highly of me." Sister Cecile stabbed a tomato slice.

Giuliano chuckled in the back room.

Martin's face turned red. He was being taken for a ride, and he didn't know what to do about it except repeat, "I want that file."

"I don't have it."

"Where is it?"

The waitress arrived with a carafe of red wine and the spaghetti.

"House wine. It's good."

"I'm sure. How much do you want for the file?"

Sister Cecile laughed. "I really don't have it. Ah, the food."

The waitress placed the main dishes before the prospective eaters. "Everything all right, Sister?"

"Fine, thank you, Loretta. It looks wonderful." She began to eat without further words. The eel had been cooked with oil and garlic and coated in bread crumbs before baking, and the two-inch pieces bore little resemblance to what they had once been. Cecile ate with relish, and Martin began on his own dish. It was a delicious concoction. Chicken, he thought, in a sweet-and-sour sauce. His onion casserole was excellent, to his surprise, and even the greens, which Cecile referred to as *trunzo,* were delicious. They reminded him of something he had eaten in Roxbury at a Cajun fast food outlet. He remarked on it.

"Yes, collards. Good, aren't they?" Cecile smiled. "And do you like the *coniglio al agrodolce*? It's pure Sicilian."

"Delicious." He chewed with appreciation. "Who's got the file?" He was beginning to lose patience.

"Not me. I never cared much for rabbit myself," Cecile continued, "but most people seem to enjoy it. You looked the type." To eat small, helpless creatures, she thought, finishing the sentence in her mind.

"Rabbit?" Martin looked at the empty plate and picked up his wine, finishing it in a gulp. He poured again from the carafe and drank again. "I've never had better," he muttered and began to wind spaghetti.

"The file is safe, and it won't be used against anyone. It's not ethical. But it's out of my hands now. You will gain nothing by threatening me, or Jane, or my convent."

"I only deal with people who deserve it," he said and sounded self-righteous. The spaghetti was spectacular.

"Extortion is a criminal act, I believe, not to mention a sin."

"Everyone in that file has done something immoral, and they're paying for it. It shouldn't concern you. I don't want the file to get in bad hands."

"Really? Why not?" Sister Cecile asked.

Martin began to feel uneasy. No one had ever been in a position to question his motives before, and he had never really questioned them himself. Like most criminals, he didn't feel he was bad at all. It was the other guy. He was just having a good time. People out there were just asking to be screwed. Inviting it. So he screwed them.

"You don't have much to bargain with," Martin continued. "All I want is the file, then I'll leave Jane alone. And the convent." Martin pushed his plate back. "What's for dessert?"

"I don't personally have the file, nor does Jane. The *crema di fichi e mandorle* is delicious."

"Translate." He wasn't going to be tricked again.

"A fig-and-almond cream."

"I'll have it. And some Amaretto di Saronno."

"Certainly, Mr. Moon." Sister Cecile signaled the waitress and gave the order as the girl cleared the empty plates. "But about the file. And about my convent. I want the convent to be left alone. Your file is safe. Consider it gone. Is that a fair trade? Nobody will use it. You certainly shouldn't be."

The waitress was prompt. The amaretto was there already, and Sister Cecile was presented with a cup of cappuccino. Martin wished he had ordered coffee too.

"We do have an understanding, don't we?" she asked.

"About what?"

"An understanding that Jane won't be injured, an understanding that my friends won't be intimidated by hoodlums, and perhaps that you won't hurt Mr. Hersey, too. I think we owe him something after all this."

"He doesn't deserve a damn thing. What did he say when you told him about Jane? You told him, didn't you? Abe Hersey is a first-class opportunist. He's been a lousy father. He'll be a lousy grandfather." Martin was red-faced.

The meeting had been one damn thing after another, and the thought of Abe Hersey was just another aggravation.

The *crema di fichi e mandorle* arrived, and they both began to eat as though there had been no words between them. Sister Cecile ate thoughtfully, considering everything, then looked up. "You want a deal," she said.

Martin didn't answer.

"We haven't told anyone we have the file. And we won't. You could be indicted by some of the material in it, something about prostitution, isn't there, Mr. Moon? Not the only offense. We could also make a good case for racketeering, income-tax evasion, and I'm sure we could get some of those people to bring extortion charges against you. But I always feel people need a second chance to amend their lives. It's very hard to forgive seven times seventy, but those are our instructions. I would suggest you make a second chance for yourself. It's a God-given opportunity."

Giuliano saw Sister Cecile's face through the peephole. Angelic. My God, she actually believed what she was saying.

"And in return for our taking care of these matters, you stop the intimidation of all those poor souls. You must."

Martin bit into an almond and chewed. It was a spectacular dessert. It didn't matter who had the file as long as certain people thought he had it. The money wouldn't stop coming. Those bastards would keep paying. "How can I know for sure you won't release that information? That you won't prosecute me?"

She shrugged. "I guess it's a matter of honesty. I'm honest. I never lie, and I'll give you my word. But I would feel obligated to inform these people you deal with that you no longer have the material." She paused. "Just in case you forget."

He stared at the nun. The damn, crazy nun wrecking all the stuff he'd put together. Ten lousy years getting that stuff, opportunities that wouldn't come again. She didn't have the file, but it still existed. He'd get it. "Fine. Just

103

fine." He forced a smile that didn't quite make it. He'd keep right on extorting. She would never know.

Cecile didn't care if he was a killer at this point. She had her own people to protect. "If there are any more problems with my convent, you'll be indicted on extortion charges and, and . . ." She stopped. "And whatever."

"I see," he said. The smile was pasted on his face now. He looked slightly sick. "I'll do my best then. And there's one other thing."

Cecile looked up, gray eyes quizzical.

"Jane."

"What about her?"

"Where is she?"

"She's fine."

"I'd like to see her."

And get your hands on her, Sister Cecile thought. No way. Martin twitched in the chair, and in the back room Giuliano looked thoughtful. There was more to this than met the eye.

"I want to know where she is."

"Sorry." She wondered if he cared about the baby at all. He hadn't really mentioned the pregnancy except in reference to Abe's being a lousy grandfather. Martin Moon was slime, she thought. A real slime.

Martin lit a cigarette. He'd quit smoking again yesterday, but the pack was still in his pocket, for security. There was a time and place for everything. He took a long drag and sent the smoke out across the room. Who gave a shit about smoking. He wouldn't quit after all. The desserts were finished, and the nun had finished her cappuccino. "Anything else?" he asked. "I mean, reason for my being here?"

"Nothing else. I think that about covers it. Really, I was most concerned about Sister Mary Aida. They say she died instantly, without pain. Heart failure can be sudden. But I don't want it to happen again. It could be called accidental, but I certainly don't want characters like that coming around. Rumors spread, and we could have more trouble attracting vocations than we do now. It's deplorable, the lack of vocations these days."

Martin fidgeted and put out the cigarette. "I see. Then I'll be going."

"Yes."

Loretta had dropped the check on their table some time ago, and Martin looked at it, wondering if it was protocol for him to pay. The nun had done the inviting. She watched him staring at it. He picked it up.

"I'll charge this to the extortion account," he said dryly. Then he stood up and nodded.

"You run along," Sister Cecile said, looking up. "I appreciate your coming." Sister Cecile was tired and trembling inside, but she owed Giuliano some conversation after all the trouble he had gone to. "I'll have another cappuccino by myself. We don't have them in the convent."

Martin left, and as his shadow vanished outside down Hanover Street, Giuliano came out and sat next to Sister Cecile. Maria watched from the cash register, and her big hands strangled the wad of bills she held. "She's a nun, a nun, a nun," Maria whispered to herself and carefully flattened out the bills and put them into the till.

"Good work, Cecile. I thought I was going to have to take him out at first. You should have found out who these *ragazzi* were at your convent. I would take care of them."

Giuliano signaled the waitress as he spoke. Loretta tripped in her hurry to reach their table. "Chianti," he said to the girl, keeping his eyes on Cecile.

"You think I don't know that? I was very careful not to ask who they were," Cecile said. She met the Italian's dark eyes. He was looking well. "Maria must be taking good care of you. You look younger than ever."

"Maria's a treasure," he said automatically. The Chianti was there, and he sipped lightly. "Special diet. One glass a day and no cholesterol. Good for the heart."

"I don't want to punish anyone," Cecile said sadly. "Perhaps they did God's will. The nun who died, Sister Mary Aida, was in considerable pain. Cancer."

Giuliano looked startled. "You'd see God in the table-cloth."

"Perhaps."

"You think that bastard's gonna just lay off? You believe that? You want another cappuccino?" Giuliano had heard it on the microphone.

She looked down and saw her hands shaking; she had not been as cool as Moon had thought. "No, not really. But there you are with that wine and it looks good. Can Maria join us? We can drink together. And no, he probably won't just lay off. But now he knows *I* don't have the file, and that the convent doesn't, and that Jane is unavailable. The rest is in God's hands. I've done all I can. Call Maria over. I'd love to see her."

That was not what Giuliano wanted. He still liked to be with Cecile—alone. But what could he do? "Hey, Maria, tell Marco in the kitchen to take the cash. Join us for a drink."

Maria bounced in response, flapping to the kitchen door. "Ay, Marco, do the money." She plopped down at the table beside her husband, showing one bad tooth in a huge grin. "Cecile, darling, how are you?"

"Two more Chianti, Loretta," Giuliano called.

Cecile settled into the chair. It would be another night when she would be saying vespers all by herself. Late.

10

Summer came softly and the days melted one into another. Fireworks bloomed over the Charles. The Boston Pops honked in the Hatch Shell. The Esplanade was filled with people. In the Public Garden the roses neared their end and the begonias burgeoned; the Swan Boats carried children back and forth for endless sunny days.

There were no more hoodlums at the convent. More frequent confessions became the norm, and love and charity prevailed, as though this very day each sister would face her Maker. Cecile had assured them there would be peace, and there was. Then she went on her fund-raising trip through the Boston Archdiocese and raised slightly over forty thousand dollars for the retirement home. It was difficult work and required speaking at as many as five Masses a day to spread the word.

On the fifteenth of June she set out for the diocese of Richmond, Virginia, where the Sisters of Our Lady of Good Counsel had a small convent. In Richmond she planned to work with several of her southern fellow sisters in order to cover as many parishes as possible during the three-month schedule. It went well: hectic on Sundays but peaceful during the week. She spent a great deal of the time praying, the rest of the time she spent at meetings and chatting with old friends. She thought of Jane often. Jane would be growing bigger now, heavier. The baby was growing. It was an exciting time, but also sweet and peaceful. Her private-detective card rested unused in her purse pocket. Abe Hersey had been informed that things were progressing nicely and that his daughter was safe. He had written Jane, by way of the Dorchester Convent, and she had responded. He had already paid a bill for six days. Sister Cecile had decided only to charge him for the days she had actually spent on active duty helping Jane. There would be more.

In other spheres, life was not as idyllic. For Howard Marshall, demoted to trashman, each day brought more disgust, self-pity, and fury. As the days grew warmer, so did the trash. Ripe meat, fetid yellow rice, and used Pampers cascaded before him as he tossed the city dwellers' bursting bags into the refuse truck. Dead rats were on the streets, glass and discarded furniture filled his life. His muscles developed as his humility was tried. He had been a driver for two years, and now he suffered the indignity of following the trucks on foot. The murder of Ray McVey had all but slipped his mind, but murderous thoughts haunted him as he schlepped trash.

The Cambridge and Boston police departments weren't happy either. Every Tuesday morning, without fail, Lyuba McVey would call Detective Limper at Cambridge Police Headquarters in Central Square. "Any news on my Ray?" she would ask.

"We're coming close," Jim Limper would say. "We're in touch with the Boston Police on this, you know. It's their jurisdiction."

"But he was killed right here in Cambridge in his own back yard," Lyuba would repeat. "Nothing's safe, not life, not property!"

"We do our best, ma'am."

And Jim Limper would call his Boston counterpart. The murder was a dead end, though. Of all the low life who might have wanted to do in Ray McVey, not one of them could be placed near the crime. To his discredit, the police detective had never really followed up on Lyuba's obscure suggestion that the death of her flower bed had any relation to the death of her son. It didn't make any sense and Lyuba

McVey didn't make sense either. Every cop in Cambridge knew about the McVeys. They were fucking nuts.

Lyuba was becoming impatient.

Paul Dorys had really planned on a short vacation in Mexico but had managed to entangle himself in a law case. He had intended to vacation in and around Mexico City with an old friend who worked in immigration law. Pedro Escribez had gone to law school with Paul in New York and now worked with immigration problems confronted by Mexicans seeking legal entry into the United States. Pedro's cases were an endless fascination to Paul, and the chance to be in on some litigation, even if only as a bystander, was too much to pass up. A few telephone calls to his partner cleared his schedule for another few weeks, and besides cooking in hundred-degree heat while chasing scrubby cattle, Paul got a taste of Mexican law. He delayed his departure from Mexico until the first week of July.

"Muy bueno," Paul said, long since purged of cool city smog, as he bade his old friend good-bye at the airport. The complete change had done wonders. He couldn't even remember what Boston looked like. Almost.

He returned to the city refreshed and ready for anything.

It was good to be back, Paul thought as he trudged up the steps to his home and took a deep breath of his neighborhood air. Not bad for Boston, he decided and unlocked the door. There was a pile of mail—bills, circulars, and an ancient postcard from Paris from Cecile. The air inside was stifling from the heat. First thing he did was turn on the air conditioner, then he checked the refrigerator. Besides three eggs and a bottle of catsup, there was a six-pack of Samuel Adams beer. He snapped one open and settled down to listen to the messages that had accumulated on his machine. He'd been in touch with his office on a weekly basis and there was work waiting, but he hadn't bothered to call in to his home even once. Nothing was noteworthy except the final message from Lyuba McVey. By the time her voice came up, Paul was on his second beer.

"That fugginassole Cambridge Police Department hasn't found out who killed my baby. Paul, you get over here."

Tomorrow he had to be at court. Old Lyuba would have to wait, he thought. He had three long-delayed cases coming to trial in the next two weeks, and it would be a miracle if he could even deal with each of them as he should. He was overextended already and only home an hour. He was on his third beer when the telephone rang. He forgot Lyuba completely.

"Paul, it's Sister Raphael."

Paul groaned silently. "Sure, Raphael."

"You've been away. I've called every day, but I won't leave a message on that infernal machine."

"Don't blame you."

"No. So I thought you should know that everything is fine now. There have been no more deaths, and Cecile's in Richmond now for a while. She put a stop to those men somehow."

"What?"

"Cecile talked to Martin Moon, and there have been no more bad men approaching the convent. It was a blessing, though. Don't you think?"

"Raphael, what are you talking about?"

"You don't know about Mary Aida?"

"No. Tell me."

Sister Raphael did. Paul's telephone cord was long enough for him to get another beer from the refrigerator. He placed it beside the telephone and methodically lined up the empties. He had finished number four by the time Raphael was done and he set it down with a gasp. "That's better," he murmured.

"What's better?"

"Uh, I understand now, Raphael. And Cecile straightened it all out with Moon?"

"Yes."

"And she never heard from him after that?"

"No, she left town."

"Good thing."

"I think so. She'll be back by September."

"Who came to the convent? These bad guys?"

"We never found out who they were, Paul, and it was well over a month ago. My Rambek Computer stock went up twelve points since then. You should pick some up."

"I'll be sure to, Raphael. Thanks."

He hung up. People were dropping like flies, and he was supposed to do something about it? An old nun and Ray McVey, both better off where they were now than where they had been. He wondered idly if there was a connection and made a note to call his stockbroker.

By the time Paul was back at work in Boston, Tom Dempsey had almost quit working at all. Not that he had wanted to quit, but he was under orders, all stemming from the incident at the convent. He didn't ordinarily intimidate old nuns, but things had been leading up to it. That grammar school principal had unearthed frustrations better left buried; the Paul Dorys spaghetti caper had driven him close to madness; and then Paul had vanished from town as soon as Tom had been sprung from jail. Tom knew he had to find Jane if he was to make the money Martin had for him, but he didn't know what to do. When he'd seen the old bag pass out on the convent floor he'd grabbed his buddy and split fast, never knowing she had died. He planned to come back and scare the shit out of them again later and find Jane. He was starting to need some money again, badly.

But all that was before Cecile had had her interview with Martin Moon. The day after the interview Moon had gotten Dempsey on the telephone and raised a stink beyond understanding.

"So an old nun croaked."

"No more, Dempsey, cool it."

"I scared the shit out of them. You want to bet they'll tell me where they got your old lady?"

"Lay off the nuns, Dempsey. I gave my word."

"They got to you, didn't they?"

111

"None of your business why. Lay off. Find the kid some other way."

"You still want the friggin' kid?"

"I want her."

"The nuns know where she is."

"You tread light, Dempsey. I hear about any more crap, I'll take you out myself."

"Okay, Mr. Moon, okay. I can find the kid. I got an idea about that lawyer anyhow. I'll check his place, keep an eye on him. He's the one's on to her. I asked around, and he's got connections with a nun. Weird. Some Sister Cecile."

Martin saw Cecile's face rising like a mist in the back of his mind, clear skin with gray eyes and a spectacular mouth telling him in that soft voice how he'd be indicted on extortion charges if he didn't lay off. She was a beauty all right.

"Mr. Moon?" The voice scratched.

"Yeah, yeah, I still want the kid, and no, it ain't so weird. You work for me, you do what I say. And shut up."

"Sure, Mr. M. Be in touch."

Martin rang off, discontented. His precious file was a thorn in his side, and his best man had become a major fuck-up. Tom had already screwed up once with that lawyer, got himself in the locker on a gun charge that took some high dealings to have dismissed. Massachusetts had a mandatory one-year sentence now for carrying a gun without a permit. Lucky for Tom, Martin had a paper on a Boston judge in that file. Lucky the judge didn't know he no longer had that file. Lucky he hadn't taken the nun's threat seriously about not using the file. Nobody knew he didn't have it anymore except the nun, and maybe the damn lawyer. Time would tell. Jane, damn her, and having a baby? It was hard to believe. He sat back in his velour rocker and remembered Jane. Her slender, white body. Skin like alabaster with all that red hair. Smart too. Too smart. Where the hell was the file? He'd love to get his hands on her. He flexed his fingers and remembered how her skin had felt— soft, young, just right. He got up and paced. Inactivity was getting him down. He'd go play some racquetball, then maybe call up a girl. He still had his address book, anyway. And he had placed a girl in the damn lawyer's office. Maybe she had something for him.

It was the middle of July. Jane Hersey had put on fifteen pounds already. She had that special glow women get when pregnant. Her face was fuller and softer, her entire body was considerably rounder and more feminine. She carried herself gracefully; the bending and stooping of being a chambermaid had been good for her, keeping her limber and confident in spite of the strange shift her life had taken. She had begun to work at the main desk two weeks ago. "Too big to bend," Mère Sulpicia had said one afternoon, "and your French is much improved. I imagine you could handle just about anyone now."

It seemed that way to Jane, too. But suddenly she was homesick for America, even though she had met Bertrand. He was planning on coming to America to meet her father. But that would come later, and she hadn't even told Mother Sulpicia. One afternoon Jane found herself invited to Mère Sulpicia's office. They began with a nice chat. Mère Sulpicia asked Jane how she was feeling.

"Really wonderful, thank you," Jane replied. "But, Mère," she asked, "when do you think I can go home?"

"When would you like?"

That surprised Jane. Somehow she hadn't thought she was free to go. "Oh, well, I'm not sure. Do you think it's safe?"

"Je ne sais pas."

"I don't know either."

"There was some trouble," Mère Sulpicia said. "But things are calm now."

"I'm sure," Jane said. Somehow nothing felt relevant. She had been thinking a lot about Martin Moon, seeing him clearly. He had really been quite horrible, objectively, and she felt she could settle up with him now. From Paris, she could see everything clearly. And she missed her father.

"You can return to America whenever you want, but would you go home? Would you have the baby there? Have you made any decision about your future?"

That was too much reality all at once. Jane tried to look inscrutable but failed dismally. "I was thinking of entering the order."

"You've changed your mind?"

"Yes. I want to keep her."

"Who?"

"The baby."

"Girls do that these days."

Jane nodded. She was under no illusions there. It would be hard.

"Would you live with your father?" Mère Sulpicia straightened her tiny pile of papers and looked up. The head of the order made a point of meeting with Jane for a chat at least once a week. They spoke often during the week, but there were always other people around, precluding any intimate discussions. Sulpicia had risen in her order because of the quality of personal contact that she now exhibited. There was nothing she didn't know about anyone in her particular orbit. She spoke with everyone regularly and personally, and she knew Jane quite well by this time.

"I don't think so. I . . . he might . . . I mean, he might interfere. Daddy, I mean. But maybe later. I actually miss him."

"How would you support yourself?"

"Maybe he would give me money. I could work."

"Difficult with a newborn."

"Welfare, then. Lots of girls do it."

Sulpicia winced. "Yes. I've spent some time in America. I went to Smith and did graduate work in California. I'm familiar with American welfare."

"I want to go on to school too," Jane said.

"You're doing well at the Sorbonne."

"I'm studying mathematics."

"Difficult."

"I like it."

"You could always marry. That might solve everything."

Jane laughed. It was almost funny. She hadn't completely regained confidence in herself.

"Really, Jane, you're most attractive and very smart. Having a child doesn't interfere with most people's considerations these days. I'm sure many men find you very lovely."

"Mère Sulpicia, you know how to make me feel good, if nothing else. But I do have a plan, more or less." Jane sighed and wiggled her fingers. Her hands had begun to look different in the last month. They didn't even feel the same.

"The plan?"

"Oh, wait until the election is over, you know? Stay out of Daddy's way until he wins or loses. I owe him that. I can take my high school finals when I get home, Sister Cecile told me. Anyway, after the baby, after everything is straightened out, I go to my father and cast myself on his mercy. He might even set me up somewhere so I can go to school. God knows Daddy's got the money. I could use the welfare thing as a threat. He'd die if I went on welfare. A congressman with a daughter on the dole?" She still wouldn't mention Bertrand.

Sulpicia shifted in her chair. It was getting late. "That would probably work except for one thing. The baby's father might wish to become involved. Have you thought of that?"

Jane closed her blue eyes, and it was as though a light in the room went out.

"I'll have to get the file from Cecile and give it back to him. Then maybe he'll just leave me alone." Her lips were set and grim. "Sister Cecile wants to destroy it, she told me. And my father's safe from him now. He used me. I'm beginning to understand what Martin was really like."

"You do love your father, don't you?"

Jane nodded. "I know what he's like too. Getting away has been really good, Mother. I love him."

115

"Fast maturity, Jane. And you do want him to win this election, don't you?"

"Yes," she admitted. "He would be good. He really would. But not with Martin threatening him. Anyone running for Congress can't afford a scandal, even from way back then. Daddy did real well in law school after that, but just that one little thing. He got a girl pregnant at the first school and wrote a very foolish letter. I don't know how Martin ever got ahold of it. Daddy got a girl pregnant. Imagine that." She looked down at her belly, definitely showing the effects of one night not too long ago.

"The father of your child really doesn't care. It's sad, really. What did he say to you?"

Jane's alabaster skin turned red. "He pretty much told me to chill out when I asked him to marry me."

"Did you talk about the baby?"

"Of course not."

"Did you talk about love?"

"Don't be silly. He never loved me." Resentment flashed in her eyes. "He just wanted me. I told you how he used to hit me sometimes."

"Yes." Sulpicia stood up. "Let's meet after dinner tonight to talk about that. Right here at eight thirty. You know it wasn't your fault, but it helps to go over things. Do you mind?"

"No," Jane sighed. "I'm learning so much about myself. Why stop now?"

"We'll never understand Martin, will we?"

"Only humans pose unanswerable questions." Jane smiled. "Sister Cecile told me that one; so it proves you're human."

"That is not original with Cecile. Saint Augustine said it first, I believe." Sulpicia looked at Jane sharply and walked to the door. "I hope she didn't take credit for it."

"Cecile?" Jane giggled. "I don't understand her at all."

"Which proves that you, too, are human. Please stay and finish the madeleines. I have a meeting to attend in five minutes."

Jane nodded, and the door shut silently behind Mère Sulpicia. Jane helped herself to another madeleine. They were delicious, a pastry Marcel Proust had made famous for some reason. She sipped her tea, settled back in the Reverend Mother's comfortable leather armchair, and stared dreamily at the wall. She was getting the most unusual education here. That etching she was gazing at, she knew now, was a late seventeenth century copy of Rembrandt's *Hundred Guilder Print*. There were so many things like that. Maybe she would be like Sister Cecile. She looked down at her stomach. Maybe not.

11

Lyuba McVey inspected her calendar. The day of the month was important because checks arrived in the mail. Unemployment and pension checks. Lyuba would work regularly for six months doing piecework and then go on a week-long drunk and be fired. She could collect unemployment for a good amount of time after that and then search for another job. Lyuba had been a widow for eight years. Mr. McVey had died in the line of duty when a subway train rolled over him. He had been a brakeman. She had his pension, and with what she brought in herself, altogether it came to a tidy amount. Of course when Ray had been alive the money had been spent much more quickly, but life had been so much more interesting.

Ray had only been dead a few months. It seemed like forever. The calendar today read August 25th. On her calendar there was a series of moon pictures showing the phases on different days: full, half, a picture of a sliver, the new moon. The full moon next month would fall on the tenth. Lyuba knew that full moons portended more alcoholic relapses, more bouts with insanity, more drunken-driver arrests. Ray had been subject to the phases of the moon. Lyuba had always watched him as the moon grew gibbous. He would become depressed, edgy, irritable, and then, finally, on the day of the full moon he would break loose and take too many pills or drink too much or do something outrageous with their cat.

Lyuba sobbed. The reminiscences were too much for her. For all his faults, Ray had been a good son, a wonderful son. Why hadn't something been done? Where was justice? She figured Paul would have an answer, but she didn't know that he had been in Mexico when she called his private number last time. He would help stir up those cops. She had left a message on his machine days ago! Where the hell was he? Where was loyalty?

Paul's parents had come from the same town in Poland that she had come from. His father had been a scientist, killed in a plane crash when Paul was a baby, and Paul's mother had gone to work as a cook on the Buddenbrookses' estate. Lyuba Brudzycki had worked as a cook then too, in Boston at a diner; and then she had married Ralph McVey, and of course she had kept in touch with Paul's mother. They had gone different ways, her son and Paul. It never occurred to Lyuba to wonder why. She didn't wonder now. Instead she poured herself another gin and Pepsi and sat down in front of the television to watch "People's Court." She knew a lot about law. And she had decided it was time to take matters into her own hands. Ray would be avenged.

Howard Marshall knew about law and vengeance too. He knew that he didn't stand a chance of being caught for the murder of that creep, but that peddling dope to DPW workers was hazardous, especially now that he had lost his prestige on the job. He wanted something different for himself, and because he was ambitious, he put his plan for vengeance against Lyuba McVey on a back burner and decided to go for bigger game.

His supplier was a Cambridge politician, a city councilman of repute who sat on the City Planning Board and wielded influence in deciding what jobs went to which contractors. He had at least one architectural firm up his sleeve and cousins who did very well for themselves on construction jobs.

Howard racked his brain trying to come up with a plan that would get him out of the dangerous end of dope dealing and make big bucks for himself. Because his normal dealings with the politician were done through drops, Howard decided to take the bull by the horns. He was expected to drop off all the money he collected for his sales. It went into a plastic bag, then into the trunk of a 1983 Dodge, left double-parked in front of Woolworth's at seven o'clock every Thursday evening for exactly five minutes. Along with the money, he would leave orders for drugs and any other message he wanted to relay. His order would appear the next Monday at the bundle pickup at Lechmere Sales. Howard had never been quite sure how it got there.

This Thursday he spent suppertime composing a letter.

Dear sir,

I don't like what I'm doing no more. I want more. I figure I need a new batch of buyers that use better stuff, or maybe I can handle some salesmen myself and be a middleperson.

He thought long and hard over that one. "Middleperson," he decided, would impress that he was no dummy. He knew what was what. He'd even killed a man. Maybe he should tell them that. Howard smiled and continued writing.

I want to meat yous and we can work something out. I'll have the money for this weeks work to give yous at the meating.

Yours very trolly,
Howard Marshall

Howard wrapped up the letter in a plastic bag, then placed it in the small brown sack he usually put the money in. It would get them to move fast if he didn't put in all the money from the week's sales. It never occurred to Howard that he had forgotten to include the order for what he would push the following week. Half an hour later the letter had been placed in the trunk of the Dodge. Things were rolling.

Councilman Daniel O'Neil read the letter from Howie Marshall with distaste. The paper was sticky and had an off smell, and poor command of the English language always offended him. He was in a lounge at City Hall reserved for the city councilmen and was alone but for his brother-in-law Barry Rizzo.

"My tame trashman's getting greedy," O'Neil remarked. Rizzo had read the letter too.

Rizzo grunted. He was lighting a long black cigar.

"He's been screwing up; almost got the can for running over some old lady's garden," O'Neil said.

Rizzo blew out smoke. "Want I should clip him?"

"No need." O'Neil shut his eyes and wrinkled up his face in thought. "I feel pretty good. I'll give him a new contact in the Square to pass stuff on to, collect from, whatever. I've had a little trouble with one of the drops. This will make everyone happy."

"Middleperson." Rizzo spat a piece of the cigar on the floor.

"Would you have him be a middlewoman?" O'Neil laughed deep in his throat. He was a student of the language, the man responsible for giving the Cambridge City Council meetings a literary twist. He sat back in the chair, looked up at the high, paneled walls and the portrait of Mr. Rindge, and breathed deeply. He loved political trappings and the sense of invulnerability they always lent to the members of that year's club. Until the next election.

Rizzo suffered from no such illusions. "I don't give a fuck, Danny, you just keep the stuff moving like it does. We got a big load coming up from New York on September nine, and I want a place to put it." Rizzo stood up and circled once around the room. Then he left.

Daniel O'Neil closed his eyes as the chamber door shut silently behind his brother-in-law. Rizzo would clip him too, if he knew he was already compromised. Daniel O'Neil was in serious trouble. He needed money to pay to Martin Moon because Martin knew all about him; he had crazies like Howie Marshall on his payroll, and he had Barry Rizzo for a brother-in-law.

Councilman O'Neil spent half of Monday at home behind closed doors working out his strategy for a new schedule of drug pickup and delivery. Marshall wanted more? He would get more. He would pick up as usual at Lechmere at eight o'clock; but at that point he would take one half of the material to distribute among his own buyers, and the other half he would pass along to two other distributors, one a candy-store operator who was new to the drug trade, and the second to a cleaning lady at the Cambridge City Hospital. Marshall would pick up cash, keep records of transactions (taking ten percent off the top of each operation), and then duplicate the sales record for O'Neil's own records.

It would actually simplify things for the councilman, and O'Neil sucked in his cheeks complacently as he typed out the order of business for Howie to follow. Howie would make another couple of hundred dollars a week off the new dealings; and that should be enough to keep him happy, not to mention busy, although it only meant two more stops a week once he got things running. And O'Neil would have good, signed accounts of the dealings—which meant that he could terminate Howard Marshall at any time, simply by holding the signed sheets over his head. It was good to have a lever on your agents, Daniel O'Neil thought, remembering the lever that Martin Moon had on him. Another payment was due tomorrow. Three hundred dollars cash in an envelope to be sent to that office on Beacon Street and put in the hands of Mrs. Parks. What in God's name did Martin Moon need with money? The man was a millionaire before he was born.

O'Neil put the order to Howard Marshall in a cheap white envelope, closed up his private office, and kissed his wife good-bye. He would eventually go to his real estate office in North Cambridge. But first he had a package to drop off at Lechmere. He sat back in his new Oldsmobile and revved up the engine. It was a beautiful day, and there wasn't a damn thing that could go wrong.

Lyuba McVey believed in direct action when she believed in action at all. She left her house on Monday morning at nine o'clock and began the two-block walk down Hampshire Street to the Department of Public Works. It was a steamy day, and the traffic was just beginning to lighten up after rush hour. Only a few years ago Hampshire Street had been relatively untraveled, but now it was a major artery to avoid the Broadway traffic coming out of Harvard Square. Unisex executives pedaled by on five-hundred-dollar mountain bicycles; they wore three-piece suits, helmets, and jogging shoes. Lyuba couldn't understand it. But by the time she was at the Public Works garage, she was out of breath and didn't care. She panted in, gasped as she was hit by the air-conditioning, and climbed the stairs to the main office where she stood, elbows supporting her on the counter, to receive the indifferent "Can I help you?" of a receptionist.

"I want to find who drove over my flowers," Lyuba said. "Eh?"

"I got the money, I got the flowers planted back. Everything bloomed nice. They didn't put up a new fence yet, but I got no complaint. I just want to find the man who was driving the truck, that's all. I think I want to tell him something, find out something, you know?"

"Oh, yes, I'll have to get the supervisor, ma'am. Would you like to sit down?"

"Right here." Lyuba saw the orange plastic chair and almost fell into it. A tropical plant grew beside her and spots danced before her eyes.

"I'll ring Mr. Jannick, ma'am. He'll be right out."

"Thank you," Lyuba mumbled and settled in. She could be in the chair for days, she knew. Lyuba McVey was used to bureaucracy. But it was only ten minutes until Mr. Jannick emerged from behind an orange door to the rear of the office. He was suave, and his waxed mustache trembled slightly when he spoke. His forehead glistened in spite of the air-conditioning. He stood, unwilling to take the empty seat beside Lyuba.

"What can I do for you?"

Lyuba's eyes moved up slowly from the pattern on the floor, up the Dacron suit to the tie. It was green and had small red fish on it. She spoke to the tie. "I would like to find the man who drove the truck that ran over the flowers in my backyard," she said deliberately. She had been practicing the words in her mind for the past seven minutes.

"And you are . . . ?" he asked.

"Mrs. Ralph McVey. I live on Elm Street."

"The flowers. Yes, the flowers." Mr. Jannick willed her eyes to rise above his tie, and they did at last. He wished they hadn't, and turned away. "We had our union man deal with the discipline. We have a very strong union here, and it's always wise in problems of this sort to let the men work these things out. Was everything satisfactory?"

"Yes."

"The flowers were replanted, I believe?"

"Yes."

"Were they satisfactory?"

"Yes. I want to find the man who drove the truck."

"I see." Mr. Jannick looked out the window. "You have some further problem then?"

"No. I want to find the man. I forget his name."

"Is there some question about the flowers?"

"The flowers? I like the flowers. I wanted to speak to the man."

"About the flowers?"

"I'll speak to him about the flowers."

That satisfied Mr. Jannick. He had to take care of his men.

"Mr. Howard Marshall is who you're looking for, I believe. I don't have the time schedule here. It's down in the yard. You'll have to ask Mr. Alsop. Would you like me to check for you?"

"Howard Marshall?" Lyuba said.

"Yes. I'll ring downstairs for you."

"No, no, I've got to go now. I'll see about it. I'll do it. Thank you. I'm glad for your help." She rose unsteadily and then smiled. She had excellent teeth, and her smile did wonders for the face. Watery-blue eyes became insignificant next to the smile, and Mr. Jannick suddenly felt he had done something wonderful.

"Well, now, I'm glad I could help you, ma'am. We're always here, you know." He nodded.

"Yes, well, thank you, thank you." Lyuba dipped and bobbed her way to the staircase, turned abruptly and edged down a step, then another, and another. She had trouble on stairs, but she made it all the way down to the heavy glass door with the logo THE WORKS in big black letters printed on it.

The yard was around to the left and back, a vast desert where space and maintenance were provided for up to twenty vehicles at a time. Trash trucks lumbered in with full loads, dripping liquids; regular trucks, for carrying equipment, sand, or lawn mowers, were stashed in corners. They were all painted orange, with THE WORKS set across them at an angle. The yard impressed Lyuba with its cleanliness and efficiency, but it was too hot and the distance across the hot tarred surface seemed unending. She walked deliberately, whispering "Howard Marshall" to herself while moisture began to bead her upper lip. Men stood in clumps beneath a cavernous opening to the sheltered parking area at the rear of the lot, and Lyuba spoke to the first face that came into focus.

"Harold Marshall. I want Harold Marshall." Her voice was raspy but clear.

The men looked at each other without seeming to look. They knew Howie did drug deals, but customers were usually more discreet.

"I think you mean Howie," one of the men said.

"Howard, I said Howard. He here?"

125

"He's out now. You want something he's got?"

"Yes." Lyuba nodded hard.

"You come by here three o'clock Tuesday. He'll deal with you. He's got the stuff then, over on the corner of Tremont. Okay?"

"What's he look like?" Lyuba wanted to be sure.

"Medium heavy. Black hair. Wears yellow on Tuesdays. Can't miss that yellow shirt."

"Good." Lyuba was satisfied, and she let loose her beatific smile and turned to begin the long trek across the yard and home. She could last another day before confronting this Harold Marshall. She needed time to think.

The men watched, stuck in the spell of the marvelous smile belonging to an old woman with thick ankles tramping deliberately across the yard.

"She want drugs?" one said.

"She want drugs," another affirmed.

"Goddamn."

12

PAUL Dorys, Esquire, had sat at his desk for weeks wanting to call Sister Cecile, just to talk. He missed her. Not a satisfactory substitute, Sister Raphael had kept in touch for her friend and had even called his home recently. Linda had answered. Linda was a lawyer with a rival firm and intelligent as hell. She had been staying at Paul's for a few days to try things out and was becoming a habit.

"Who is that odd voice?" Raphael had asked.

"Linda."

"Oh."

That had been almost enough to convince Paul that there was something wrong with Linda's voice. Raphael had gone on to say that Cecile would be back on August twenty-fifth, a few weeks early.

"Good," Paul had said.

"Did you buy the stock?"

"Yes. It went up three points yesterday."

"I know."

"Raphael, where do you get your tips?"

The old nun had just laughed. "Cecile inquired about the file, but I told her things were on hold. Is that true?"

"Yes, Raphael. The file and all copies are safe. Mr. Hersey got his letter back months ago."

"Good, just checking. Thank you, Paul. 'Bye."

Now, one week later, Cecile had to be back. Paul wanted to hear her voice. It was one of the things he loved about Cecile. Damn her. He loved a lot about her. Raphael had been right about Linda's voice. It wasn't a voice you could

127

live with. He dialed the convent number before he could change his mind.

"Sister Cecile, please."

"Just one moment. Who's calling?"

"Mr. Dorys."

"Just a moment, please."

The moment grew. Paul began humming, then he began an elaborate doodle. Five minutes passed before Cecile's voice came across the wire. "Paul?"

He didn't speak for a space, letting the sound warm him. "Cecile, how are you?"

"Tired. I picked up a touch of something on the road. But fine, I guess."

"I have a little job for you." He wondered if this were only an excuse or if she could really help his problem.

"Anything, Paul."

"Anything?"

She laughed. "You know."

"It's Lyuba McVey. Remember her? She knew my mother back somewhere, and she thinks she's family. She's all right, drinks now and then; but she has a more serious problem."

"Yes?"

"Her son was killed last spring. He'd been in and out of Billerica, one stint in Westboro. A criminal, maybe, but definitely not bright. They found him dead, shot and in a dumpster, or rather on a barge in the harbor. Initially he was put in the dumpster, in Cambridge, they think. There have been no leads in the killing, and Lyuba is impatient. She needs someone to talk to, a little emotional support. Actually she thinks she knows who did it, but it sounds so crazy I've let it slide."

"Bereavement is difficult. I'd be glad to see her, Paul. But knowing you, there's got to be more."

"Ummm."

"Paul?"

"She's gunning for someone. She left a message on my

128

machine that hints she's got the answer. See if you can discover what she's talking about, but be careful."

"How old is she?"

"Her sixties somewhere."

"I'll see her. I'll give her a call. Or do you think it would be better if I just went?" Cecile was consulting a calendar as she spoke. Meetings . . . she had five scheduled for next week, four this weekend. And Jane was coming home. Maybe she could fit Lyuba in right away. "Tomorrow. I'll do it right away."

"That's great. You'll love her, she's really an amazing character," Paul said. He gave her the address, "Just stop by. Don't give her a chance to make a getaway. Tell her . . . something."

"Tell me about her, Paul." Cecile settled the receiver more comfortably against her ear.

"She knew my mother, that's all really. Not exactly girlhood friends but acquaintances of some kind. My mother would never say exactly, she didn't dare, I think, but Mom felt an obligation to keep up ties with the old country one way or another. Lyuba drinks. She smokes. She has a mouth that might shock you."

"Me?"

"Even you. But she's kind. I've never seen her take anger out against anyone except Ray. But she might. She might do anything to seek revenge for Ray's murder. I think it's simmering, about to blow."

"I'll be balm in Gilead," Cecile murmured into the receiver. "And I won't even mention I'm a private investigator. She probably couldn't afford me. Although business is slow."

"Good girl. Any word from the teenager?"

"Jane's doing fine. She's coming home. I'll be able to send Abe another bill."

"She's lost her religious vocation?"

"We suspected she wasn't really cut out to join the order. I don't know what she wants to do about that file, though, and it has to be dealt with."

129

"The whole thing may blow up, Cecile," Paul said.

Cecile shrugged. "Maybe. We're praying."

"Don't say I never warned you."

Cecile laughed. "I'll call you after I see the bereaved."

They rang off. Paul felt better. Cecile could straighten out Lyuba McVey if anyone could.

Tuesday the Red Sox played the Yankees at Fenway Park. The pennant race was heating up and bets were high. The sun was hot and had no trouble cutting through the city air to create little mirages of heat patterns. The Sox had been ahead in the early innings, but the Yankees were ripe for a win. Bets were on when Lyuba started out for the Public Works yard. Cars were pulling up at the little store on Hampshire Street; men with cigars and checked pants listened to the score. By the time she arrived things were already looking bad for the Sox. The game was half over, all over for the Red Sox. It was one of those days when the Sox didn't really stand a chance.

Lyuba had bet on the Yankees, and she felt good. Ray's spare Saturday-night special felt pretty good too. She had it in her raffia bag along with some of last year's apples. When Lyuba wasn't drinking she ate a lot of apples.

She arrived at the corner early, in time to see a heavy man wearing a yellow shirt and dirty dungarees cross the street from the yard. She stood under the street sign and waited. He was handing someone a bag, taking something in an envelope. Probably had the man's lunch, she thought and began wishing for a steak-and-cheese sub. Cars passed by and then the street was empty. He crossed to her side.

"You want to buy?" He had already looked her over. The men at the yard had told him he had a new customer. No way this lady was a cop; so he could afford to be direct, and he liked to deal fast.

"Buy." She repeated the words and reached into her bag to feel the gun's surface. "You're the one," she began.

"I'm running short this week. Supplier's off, but I'm getting crack in. Good price. I've only got a little of this to-

130

day." He flashed a handful of red and blue capsules and one white bag. Lyuba knew what it was, all of it. Ray had brought that stuff home all the time. Suddenly her path to revenge was clear.

"Some of that stuff," she gestured to the reds, and he quoted a price. It was more than Ray had paid, and she repeated the price Ray had mentioned. "I get it for that."

"Where?"

"Downtown."

"Gimme ten bucks," he said.

She smiled and shifted her hand in the bag to bring up her change purse. She located a crumpled ten-dollar bill and stuffed it into his hand. He pulled out an envelope from his pants pocket and checked the contents. "Enough?" He held it open for inspection. She nodded, took it, and pushed it down into her bag.

"Next week I want twenty loads of the new stuff. Get me some pipes too. Can you get that?" She heard her voice shake, but apparently he didn't notice. He only saw his commission going up.

"Yeah, I'll be here." He turned. There was another customer walking up very slowly, waiting for Lyuba to finish business. Her eyes moved from Howard to the other figure, and she wiped a wet streak from her face.

"Okay," she said and walked on, going in the direction away from her house. Then she turned, came back, and passed him by in time to see him showing his wares again. She continued to Windsor Street and took a right. She was devious. She would go home another way.

Sister Cecile knew it was still baseball season when she walked by Linwood Court in Cambridge. Fans lolled on their cars with ghetto blasters roaring. She saw the dust and a dozen local kids playing ball on Market Street. She had to walk through the middle of the game, but it didn't seem to matter to the kids. She wondered whether, if she had been wearing a habit, they would have noticed. Probably not. Times had changed. Counting off street numbers,

Cecile noticed an older, dazed-looking woman walking down the street too. The woman turned in at the house Cecile had decided was probably her own destination. Cecile kept coming as the woman unlocked the door.

"Mrs. McVey?"

"Eh?" The woman turned to eye her suspiciously.

"I'm a friend of Paul Dorys. Are you Mrs. McVey?"

"Paul's friend? You know Paulie?"

Lyuba stood on the top step and looked down. Her hands were shaking.

"Can I come in and talk to you? Paul asked me to stop by."

"I've got to get in."

"Of course." Cecile smiled and followed the older woman inside.

Lyuba forged ahead, straight through the small hallway to the musty, green living room on the right, then through to the kitchen, where she opened the refrigerator door and pulled out a bottle of Welch's grape juice. She hooked her hands around the bottle and drank directly from it. It had no cap.

Cecile followed her to the kitchen, sniffing. The house was dusty and full of cat hairs. The cat was sprawled on the kitchen table where it surveyed Cecile through one green and one blue eye. It rose slowly, twitched its black-tipped Siamese tail, and made a noise like a baby crying before jumping off to the floor with a thump.

"There." Lyuba replaced the bottle and smiled a purple smile. "I get hot. Want a drink?"

"No, thanks."

"This house is real big with Ray gone. We can sit almost anywhere and talk about Paulie. You know Paul?" Lyuba wandered past Cecile and back into the living room where she sat heavily on the couch, raising a small cloud of dust and cat hairs. Cecile followed and perched on the edge of a green chair decked out in yellow antimacassars.

"I always knew Paul," Cecile began. "We grew up together. I'm Cecile Buddenbrooks, Sister Cecile now."

132

"Oh, them."

"I'm the last of them."

"Had a brother, I remember."

"Once," Cecile said patiently.

"Paul said look me up?"

"I was just passing by. He'd said you were a dear friend and that your son had just died."

Lyuba McVey sighed. "I told Paul the cops weren't doing nothing about Ray getting killed. Paul's such a hot-shot busy man he sends you? What the fuck good's that do?" She pointed at the gold cross around Cecile's neck. "And what can you do? Nobody's doin' nothin', so I'm fixin' it myself." She huffed and puffed and wondered where she had put her purse with the drugs in it. "Where's my purse?"

"The kitchen? You went right in there. I'll look." Cecile began to move.

"Sit! Sit, sit, sit. I know who killed my Ray. I know why they killed my Ray. And I know I'm gonna get him. He's gonna suffer for what he done. Got a cigarette?"

Nobody ever asked Cecile that. She opened her purse and pulled out a small gold cigarette case half-filled with Kents and offered Lyuba one.

"I'm a Catholic, see," Lyuba said. She picked up the matches on her end table and struck one. She spent a long time lighting the cigarette. "My Ray made his First Communion at St. Mary's."

Cecile nodded.

"Now he's dead. You want to know why they killed my Ray?"

"Yes."

"He went to get the man who ran over my flowers. He did it for me, Ray did. He said so. Ray went to get him. I met the man too, and I know he killed my boy." Lyuba was blubbering now, taking long drags on the cigarette between hiccups.

Cecile moved over to sit beside the distraught woman and patted Lyuba's free hand. "I'm so sorry, so very sorry

133

for you," Cecile said. "Ray must have wanted to help you so . . ."

"Howard Marshall killed Ray," Lyuba said. "He drove that truck over my plants all hopped up on his own stuff. I seen people like that. They take the stuff and they fly."

"Drugs?" Cecile asked. Lyuba's hand seemed to grow stronger in her grip. The hiccups stopped.

"Drugs. He deals. That's why Ray is dead."

"I see," Cecile said.

"I know drugs. Ray showed me drugs. Get my purse from the kitchen."

Cecile jumped up and got the raffia bag. It was strangely heavy. When she put it on the couch beside Lyuba, several apples and the butt end of Ray's gun appeared. Her estimation of Lyuba McVey was changing fast.

"I just bought some stuff from Mr. Marshall," Lyuba said and fumbled in the bag. She pulled out the envelope and showed the contents to Cecile. "Some of these make you feel good," Lyuba said. "Howard's getting real stuff in next week. Big stuff. He's making hard money. I'm gonna fix him."

"How?" Cecile asked.

"I'm working on that. Maybe buy real stuff next week, set up for a big buy and have the cops?"

"So we work something out," Cecile said, catching on fast, "and set this Herman Melville up."

"Name's Marshall," Lyuba corrected. "Howard Marshall."

"Right. We have to figure out a plan. Maybe we can get his supplier too. Make a big sweep." Cecile was getting into it. "We'll need a lot of cash," she added.

"A thousand bucks, maybe more. Crack. Crack next time. Marshall's gettin' into the heavy stuff."

"I wonder if he takes credit cards," Cecile mused. She absently removed another cigarette from the gold case and handed it to Lyuba, rolling it between her fingers before she let it go.

"Paul can get some money," Lyuba said. "He's got

money. You tell Paul what I know. I kept telling Paul, but he don't listen. Paul's no help at all. Cops don't listen, either. I gotta do it all myself."

Cecile was thoughtful. "Now, Lyuba, a drug charge is nothing next to a murder charge. Somehow we have to prove he killed Ray. How did he do it?"

"Ray was shot but I know Ray had his knife on him when he left. He didn't when they found him. Bastard must have killed him, taken Ray's knife away."

"Where was he killed?"

"Cops say they think the dumpster was the one from back there." Lyuba tipped her head back toward the rear of the house. "Norfolk Café's dumpster. I think they went back there and had a fight."

"A fight. A motive." Cecile nodded. "So the knife might still be there?"

Lyuba shrugged. She was growing tired, and it was way past noon. She'd already missed her show on TV; she wouldn't miss her drink. Not even for a nun.

"And you say they never found Ray's knife?" Cecile asked.

"Never. It's out there. Cops can't find nothing." Lyuba was thirsty. Her fingers began to tingle.

"Let's go find it." Cecile jumped up.

"I'll have a little drink first."

"Oh, yes. I'll wait."

Lyuba got up from the couch with an effort and went to the kitchen where she poured two drinks. Scotch, neat. The glasses were dirty, and Cecile's "thank you" was barely believable when she accepted her drink from Lyuba's shaking hands. The nun eyed the dying ivy on the windowsill; it didn't deserve any more trouble than it already had. She spotted the cat's bowl in the kitchen; its crusty edge seemed to demand an alcoholic swab. But no, she couldn't do that to the cat either. "I'll take a little water with mine," she said at last and went to the kitchen where she dumped the stuff down the drain, added water to the glass, swished it around, and dumped it after the Scotch. "Ahh," she said and placed the empty glass on the drainboard. Cecile returned to the living room under Lyuba's disdainful eye. The older woman drank slowly, but then she had poured twice as much into her own glass.

Ten minutes later they went out into the backyard and across the new flower bed. Cecile stopped to admire the miniature roses. There were several pink blossoms still blooming on delicate thorny stems, and a second bush had lovely white flowers. The coreopsis were doing well too, abundant yellow flowers spraying the area with sunshine. The fence through which Howard Marshall's truck had plowed was still down, allowing easy access to the parking lot beyond. The two women stepped through the garden, avoiding the new plantings, then up a slight grade to the parking lot. The café was off to the left, bordering on Hampshire Street; and there was the dumpster, dented and blue beside the café. In one corner was an abandoned 1967 Pontiac without tires, beside it several live cars, and further down a large orange truck wearing the logo THE WORKS.

Aside from that the lot was empty but for loose trash: empty potato chip bags and the leavings of discreet drinking, several brown bags turned down at the edges. Summer was turning into autumn; somewhere in the scraggle of ragweed along the edge of the lot two crickets chirruped.

"I think we should look along the edges closest to the dumpster," Cecile said. She was frowning. It was a filthy place with the pent-up dirt of the past summer languishing in the corners.

"He's a bum, this Marshall. Lazy," Lyuba said. She was puffing for breath. "He wouldn't have taken it far." She began to kick at the dirt bordering the blacktop. Cecile followed her, kicking a few inches farther in. Cecile was wearing lizard Etta Jennicks that she had charged at Filene's. Lyuba McVey was wearing Nike running shoes and was kicking nicely, raising a cloud of dust.

A car pulled into the lot, and the two women kept kicking on like two chorus girls in rhythm. Dirt scuttled side to side, and the sun sent a burst of light reflecting from the car window into Cecile's eyes. That was when she kicked up the knife, first seeing its glinting edge. She stopped, kicked deeper, then reached down and scooped it all up, using the edge of her skirt, just in case there were still fingerprints. "I found it," Cecile said. "After all this time."

Lyuba stepped up, her face dripping. "Ray's" she gasped. "Yes, yes." Lyuba was wringing her hands. "Ray's."

Cecile beamed triumphantly, but then she frowned. "Well, it proves he was here. I guess." But it didn't do much else. It didn't even prove why *she* was here. "Let's go home," Cecile said softly.

Lyuba stood immobile, then turned abruptly and began to march back toward her house. The house offered security from a hostile world—another drink, a nap, the television, and what was left of some Lithuanian cookies Lyuba had bought at the church fair on Windsor Street last Sunday. Her desire to be in her own house was so great that her words barely made it. "I have everything," she said, "in the house."

Cecile followed the old woman carefully through the tangled web of the end of summer heat and trash. The air was thick with warmth and dust and the scent of beer from the café. She had found Ray McVey's knife for his mother. She would take it to the police for whatever good that might do. Probably no good at all.

She looked sideways and saw Lyuba McVey's fabulous smile. She had done good, after all.

13

LYUBA McVey slipped off into her Tuesday-style oblivion shortly after she and Cecile returned to the house. The television came on, the drinks were refilled, and Lyuba sat back on the couch with the cat firmly on her lap. "It's all over. We've got the goods," she said. "Not only that, I got this plan that's gonna bust this whole thing sky-high. You get Paulie for me. Do that. My show's on now." Her eyes almost closed in bliss as she clicked the television remote control. Sound blasted the room.

Sister Cecile was more thoughtful. "I don't actually see what good this knife will do us. We should give it to the police to prove Ray was there. That will at least place him." She was speaking to Lyuba, but the cat appeared more interested. She began writing down things on a scrap of paper from her bag. "The knife and our names, and maybe the date and time." Lyuba began to snore.

"Oh, sleep," Cecile muttered and stood up. She picked up the second drink Lyuba had thrust on her and dumped it down the kitchen sink. She located the telephone underneath last Saturday's *Herald*, dialed Paul's number, and was put through to him immediately.

"Just leaving, Cecile. Did you see her?"

"I'm here now, Paul, and I have something for you."

"What?"

"Ray's knife. Lyuba and I found it at the scene of the crime. It proves Ray was in the Norfolk Café parking lot. He had the knife on him that day, Lyuba says. I think you should turn it in to the police station.

"Knife?"

"Ray McVey's knife. Plus, Lyuba has some plan, she says. Something she says will blow everything out of the water. What do you think?"

"I'm hardly thinking." Paul had his feet up on his desk and he exhaled in a huge yawn. It had been such a lazy afternoon, and now look at it.

"I suppose I'll have to turn it in," he said, "along with some contrived tale of how you got it."

"No need to contrive. We decided it might be in the parking lot and went and looked. Simple."

"All neat and tidy," Paul said. "You leave me no choice, as usual. I can take a cab over to Cambridge right now, and we can bring the knife to the station. What about Lyuba?"

"Asleep." Cecile eyed the bottle of Scotch on the table. "Poor thing."

"How well do you know this woman, Paul?"

He laughed. "I'll be along. Pour yourself a drink. She keeps a good bottle next to the Lysol under the kitchen sink."

"Thanks." Cecile hung up. She could hear snores from the living room and the television roaring. If she turned the TV down it would probably wake Lyuba up, Cecile thought, so she tried to ignore the sound. She could either wait here in the house or sit on the front steps. There was nothing else to do and it would take Paul at least half an hour to get there from downtown Boston. He was probably parked in some abysmal parking lot half a mile from his office. On the other hand, he had said "cab." Maybe he had walked to work and needed a cab now.

She looked under the kitchen sink and discovered the bottle. Chivas Regal. How had Paul known?

All the glasses in the cabinet had a greasy film on them. Cecile took one out and ran water until it was hot. She soaped and rinsed the glass, shook it carefully, and wiped it dry with a tissue from her purse. She set it on the counter and poured, then took her drink and went out the front door to wait on the wooden steps. The house had a smell and it was dark and noisy. Outside she felt only the loveliness of a summer afternoon. All up and down the small street, trees of heaven filled the area with drooping, cracking branches and feathery leaves. Children laughed and shouted words children didn't used to know. Sister Cecile sat down and settled her feet on the next step down, leaned back, and sipped. It was almost genteel.

She didn't hear the yellow cab as it pulled up. Her eyes were half closed, the glass empty beside her on the step. Paul stooped down and lightly kissed her cheek.

She screamed, "Paul, you fiend!"

He stepped back and laughed.

Cecile straightened her skirt and sat up.

"Nuns shouldn't sleep on the porch steps," he said.

"Shut up and sit down."

He sat beside her on the step. "Don't I always do just what you ask?" He grinned.

She ignored him. "Lyuba says the killer is the man who ran over her flowers."

"No shit. Howie Marshall. She's been hinting about that to me all along."

"But no proof." Cecile fingered her glass. "I found the Chivas. Will she miss it?"

"Probably. Where's the knife?"

"In the kitchen. It's ugly. Take it down to the police station. Lyuba says it's this Howie Marshall who killed Ray. Maybe his fingerprints are on the knife. We should tell the police, right? When we give them the knife."

"Sure, Cecile. It's not going to be easy to prove. The cops don't want a knife. Ray was shot. They want a gun."

"The police should still be told and given the knife. I don't have to come, do I? I mean, it's not my case."

"Sure, Cecile."

"You can be my plenipotentiary."

"Sure, Cecile. Let's go shake Lyuba and check our strategy with her. She's the chief. But don't delude yourself. The police aren't going to arrest somebody on her say-so. Not even if he did do it. They need proof, and so do I."

140

"I think she may want to use thumbscrews on this man to get even. It might be better for him if they arrested him."

"Much better," Paul agreed. He helped Cecile up by the arm.

Inside, the television seemed even louder than before. Paul flipped it off casually as he walked by. Lyuba sat up with a blink.

"Paulie, you come too?" Lyuba asked, not making a great deal of sense.

"I come too," he said and settled down beside her on the hairy couch. "So we have a knife. What would you like to do with it?"

"I've been thinking about that," Lyuba said, and Cecile stared in wonder because the woman talked as though she actually *had* been thinking about it.

"I think we should give Ray's knife to the police," Lyuba went on, "but not mention that we know who did him. Let them run around a little. That will give me time."

Cecile sat in the armchair, an invisible third party. Paul and Lyuba were like practiced conspirators.

"Time for what? Private revenge?" Paul asked.

Lyuba nodded. "He sells drugs, that man. He's made people suffer. He's gouged them for money for the stuff. He's the one killed my Ray, all right!"

"How do you know?" Paul pulled out a cigarette and lit it. "How do you know he did it?"

"I made a little drug buy. And he ran over my flowers. That's why. Howard Marshall. I know my Ray saw him. I know."

"I see." He blew a smoke ring. Lyuba's reasoning was hard to follow, even on a good day. On the other hand, Howie Marshall sold drugs. Maybe there was something there.

"I'm setting up a big buy next week. I need some money for that. How about a grand?" Lyuba asked. "How about ten grand. Really big-time. Pull in all the shitheads."

"How about it?"

"Can you get it?"

141

"For you, Lulu?"

"For Ray."

"I'd rather do it for you."

"You don't like my Ray?"

"Come off it, Lulu. You know how I feel about Ray. You know I always speak ill of the dead."

Lyuba laughed seductively, giving Cecile a glimpse of the charm she once had. "Son of a bitch, Paul, you old fart," Lyuba said.

"Watch your words. There's a nun here."

Lyuba roared and slapped her thigh. Cecile could see the flesh jiggle under thin cotton. "Don't, Paul," Cecile said quietly.

"Don't, Paul," Lyuba mimicked. "That one's a sometimes nun. She don't act like no nun I ever knew. Where'd you find that nun, Paulie?"

"She's my old friend, Lulu."

Lyuba looked from Paul to Sister Cecile and back to Paul. She must have seen something because she sat up straight and became serious. She even brushed her wrinkled skirt down to cover her knees, and when she spoke her voice sounded old, weary. "I have a plan to send this man so far upriver he'll never come down," she said. "That bastard killed my son, Paul. I want to set him up so they pick him up for drugs. Then we spring Ray's death on him. He done it. I know because Ray said he was gonna see this man the day he died. This drug pusher Howie Marshall, he saw my Ray last."

"I'll turn the knife over to the police, Lyuba, and I can mention that you suspect Howie Marshall, but that's it. I'm a lawyer, remember? And the thought of your setting up a drug buy doesn't feel good. What if you're arrested too?"

"Not if you set it up with the cops, Paulie. You could do that. I know you got friends with them cops. You got Ray out all the time."

"Some of the time," he corrected. "Sure, I know Jones and some of the vice squad. I could talk to someone. I'm still a lawyer, though, and they don't like lawyers too much. I'm usually getting out the ones they put in." He stood up and walked to the front window and pulled back a filmy curtain. It wasn't clean, and a puff of dust rose at the rare disturbance. Paul turned back. "They'll be glad to see the knife you found, and I'll have to mention Howie's name. But you know cops. They like hard evidence."

"I'll do my drug deal." Lyuba sat, eternally complacent. "Just get me the money, and set it up with the cops. I'll wear a tape recorder. I'll get him with big stuff. Maybe I can get him to name his source."

"How do I get my money back?"

"If it's set up with the cops, they'll know it's your money. I want to get the supplier too. A couple of good buys, then I ask for the boss. Maybe we clean up the city."

"Not likely," Paul said.

Lyuba shrugged. "More comes in, but we get some revenge. We get him twice: dealing, murder. Makes it better. They won't let him off so fast. We get the big man on top, we got a big case. We make sure he's wrecked, then he won't kill no more kids like my Ray."

"Sounds good," Paul agreed and sat back down. "I trust you, but the cops know you're crazy Ray's mother. It's not going to be easy."

"You can do it." Lyuba had total confidence.

Cecile couldn't remain silent any longer. "You could actually do it, Paul. Lyuba knows the area, and with police backup ... Well, I know it sounds wild, but do you have a better idea?"

Paul grimaced. Two crazy women. One was bad enough, and Cecile should know better. "Shit," he said. And the cops would probably even go for it.

Sister Cecile's eyebrow rose. She knew exactly what he was thinking. "Let's try," she said quietly, her dignity restored. "But we'll worry about you, Lyuba."

Lyuba shrugged. "Nothin' ever happens here now my Ray's gone," she said. "Ray always had friends, music. They stayed up a lot, made me mad. We had fights. Cops would come and take him to lockup for the night. I'd call you, Paulie. I gotta do somethin' now he's dead." She looked mournful. "How long you think I'm gonna sit around like this? This ain't no fuckin' life."

"I'll take the knife up now, Lulu. See what I can set up with my buddy on the force, Jonesy. But I don't think he'll go for it. Let's go, Cecile." Paul patted Lyuba's arm and beckoned to Cecile. "Where's the knife?"

"I'll get it." Cecile hurried to the kitchen where she put the weapon in a plastic Tello's bag that was stashed beside the sink. Three minutes later she and Paul were outside, breathing the late-day air.

"Hard to believe," Sister Cecile murmured.

"You should have known Ray."

"No, thanks."

It was only slightly more trouble than Paul had expected to turn the knife over to the Cambridge Police Department. Detective Limper took the knife and wrote something on a paper and attached it to the handle. He looked doubtful.

"The knife belonged to Mr. McVey," Cecile explained carefully to the policeman, "and he had it with him on the day he was killed. I found it myself, and thought you should have it as proof that he was there. It may have my fingerprints."

"This places him, I suppose. But it's not going to change anything," Detective Limper said. Mr. Dorys had an excellent reputation. And a nun? How the hell had these people become involved with the McVeys? He would follow up on it, recheck the parking lot, recheck the dumpster for blood, if they could locate it. He had no choice.

"I'll have the lab go over the knife. We may even get fingerprints. There are ways of drawing up latent prints even after this long. If we're in luck, we'll get a match with a set of prints on file. But he was shot, don't forget. This knife doesn't mean a great deal. You'll have to be finger-printed. Later."

"It's better than nothing, and it was there," Cecile said, determined to have her say. Then she backed off a few steps to let Paul finish with a man's point of view. Men needed that one-on-one stuff with each other sometimes.

Paul spoke with the officer for a full ten minutes; he gave surprisingly few facts for so many words. But he was a lawyer. He did mention Howard Marshall's name, though, and, as expected, got a minimal response.

Then Paul asked to see Detective Jones. Lyuba's idea about a drug buy probably wouldn't fly, but he might as well ask.

"Jonesy's off. He won't be in until later tonight. Around nine you might find him here."

"I'll come in then," Paul said.

"Can I give him a message?" Limper was suspicious. He was suspicious of the knife and suspicious of the nun. There was something odd about her, yet she certainly had a way. Pretty, too.

Paul saw the detective's eyes travel over Cecile, and he didn't like it. "No message. I'll be back." He turned to Cecile, grabbed her arm, and practically shoved her out of the station house. "I don't like you being in that place," he muttered, dragging her down the cement steps to Western Avenue.

Cecile regained her balance and pulled away. "Really, Paul, I thought we were doing nicely. Mr. Limper was very helpful."

"Very helpful. I'll deal with him by myself next time."

"You don't need to go all protective on me."

"Don't I? It's one of the few things I can be with you."

"Well, maybe. I've got to be getting back, anyway. I missed vespers again."

"And dinner. Let's get something to eat. I'll send you back in a cab, and by then it will be time to see Jonesy. You can pray later."

It made sense. Dinner had been over for an hour; the nuns were in chapel now. The kitchen would be bereft of food, and she was starving.

"Feed me, then," she said.

"Got your credit card?"

"Cheapskate!"

They ate at a new Chinese restaurant. There was always a new Chinese restaurant in Central Square, Cambridge. The food was greasy and contained ample amounts of monosodium glutamate. Sister Cecile's fortune cookie predicted a long, happy marriage, and Paul's suggested that he should be careful with his tax forms that year. They emerged from the Oriental ambience feeling groggy, either from the experience or from the Hong Kong beer.

"I don't think I'll try that again for a while," Cecile murmured. The evening was cool and the street well-lighted. "Where are the taxis?"

"My innocent child, next time we'll do the Indian restaurant and see how that makes you feel." Paul directed her to the left. "Taxis are in front of Woolworth's. Come on. I'll pick you a good one."

Minutes later Cecile was in the back seat of a yellow cab. Paul stuck his head in the front window. "Adams Street. Our Lady of Good Counsel. Know where that is?"

The cabby nodded as Paul twisted his head in to see the name: Jacob Zuber. "I been there before," Jacob said with a half-smile.

" 'Night, Cecile." Paul waved and went out into the street again, ducking between a Harvard Square bus and a motorcycle. He was gone in a moment and Cecile was swept into a U-turn to begin the journey back to Dorchester. She settled back, eyes closed. The day had left her drained.

They drove in silence for some time, passing out of Cambridge and into Boston. Eventually Cecile opened her window enough to let in a nice breeze and began to enjoy the ride. The cabby began to speak.

"I took a kid out your way back last spring. Young girl. Always wondered what happened to her." Jacob had slipped the bullet-proof plastic window that separated them to one side so that Sister Cecile could hear his words clearly. "Late one night. She was scared stiff about something."

146

"Oh!" Cecile said.

"You know about that kid? Same convent, right?"

"Yes, she . . ." Cecile paused. What could she ever say about Jane? "She came for help and we gave it."

"So what happened? What's she doing?" Jack Zuber didn't want to betray his interest but he hadn't been able to get the red-haired kid out of his mind. He'd even told his wife.

"Well, everything is fine now. She's safe and happy. She's having a baby." Cecile didn't usually tell taxi drivers personal things, but he seemed to know Jane somehow—really seemed to care.

"No kidding. Won't I have something to tell the wife tonight! Wife's always wanted kids, see. We always wanted to do something for a kid like that. Real young. Not married, right?"

"Right."

He shook his half-bald head, spotlighted by lights as he drove through Boston toward the other side. It was a bumpy ride. Boston had potholes big enough to swallow taxis the size of his.

"Wife always wanted to get in that program taking in kids like that till they have the baby. Make herself something like a grandmother, you know?" Jacob blasted the horn at a van blocking half the street, then swerved into the left lane. "My old lady, she always wanted a daughter." He shrugged eloquently. "She was asking at Saint Ann's about that, giving a room to someone with troubles, giving the kid a chance. She even took a course at the parish hall last year."

"You go to St. Ann's in Dorchester?"

"Sure. Father McGee's," he said with a mock brogue.

"Would you be willing to let her stay at your home? For pay, of course. Without anyone knowing?"

"Secret-like? Sure, wife would love that."

"She's in a nice place, but she's returning here this week. St. Ann's parish isn't quite home, but close. The baby's due soon."

"The wife would be thrilled." The cab pulled up in front of the convent. It was still twilight and traffic was light. The old building looked welcoming after a difficult day.

"I'll take your number, if I might, and perhaps be in touch," Cecile said. She pulled out a scrap of paper from her bag, this time an envelope. She pushed it through the space and into Jacob Zuber's hand. "Could you write your name and address there?"

Jacob wrote quickly in heavy strokes. "I'll tell my wife. There was something about that girl. I been thinking about her ever since." He slid the paper back.

"Thank you." Sister Cecile spoke quietly, pulled out a ten-dollar bill for the fare and tip. She handed it in through the space. "Thank you, Mr. Zuber. You may be hearing from me. I'm Sister Cecile."

Vespers was long over when Cecile finally let herself into the silent chapel. On the way in she had left Mr. Zuber's name and address with Sister Raphael, asking her to check up on the man through Father McGee at St. Ann's. Jane was arriving in two days and having her stay in the convent could be difficult, particularly for Jane.

Tom Dempsey was restless, depressed that Jane had vanished, and very low on funds. He had come to a dead end in his search for Jane Hersey. Martin Moon had been no help at all and had become sullen each time Tom made mention of Jane's name. "She ain't come home, not once. I got a friend watching the Hersey place," Tom complained.

Martin would growl every time he saw Tom. "The nuns got her stashed, that's all. You find her, you get the money. And stay away from the damn convent. She's not there." He was treading on water with the nuns. Sister Cecile had scared him badly, but not enough to make him stop his extortion. She would never check up on him. Besides, he was busy creating an entire new file. Damn crazy nun would never know.

Dempsey was ready to quit. He had followed Paul Dorys everywhere and discovered nothing. His break-in attempt

148

had failed when no less than six alarms had gone off. A week later a professional friend of his had gotten in undetected, somehow, and gotten out again with word that the lawyer had a great CD collection and some good wine, but no papers resembling those in the file and no safe in the place. It cost Dempsey two hundred dollars for that job and it came to nothing. Then Tom Dempsey had called Richmond and checked out the order of Our Lady of Good Counsel there, but they didn't deal with unwed mothers and had never heard of Jane Hersey. They had mentioned that a Sister Cecile from Boston was traveling in the diocese doing fund-raising, but that meant nothing to Tom.

By the end of August Tom's advance was long gone, and Moon had no more jobs for him. Things were not jelling. The IRA was lying low until the late fall and didn't need any new gun deals, and Tom was still feeling humiliated from the spaghetti fight with Paul Dorys. He was itching to get into something new, something that made money. Big money. What he could really use was a new drug connection. The market was good, the money better, and the attrition rate of dealers high. He'd have to look around.

Barry Rizzo operated out of an insurance agency in the South End. He would have preferred the North End or even East Cambridge; but territory was assigned, and that was that. Unless he moved up. And he had never been quite sure if he wanted that. Triple Crown Insurance Company was safe and comfortable and had a good color TV in the back room along with a small bar. He had a solid distributorship in marketable drug products, and it was a bull market. He had just made an appointment for that afternoon at three o'clock with a new man who had come knocking on his door two days ago. An Irishman named Tom Dempsey.

Barry didn't like Irishmen much. It was his bad luck his sister had gone and married O'Neil, but O'Neil moved a lot of drugs now, and that meant money. He had researched Tom Dempsey already and Dempsey had checked out as a regular local tough who did anything for a buck, and that meant more money for Barry. Barry had just bought a new Cadillac for himself, and now his wife wanted a new car of her own. Equal rights or something. Barry thought and mixed himself a gimlet. He always needed more money. The front office was busy; they actually turned a good profit selling insurance, but he had that Mick coming in half an hour and could use some relaxing.

Tom Dempsey was early. He walked up and down Tremont Street eyeing the gay bars and the liquor stores and the drunk Indians. Gentrification was tough on the Micmacs. They'd be pushed right into Roxbury soon and vanish. Another Indian tribe gone. Finally Tom pushed open the insurance-agency door. It was cool inside, eighty outside. "Mr. Rizzo? I have an appointment."

The young man behind the counter blushed. It was a trait that endeared him to many patrons but not to this one. Tom merely wiped a trickle of sweat off his chin and licked it off his finger.

"Mr. Rizzo is in the back office. I shall ring," the young man said carefully.

The young man rang and smiled at Tom. Two beeps answered the ring and he waved Tom into the inner area. The rug was thick and blue, too thick for a hot day.

"Go right on through, sir. The beeps unlock the door."

Tom marched in, his feet having trouble on the heavy pile. He opened the door and heard it click firmly behind him. Barry Rizzo was working on his second drink and just beginning to relax.

Tom Dempsey eyed the drink, the small bar, and Rizzo, in that order; he shuffled a little on the rug, and began his speech. "I got good references. I want some work. Sales?"

"I mentioned sales." Rizzo nodded. "You check out. Sit down."

Tom was waiting for the offer of a drink as he sat. The only chair not covered with stacks of insurance forms was wooden, though not uncomfortable, and looked directly on the bar and its row of mouth-watering bottles.

"I did some sales up in Lynn," Tom said. "I been doin' work here in town, but it's slow."

"Ever cut somebody?"

"Sure." Tom Dempsey smiled. The old nun had croaked because of him. That must count.

"I got some new territory opening down Savin Hill. Dealer there overdosed, and good help is hard to get. We've thrown in some subs, but they got more than they can handle." Rizzo didn't mention that the subs were both so hooked on their own product they could barely make their deliveries. They only worked to keep their own habits going.

"I can handle it." Dempsey swelled a little, his eye wandering to the bottle of gin and the small open jar of cocktail onions beside it. He could almost taste a drink, and his mouth began to water. He swallowed and made a peculiar gulping sound. "Ain't nothin' I don't handle," he said.

"You do drugs?" Rizzo asked.

"No hard stuff. I like to drink now and then." He tore his eyes away from the bottle. "I like a drink in the evening sometimes," he said, looking at Rizzo's glass. "Drugs, they give me no problem. I pass on drugs. Sometimes I smoke now and then. No big thing. I'm cool."

"Tom Dempsey, you're cool. We'll try you." Rizzo spoke softly and Tom nodded quickly in agreement. Rizzo was damn smart and he knew it. "So I set you up with my sub in Savin Hill tomorrow. We'll arrange a meet. He'll show you the deal. You pick up the wares at a grocery store on Sidney Street. You take them around. We got a regular run. You make collections, deliveries. Anyone give you any trouble, what you gonna do?"

"I'm gonna straighten them up. No guff, man. I don't take no guff. You want I should take 'em out?"

"Nothing like that. No cops nose around if they all keep breathing."

Tom nodded. "They all keep breathing."

Barry pulled out a long sheet of paper that could have passed for an insurance policy. In fact it was modeled on one as far as form went. The words specified certain expectations for Rizzo's employees and certain obligations. At the bottom of a page of fine print rested the proverbial bottom line: the money each agent would receive for the work rendered. Barry filled in a few of the blanks, then thrust the sheet at Tom.

"You check this out. Tells what your job is, specifies payments and percentages. Read it. Sign it. You mess with it, you mess with me, you won't be walking. Understand?"

Tom managed a weak "Yeah," and accepted the paper, noticing how his hand shook. Damn it, couldn't the man see he needed a drink?

The contract made for tough reading. The words were designed to be understood by someone with an eighth-grade education, rather like *The New York Times*. Tom had never read *The New York Times* and he couldn't read this. He stared at the fine print for three minutes while Rizzo mixed himself another drink and sat down. Finally Tom found the blank at the bottom where the percentage had been written in. Next to that was the week's expected take. That he could understand. Almost. He took the pen that Rizzo had slid to the edge of his desk and signed the blank. "Thomas F. X. Dempsey, Jr." It looked good. He handed the paper back to Barry and felt himself an equal. "How about a drink?" Tom said expansively.

Barry Rizzo leaned back in his chair. "Harp," he said. "Terry's sells Harp. Half a block down." He folded the contract and put it in a drawer. It was worthless, but he liked the formality. "I'll see you tomorrow night, corner of Grampian and Savin Hill. Eight thirty."

"Yeah." Tom could feel the dismissal in his bones. He could feel everything in his bones, he needed a drink so bad. "I'll be there." He stood up, tried to smile and failed, turned and left. Harp. Damned if it didn't sound good. The bastard knew his men. Tom covered the block to Terry's Bar and Grill in half a minute flat and had a Harp in his hand in another three minutes. By the time the beer was three quarters gone, the only thing Tom Dempsey could recall from Rizzo's office was the bottom line of the contract and the time of his meeting for the next night. He finished off the first beer and ordered a second. By the time he was on his third he was murmuring to himself about Italians. "I think I like that Guinea," he said out loud.

The bartender slapped up a Guinness Stout.

14

Sister Cecile was engulfed in paperwork. Pledges for aid required follow-up letters. She wrote more letters to other religious orders. Annuities and pensions had to be considered. Sister Cecile wasn't just dealing with the present, she also had to plan for the future and make an accounting for a past that had been badly planned. She had already met with the Cardinal's stewardship officer, met with the provincial head of the Sisters of Notre Dame, read insurance company brochures on retirement planning and added up the pledges she had collected all summer. There was not enough money, real or promised, to establish and support a retirement home. And Jane would be home tomorrow.

Paul called on Wednesday afternoon. "Cecile, how are things?"

"I'm just waiting for the Lord to provide. Our Florida community is looking like a pipe dream."

"Pick up something cheap in central Georgia."

"Would you retire there?"

"No. Heard anything from our itinerant teenager?"

"She's coming home. We've got to deal with that, Paul. She can't hide forever."

"No," Paul agreed. "Any ideas?"

"Her father's running for Congress." Sister Cecile began a doodle, a giant cross with tiny roses at its base. "It's not easy to make a decision and stick by it," she said. "But Jane has, and now what?"

"Freedom," Paul said, "is one of those elusive things,

particularly for a pregnant teenager. I don't think Moon would dare touch her now."

"Maybe, maybe not. Can we risk her life?"

"Has she ever written her father?" Paul asked.

"Oh, yes. I gave her some neutral stationery. She mailed his letters to me, I put them in clean envelopes and sent them along. And vice versa. Abe is ready to welcome the grandchild now and everybody is happy. Abe has been thrilled with everything since he got that old letter back. Case closed. Almost." Cecile doodled a particularly heavy rosebud. "Of course I check Jane's letters over. There have been several. Actually, Jane herself suggested I check to make sure she doesn't let anything slip that she shouldn't, like where she is. The letters are pathetic. Abe has responded twice. I believe they really care for each other, but they don't really know each other very well. That will come eventually or maybe never. One's own parents are always hard to know."

"Some things defy heaven and earth," Paul said.

"You're cynical."

"Realistic. I live in the real world, Cecile. Unlike you."

"It's all relative to the truth. Tell me what happened with the police officer? It didn't work, did it?"

"Jonesy? In Cambridge?"

"That one."

"Jonesy actually went for it. The drug bust is shaping up. Next Tuesday, Lyuba will make a good-sized buy and suggest a major purchase for the following week: heroin, dust, crack, and pretty pills all colors."

"Unbelievable."

"We're hoping. Jonesy thinks it may be Cambridge's big supplier who's behind it, and if Lyuba can get to him some way, insisting on speaking to the boss or no deal, it might be good. It's big bucks. We're going all out. I was surprised with the enthusiasm the cops worked up, considering Lyuba. They all knew Ray. Poetic justice or something. But she won't go in alone. She'll have serious backup."

"Lyuba? Nobody would sell her any sizable amount of

drugs, would they? She's unreliable, isn't she?" Cecile's doodle was sprouting angels with detailed feathers on their wings.

"Don't be naïve. Lyuba's ideal for a player. She's totally beyond suspicion. Will you be there?"

"Wouldn't miss it. How will I manage?"

"Come, come, Cecile. I know you better than that. You'll manage."

"Don't tease, Paul."

Paul laughed. He was calling from his apartment and was stretched out on the couch with a bottle of Samuel Adams in his hand. He rubbed his thumb up and down the wet side, making a clear spot. "Truth is stranger than fiction, Cecile. I'll be in touch with you about the go-down time."

"Do that, Paul."

Cecile crumpled the doodle and tossed it into her wastebasket. The basket was ten feet away, and she never missed. At least there was some satisfaction in life.

And, in general, things were picking up. Jane was coming home. What on earth could she do about Jane? Why didn't Paul have any ideas?

Sister Raphael was in the hall holding a dust rag in one hand, a book in the other. She was standing and reading while the dust rag made aimless swipes at a small mahogany table when Cecile emerged from her office.

"Oh," Raphael said. "Cecile, you must read this. It's the latest theory on computerized stock swings. It explains how we could hook on to the stock computer network and actually anticipate the swings if we could just get the right program."

"We don't have a computer." Cecile took the dust rag out of Raphael's hand and began methodically polishing a brass Madonna on the wall. "And who could ever work out a program like that?"

"My nephew."

"He has the computer?"

"Very smart, my nephew. He has a new one. He's been

explaining it to me on my day off. He'd love to do it. You know how computer trading works."

"I do?"

"I'd like to try, Cecile. May I?" Sister Raphael always asked permission before she set out in wild pursuit of a new idea. It was another compromise with humility, and Sister Cecile was her superior.

"Of course, Raphael. Let me know." Cecile was ready to walk on when she remembered. "Did you check up on that cab driver, by the way? We don't want Jane to stay in the convent any length of time."

"Mr. Zuber." Sister Raphael took the dust rag back from Cecile's grasp. "Yes, Father said he was a wonderful parishioner and that his wife is the salt of the earth. He actually said, 'salt of the earth.' I didn't think real people said that anymore. She's been running the Confraternity of Christian Doctrine program for the past five years and is wonderful with the children. Never had any herself; so she comes in fresh, unjaded. They don't have a great deal of money. Jake lost his deli job a few years back, and he's been driving a cab ever since.

"And," Raphael added, "you were right, she's already taken some counseling course the diocese offers through Catholic Charities. They run outreach programs to young mothers."

"Perfect. I suppose we should arrange for Jane to stay with them. I'll get right on that," Cecile said. "And I must get in touch with Abe."

Sister Raphael nodded. She began to dust the table all over again. "Paris obviously isn't the whole answer. Things must be dealt with. Jane may still be in mortal danger."

"Of course she is, but it's the file that we must settle. Nevertheless, Jane is arriving imminently."

The younger nun vanished back into her office. She had Mr. Zuber's telephone number and she dialed it quickly. She needed them. Thank God, Raphael had cleared the Zubers to everyone's satisfaction, and the Father, she discovered, had already spoken with the family. It appeared that things were going to work out perfectly for Jane. Cecile had a wonderful talk with Mrs. Zuber. Edith Zuber was anxious to take Jane in immediately. "We have a spare room," Edith said. She was thrilled. "It has lace curtains already. I can't wait to tell Jacob how soon it will be. He told me, and Father McGee, of course, and I spoke at length with that wonderful Sister Raphael, but I couldn't quite believe it."

"Father McGee speaks highly of you both," Sister Cecile murmured. "As for money, I'm going to be in touch with the girl's father and it will be forthcoming. He's not to know where she is. We'll have to work out something, dye her hair brown maybe. It's important nobody knows she's there, or who she is."

The next call was to Abe Hersey. "Abe, it's Sister Cecile."

"Jane? Is everything all right?" Alarm in his voice. The baby was coming soon.

"Jane is doing well, Abe. I have wonderful reports. The problem now has to do with the rooming and delivery. I'm afraid it's going to cost. She's had a job where she's been, but now Jane will no longer be able to pay her own way. She considered AFDC, but I felt you would object to welfare. Plus, she needs seclusion. Jane plans to board with a lovely couple, but they can't afford to keep her for free."

"I see."

"And you do understand why she wants to remain hidden?"

"My campaign. Of course." Abe sighed, torn by thoughts of his daughter and his politics.

"And the file," Cecile added.

"What file?"

Cecile's eyebrow rose. "Oh, nothing. Teenagers are always into something. Yes, well, she is concerned about the campaign. She does want you to win. And she realizes she could be an embarrassment."

"She always was a good girl. You know, I miss her. Listen, that's thoughtful, isn't it? I don't understand this entire

158

business. That Martin Moon. He's called me several times trying to find out where she is. I didn't say a word. Don't trust him an inch. Well, I'll send some money for Jane. She's staying with a couple? Would a hundred dollars a week suffice? Room and board? That's cheap, isn't it? I could manage one fifty. How should I send it?"

"Send it to me here and I'll take care of it." Sister Cecile said. "My fee is separate. I'll send a bill later."

"Yes, fine. Hard to believe," Abe said softly. He was sounding quite unlike the man who had stormed the convent in April. Incipient grandfatherhood did that now and then. "I wonder if the baby will have red hair," he murmured. "She's all right, you say?"

"Now don't you worry, Mr. Hersey. She's fine. Jane would love to see you, but it might cause problems right now. You know how the press is. We're thinking of St. Margaret's Hospital for the delivery."

"I can see her there?"

"Of course. Now, her stay with the couple will begin soon; so send the money to the convent here, and I'll see to it that it goes to the people immediately."

Abe spoke quickly. "I'll take care of that today. Thank you, Sister."

"Jane will be terribly pleased."

Moments later Cecile hung up. Everything was settled. She went straight to the chapel and gave thanks. Abe was mellowing.

Logan Airport was suffering from the heat when Jane Hersey's flight settled down on runway four. It took an hour for her to make it through the line at customs and out the door to Cecile's waiting arms. Jane wore a pale blue smock that danced around her pregnant figure; she looked beautiful. Maternity became her. Even her limp red hair had a fresh look.

"I'm so happy to be back," Jane said with a sob. Cecile felt like a grandmother herself as she hustled Jane off to a cab and a quick ride to the Zubers' three-family wooden house on Arcadia Street near Ronan Park, Dorchester.

Four days later the heat had lessened only slightly, but an inversion had caused a sickly haze to settle over the city, Cambridge included. The weather reporters all warned people with breathing problems to stay indoors in air-conditioned rooms. September shouldn't be this way, but it was. Hampshire Street stank of its own car exhausts. Lyuba McVey gulped for air on her corner where she waited for Howard Marshall. She was wearing a house dress that cut her swollen legs at their puffiest point. The dress had one large pocket that held one thousand dollars in hundred-dollar bills. She was mumbling to herself, "Herbert Marshall, Howard Marshman, Harold Marshwell," over and over as she tried to remember her supplier's name.

She would show him she had bucks, she thought with a grunt. Big bucks. Once he had the money in his hands he'd be caught in the greed trap. She knew all about it from watching Ray. And next week she'd get her revenge for the memory of that dear boy. A tear slipped down a crease in her cheek.

Howard Marshall had already fallen into the greed trap. He knew his new setup with Daniel O'Neil would make him rich. More drugs, more setups, more sales, more money. It was as simple as that. The old lady he was meeting today would add to his take. She was buying so much, she had to be reselling it somewhere else. Free enterprise. The American way.

Immersed in his dream of power and glory, Howard was five minutes late. Lyuba had her money out when he was half a block away. She waited to speak until he was closer. "I got it. Count it," she said.

Howard did. His yellow shirt stuck to his balloon of a stomach, and he breathed through his mouth, counting aloud in gasps. The money felt real good, and it was right. "Your order's in the bag," he said. "Check it."

She did.

"Next week I want more. I got ten grand. I got a list."
Lyuba produced a paper and handed it to Howard. The
drugs had been listed with weight and price, reflecting the
current market value. Detective Jones had given Paul a list,
Paul had agreed to front the money, and Lyuba had
recopied the list in her own style.

"Too much for you to handle, I bet," she scoffed at Howard. "I want to deal with your boss. We need a safer place,
too. I got one in mind."

Howard didn't know what to say. He looked first at the
list and then at Lyuba. She was a fat old bird with thick ankles, not a drug supplier. She couldn't be. Maybe she was
supplying the Sweet Adeline's International. Or the sewing
club. "You going big-time?" he asked suspiciously.

"Big," she said. "I want the horse's mouth. You're the
bottom. I want the top. I want you, your boss, and me to
work out some big deals. Fuckin' big."

Howard didn't hear the tremor in her voice because his
own brain was quivering like jello. He was counting his
percentage in his mind. He could retire early.

"You deal with me straight," he said. "No boss."

"You don't got guts enough to carry that much," she
said. "You and your supplier show up together or no deal."

Howard looked at the paper again. That meant O'Neil,
and O'Neil wouldn't be seen. But the money! So much
money—he'd be rich. "I gotta think about it. I gotta talk to
somebody. How'm I gonna reach you?" Sweat trickled
down his chin and dripped off.

"Call me up," Lyuba cackled. She loved it. "See that
number on the list? Last one on the right? That's my phone
number. Try it. You tell me the man's coming, I'll have the
money."

"Hold on." Howard fingered the money in his pocket. He
got a piece of that already. He wanted a big piece of what
was coming. "I'll do it myself. Guaranteed."

"Nope. You and the big man, back of the Norfolk Café,
one thirty next Wednesday. Everything on that list. You call

161

me and make sure you're going to be there with the boss. I got a lot of plans. I got money."

Howard believed it. Money. He loved it. "I'll do my best," he said. "I'll try and get him."

"You get him," Lyuba said, "or no deal. I got a future to think of." She cackled again and turned, knowing he was caught. She waddled away, the bag of drugs swinging from her arm like a basket of apples. She would hear from that Hubert Martin. She was sure.

Howie Marshall had another buyer after Lyuba. Then he hurried off, his mind reeling from Lyuba's proposal. Ten grand. He knew it wasn't really much. Drug money was big but he was new to deals beyond nickel-and-dime stuff. He had to talk to O'Neil, and fast. The old lady really meant no deal if she wasn't in touch with the big man. All that money could vanish. He wanted money. He wanted to quit the job behind the damn trash truck. The connections were good, but it stank. He wanted money fast.

It took Howie the remainder of the afternoon to clean up three trucks at the department. Foul, stinking trucks, but he could only smell money. In hot weather the maggots were bad, little white things that dropped like heavy snowflakes into his pant cuffs. He imagined them as cocaine, as crack, as drops of gold, white gold. He hummed "Red River Valley" over and over, and he laughed at Al Beasley's jokes. The rest of the crew raised eyebrows and assumed with one mind that Howie had been dipping into his own supplies. It had been known to happen. When Howie left he was still humming, and he hummed all the way across town to his Cambridgeport apartment where he lived with a woman who had made a career of jobs in Central Square and late-night drinking. He wasn't sure she loved him, but they split the rent and kept each other warm on winter nights.

She was out when Howie got to his place, which meant the bathroom was free for the duration. He took a long shower, smoothed on hair gel, and dressed in a clean green shirt and tan pants. He looked for a tie and found a wide, yellow one with an eagle in the center. He knotted it carefully and looked at himself in the mirror. Cool.

Dan O'Neil lived in North Cambridge. He could take a cab there. This was a time for real class.

15

DAN O'Neil had gone badly into debt to finance his house on Haskell Street, but he fancied he was modeling himself on Tip O'Neill, who was no relation at all. Dan had vague dreams of becoming the most powerful man in the United States. His wife, Merle, was no Millie, though, and she had declined to have five children. "No children. I hate kids," she had told him twenty-seven years ago on their wedding night. At the age of twenty-two she had gone in for a tubal ligation and had never regretted it. Dan O'Neil had never regretted it either. Kids were messy creatures who grew up and got into drugs.

The O'Neils spent their vacations in expensive resorts around the world. Money went fast: cars, clothes, food, repairs to the house, new furniture to replace unfashionable furniture. Merle had a job as a receptionist in an architectural firm. It paid very little but provided a lovely background for displaying her clothes and hairstyles. The O'Neils dined out frequently, but tonight they were home, drinking martinis and eating gourmet frozen dinners in front of *Rambo,* which was playing on channel 38. Neither of them heard the cab drive up, but they both heard the door chime.

Neither made a move to get up. It was a game. The power figure of the day remained seated. Tonight Dan was feeling confident. He had had a good day, and Merle knew it. When the door chime was repeated, she made a resigned face and rose slowly to show she didn't really care. She moved gracefully through the hall, her long skirt swishing against the sculptured carpet. It was a new carpet.

Merle hoped it was someone really important at the door. That would show Dan, sitting there like some animal, stuffing his mouth in front of the television. She opened the door and smiled, her eyes dropping in shock to Howard Marshall's eagle. He did not look important. "Yes?" The smile disappeared.

"I gotta see Mr. O'Neil," Howie mumbled.

Merle O'Neil was an imposing woman, close to six feet tall, with pale-gold hair piled high. Howie couldn't meet her eye without looking up, and he made it a point never to look up at a woman. So he stared at her neck, a piece of anatomy tanned at the local Tan-O-Rama four days a week until it was a crisp, dried column with tight wrinkles that ended in collarbone. "I gotta see him," he repeated to her neck.

She didn't like the top of his head. Not enough hair, too much goo. She could smell it. "Who are you?" she asked.

"Name's Marshall."

Harrumphs came from the other room above the chatter of the television. Daniel had been straining to hear who it was, and he had a picture of what was going on. His wife and Howie Marshall were not soul mates. He finished chewing the soggy asparagus in hollandaise sauce and wiped his lips, missing a drop of yellow on his upper lip. "Marshall, what the hell are you doing here?" He was out in the hall, graceless but unrushed. The day he would rush a meal was yet to come, even frozen asparagus.

Howie flinched but stood his ground in the doorway.

"Let him in, Merle, before all the goddamn air-conditioned air gets out. Costs us a goddamn fortune cooling half of Cambridge."

Howie was in. The door shut tight behind him. Merle stepped back and Dan kept talking. "What the hell are you doing here in my house? You know you can't come here."

Howie looked at Merle. It was easier to see her face with a little distance between them. Ugly, he thought. "I got

165

something big." He looked at Daniel. "I got something real big. Couldn't wait."

Daniel O'Neil nodded to his wife. "We'll go downstairs, Merle. Be right back." He gestured Howie along, and Merle stepped back.

The O'Neils' basement had been carpeted, wall to wall, in pale, tasteful green. The curtains covering the slits to the outside were rose damask. The bar was mahogany and very well stocked. The pool table was expensive; the green-and-pink patterned chairs and couch were comfortable. Soft lights came from invisible sources, and music began at a touch of a button. There were no books, no art; but behind a glass sliding door was a large green-tiled room with a huge pink hot tub. Howie's eyes bugged out. It was exactly the kind of room he wanted. When Dan made the automatic offer of "Would you like a drink?" Howie gulped a "Gimme a beer." His mouth was like cotton.

The beer helped. Howie sank into the couch. O'Neil leaned against a barstool, waiting. It had better be good.

"I got this buyer," Howie began. He wouldn't mention it was an old woman. "She wants a lot of stuff. A real lot. She made a big buy today, took everything I got 'cept what I saved for Francis. I got the order she wants here." He shoved the crumpled paper Lyuba had given him into view. "It says here . . ." He stopped. "You read it." And he held it up.

Dan took two steps away from the barstool and accepted the paper. He examined the detailed price list and was impressed. His cut from it would be bigger than Howie's. A lot bigger. And Merle wanted to have the living room redone. It was damn tempting.

Howie could see that he was impressed.

"She says it will be a steady thing," Howie added.

Dan sucked in his cheeks and nodded. "Wants it next week?"

"Wants it next week," Howie agreed, "and wants you there with me."

Dan blew out his cheeks and released the air with a popping sound. "Sure, it's a lot of money. She? You say it's a she?"

"A she," Howie affirmed.

"She cops?"

"No way." Howie laughed. "Old bag. She's starting a candy store. She's steady."

"I see. Where's she want the meet?"

Howie paused. He didn't want to say yet. "She wanted me to call her once I got the go-ahead from you. Wants you to be there because it's big and she wants assurance from the top brass. Wants me to be there because I'm the source." Howie made sure to include himself. He knew about being cut out, and it wasn't going to happen to him. Not with all the money this deal involved.

Dan was thinking along the same lines. Too bad he couldn't cut out the middleman. "It would be simpler with just me," he tried.

"She said me and you. She was very definite." Howie was starting to panic.

"Less danger, just one of us," Dan said.

"She knows me. She trusts me."

"Sure." Dan leaned back on the bar, fingering the list of items. He had been doing some addition, and his cut would be enough to get a start on the living room. But he didn't like it. He never went public on deals. He'd set that up with Rizzo a long time ago. It was part of their agreement. He couldn't cross Rizzo. Damn. "I can't do it, Marshall," he said.

"You gotta. It's bucks, for God's sake. She won't do it without you."

"I can't go public." Dan sounded as if he might cry. He turned to the bar and reached for a bottle of gin. He poured some into a glass that had been sitting there since last week. He drank.

Howie stood up. Shit. The deal was off. "Okay. Give me the list. I'll call the old bag and see if we can sell less without you coming."

"Do your best."

"She might start lookin' for another dealer, maybe go somewhere else," Howie said mournfully.

"Yeah. I'll see you out." Dan drank off the rest of the gin. It burned down his throat, then up into his mind. "I might want to take the risk. I might. But I got people to think of. The wife, you know?"

Howie moved up the carpeted stairs in a cloud of depression. How could O'Neil pass up all that money?

Howie didn't take a taxi home. He walked two blocks over to Massachusetts Avenue and took a bus all the way to Harvard Square, then a subway to Central Square, and then walked deep into Cambridgeport to his apartment on Erie Street. There was a frozen burrito in the freezer compartment and some beer below. He put the burrito into the microwave and turned it on, then snapped the flip top off the beer. He had remembered to get the paper back from Dan, and as soon as he had something to eat he would call her up and see what they could work out.

The burrito was hot and pale and still frozen near one end, but it went fine with the beer. Howie lifted a loose bean off the plate with his index finger and ate it. He threw the empty plate on the counter and dialed the number.

"Howard here," he said to a crabby "hello." "This the lady wants to buy?"

"Yeah." Lyuba's heart began flapping. This was it.

"Identify yourself somehow so I knows it's you."

"Like say something about you? You got a stomach," Lyuba chuckled, feeling better. "Yellow balloon stomach, how's that?"

Howie didn't like that at all, but it served the purpose. "My boss says I handle the deal myself. It's not such a big deal. Where you want to meet?"

"No meet," Lyuba said defiantly. "No boss, no meet." Those were her orders. If they didn't get beyond small dealers, she couldn't get the ten grand she needed to complete the deal. She would get Howie one way or another for

168

killing her son. This was just one way. If it didn't work, she'd figure out something else.

"How about if we just deal half the stuff. Just the powder, no pills?" Howie tried. "Not such a big deal then. Maybe we can spread it out over a couple of weeks."

"No way. I'm gonna want more the next week. Another big order. I want to deal with the big man. I want you there to verify he's okay. That's the way it's gotta be. If he ain't interested I'll look into Southie. I heard about a man there deals from the top, no small-potato man like you," Lyuba said. She was riding high, feeling her own power as she sensed Howie squirming. She pictured his face, cringing, anxious. He'd be real anxious before it was all over.

"I'll try again," Howie muttered. "I'll call."

"Do that." Lyuba hung up wearing her broadest grin. This was fun.

Howie didn't call anyone else. Instead he opened another beer, drank it, turned on the television, opened a third beer, and fell asleep in front of some wavy lines. When his girlfriend came in an hour later she flicked off the television set and locked up for the night. Howie was such a slob.

The O'Neils finished their gourmet frozen dinners in silence, then Merle heated up some Sara Lee coffee cakes, and Dan made more drinks. They were a compatible couple in that they enjoyed the same things. That may have been the secret to their long marriage, that and sheer inertia.

Councilman O'Neil set the drinks down on the coffee table and sighed. He could almost see that money flying away. It was a crying damn shame but it was a relief too. He'd never touched the drugs yet and he didn't want to. Dirty, filthy stuff.

"We need new batteries for the remote," Merle said, flipping channels. "You gotta hold this thing straight up and at the damn box or it won't work. So, what did that man want?"

"What man?" He picked up his drink and looked guilty, keeping his eyes on the TV.

"What man? You know what man. That ugly man you took down cellar."

"That one? He sells stuff for me."

"What stuff?" Merle knew her husband moved stuff through Barry. First it had been some hot merchandise to friends. A good buy on a stereo that was irresistible. He had to be very careful whom to sell the stuff to. Merle knew they had gone into other things, although she had never had the nerve to ask exactly what. She liked the extra money, and what she didn't know couldn't hurt her. But she was curious.

"Just stuff. He has a buyer for a lot of stuff, wants me to come along for the deal."

"So?"

"Can't do it. I told him I couldn't appear in person. He's my man, you know?"

Merle nodded. It made sense. "How much money?"

"A lot."

"You're turning down a lot? On principle?" Merle's voice rose dangerously.

"Barry wouldn't like it, me going public. You know how he is," Dan muttered.

"Barry? Barry won't like your turning down money. I know how Barry is more than you do. He's *my* brother." Merle took a vicious bite of coffee cake.

"If you don't tell him, he won't ever find out." Dan was feeling sorely tempted. His wife could always rationalize making more money. "You want me to end up in jail? No, thanks."

"Poor baby," Merle sighed. "You could probably pull it off, wear a disguise, whatever. It's a shame to let good money go by."

Dan shrugged. He'd think about it.

Barry Rizzo was worried. Even with his new man, Tom Dempsey, moving more dope, he wasn't able to keep it go-

170

ing out fast enough to suit the boys in New York. And he had a big load coming down next week. A real big load. "Get it out there, Rizzo," they'd told him when he protested. "Get it moving. We got others pushing faster. Get it rolling."

Barry didn't like it. The drugs were like weights hanging around his neck, each new kilo of the white stuff pulling him down more. Maybe he could sell it off in big pieces, he thought, get out of the candy-store business and sell to the suburban dealers. That was where the market was growing. Here in town it was all but saturated. But he knew the drugs were sold in certain areas by certain people. You start crossing those lines, you were looking for more than a white kilo around the neck.

He was depressed. What was worse, he had to go to the O'Neils' for supper tomorrow night, sit at that big mahogany table with that frigging sister of his and eat potatoes and talk to O'Neil. O'Neil wasn't so bad. He just wasn't too smart. Too bad he couldn't handle a really big order, but he was in politics. Politics was a waste most of the time, but it never hurt to have a brother-in-law somewhere public just in case you needed something. No sense screwing up that relationship. And O'Neil did move some stuff. Not much, but it helped.

When next evening came, Barry dressed in his best black summer suit and new white moccasins. He always liked to show them how to dress right. North Cambridge thought it was "cool city." It certainly wasn't. Barry knew that. At least they were having lasagna tonight. Dan hated it, not being the right nationality; but Merle could do the tomato sauce right. It might not be a bad evening after all. If only that big drug load weren't coming, he'd be real pleased with the world. Real pleased.

"Barry!" Merle gushed and kissed her brother on the cheek. "You look grand." Merle spread the scent of something expensive but unsubtle, like a gas leak, wherever she went; and Barry, from long experience with an asthmatic

171

reaction, held his breath during the kiss exchange. He backed off hurriedly and shook Dan's hand.

"How you doin'? Lookin' good this week ..." Barry was excruciatingly polite.

"What will we have? Vodka Collins tonight?" Dan already had one in his hand, and Merle had a piña colada waiting, half gone, by the kitchen sink. "Merle's got a PC. What'll you have?"

"Oh, sure, give me one of those." Barry gestured toward the drink Dan held in his left hand and wandered into the living room for a breath of fresh air. Tinged with the blush of garlic and tomato sauce, it was a lot better than the hall where his sister's perfume still lingered.

Halfway through dessert Merle dropped her bomb. She looked up from the caramelized pears with a beguiling smile, and Dan saw it coming.

"Danny's got an offer of a real big buy," she said.

A hundred tiny pear fragments caught in Barry's throat. "You don't know nothin' about his business, Merle. What'd you tell her, Dan?"

"Nothing. Honest, Barry. She listened in. That fool Howie came by last night, right up to the house, looking for me. Wanted me to go make a sale personally. You know I don't do that. You told me it isn't worth the chance of losing it all for a personal appearance." Why couldn't Merle keep her mouth shut?

"Say that again, Dan."

"Howie's got a customer who wants to buy ten grand worth of stuff next week and more after that. She won't play unless I come along. She doesn't think Howie's big enough to pull it off."

"Makes sense," Barry nodded.

Merle was nodding and smiling and eating more pears. The money was better than she had imagined. She really wanted to buy a nice condo in Miami. Not a cheap one, a nice one.

Barry stirred the pears. "Ten grand worth of stuff. She says she's gonna make a habit of this?"

"Howie says yes. He's feeling her out, seeing if she'll deal without me. Hate to lose a good sale, you know?"

"Sale like that might be worth goin' to," Barry said idly, thinking about how he had more stuff to move than he could handle. "Maybe you should go."

"See, Dan, see? What did I tell you?" Merle was gleeful.

"You didn't tell me anything, Merle," Dan said gloomily. "So do you want me to go along, bring the stuff, make the big sale, and check this buyer out myself? Is that what you want, Barry?"

"Sure. Why not?"

That was an order. Everybody knew it. Barry had lent Dan the money for the last car, and Dan was still paying it back. And there was the loan for the new rug in the den and the garage doors they'd had installed last month, not to mention the Filene's charge account they'd run into trouble with and with which he'd helped them out. Maybe with this new money coming in they could finally get things squared away.

"I'll call Howie up tonight. He's got a list of what the old lady wants," Dan said.

"Old lady?" Barry asked.

"Yeah. Howie described her as some old bag. She's safe, anyway. She's got to be selling it somewhere, but as long as she doesn't get in my way, it doesn't matter."

Barry nodded. "I'll need the order and the money for New York. Six grand."

"I can get the order. I need a little credit on the money," Dan said.

"You want I should carry the cost? I got to give the money to the New York broker when he makes delivery. This is strictly COD." Barry was wearing his stern Italian face.

"You've got cash, Barry. Where can I come up with that kind of green?" Dan was getting nervous. "I don't have friends with that kind of loose change."

Merle's head was going back and forth from her husband to her brother, as though she were at a Ping-Pong tournament. Six grand was a lot of money to raise in a few days. Then Dan snapped his fingers. "I got an idea. I know this guy with a lot of cash. I only need it for a couple of days, right?"

"Right," Barry nodded.

"Martin Moon. I deal with him now and then," he said modestly. God forbid these two would ever find out why. "I tell him I need a loan for someone in the constituency, no more than a week, the money's back to him. Foolproof."

Merle didn't like the look on her husband's face. Maybe this whole thing was a mistake. Her mistake. Then she thought of Miami and a fabulous condo on the beach.

"A week, max," Barry said. "I mean, you meet with the old lady on Wednesday, get the money from her, and take it right back to Moon." He grinned. Dan didn't think he knew Martin Moon? What a fool.

"Martin Moon," Dan repeated, wondering if he was really nuts. He knew this deal was going to cause him trouble the minute that damn Howie had shown up at his door. "I could tell Moon it's for an operation," he said thoughtfully. "We've got house equity. I could tell him I couldn't raise the money for a week, and the kid needs it right away and the doctor won't operate without a guarantee or something. How does that sound?"

Merle's head bobbed up and down rapidly. "Good. Right, Barry?"

Barry Rizzo shrugged. He didn't care where Dan got the money as long as he got it. It would solve a lot of problems. "Sure. Sounds real good." He finished off the white wine. It went well with the pears. They'd had Chianti with the lasagna. "You get it set. Tell me what she wants, I'll get you the order, and it should all work out just fine. You find out what your big buyer wants every week after, and I'll keep it coming. We got math to do, though. Percents. The price to her is ten grand, to your dealer less so he gets his profit, and to you less so you get yours."

"And less to you, Barry," Merle said with a giggle. "How much will you make out of this, Barry?"

"Shut up, Merle. You always talk too much."

Barry Rizzo left his sister's house with a sense of well-being that was not due solely to the drinks. He had found the solution to his drug problem. Now he could handle enough to keep the New York boys happy.

He walked down the steps with a pleased look on his face and a good dinner in his stomach. *"Molto bene,"* he muttered and slid into the driver's seat of his new pale-blue Cadillac. *"Molto bene."*

It was great to be Italian.

Dan O'Neil was frowning. "Martin Moon." He shook his head. "I don't know, Merle. I might better have kept my mouth shut."

"No problem, Danny. He's your friend, you said, didn't you? You'll get the money back in a week, we'll be making a mint on this, won't we? A thousand bucks, maybe. And that's just *this* week." She giggled and picked up a napkin that Barry had dropped on the floor. "It's not like you have to work for it. Maybe fifty thousand dollars a year, Dan. What's the problem?"

"From Martin Moon? That man scares the shit out of me. I see him all the time, he scares me to death, Merle." Dan was eating more pears. He had a weakness for them.

"Oh, pish. He's a nothing. Tell him anything. He knows you'll give it back."

"He knows too much already," Dan sighed. Martin Moon was expensive. Three hundred dollars a week that Merle didn't know anything about. If Martin ever got wind of what the loan was for, he'd up his charges to Dan. Everyone knew Moon hated drugs. "I'll call Martin. First I'd better call Howie Marshall and make sure everything is on."

Merle smiled and nodded and went into the kitchen with the last load of dirty dishes. It was a rare moment when she knew enough to keep quiet, but this was it. She stacked the dishes neatly in the sink and thought about a condo in West Palm Beach. That was one step up from Miami.

16

IT was on.

Martin Moon agreed to the cash loan to Dan O'Neil. Dan could pick it up from Mrs. Parks on Monday at eleven o'clock at Moon's office. Dan called Howie to confirm their side of the deal, and Howie called Lyuba to finalize everything with her. Everything was in place.

The drugs would change hands on Wednesday afternoon at one thirty in the parking lot behind the Norfolk Café on Hampshire Street. That was the part Dan didn't like. It was too public. But Howie assured him that such was not the case. Things happened in that parking lot that were bad. Real bad. And the cops knew nothing about it. Of course, Howie was thinking of Ray McVey's murder, but Dan O'Neil would never know.

Lyuba McVey called Paul Dorys to tell him the word was GO. The big drug man was coming to the drug buy, and so was Howie Marshall. All she needed was the ten thousand dollars for the buy. Lyuba was flying. Ray's killer would be caught red-handed selling drugs. Lyuba herself was going to get him to confess to Ray's murder. She wasn't sure how, but she would. Somehow.

Paul himself was pleased but worried. Lyuba would have the Cambridge police force behind her, but the whole thing depended on what she did, and that was a very scary thought. If Lyuba blew it, he would never live it down. And the Cambridge police were very wary about their ten grand. If the money vanished, Paul was going to be held responsible. Paul wasn't quite sure that the bust would work. Almost, but not quite. Maybe he should recheck everything with the police. Just in case.

Paul arranged a meeting for that night between himself and Detective Jones.

But before all that he had to deal with a more immediate problem. His office had been broken into on Sunday night and the safe had been rifled. Monday morning he found himself sitting on the office floor surrounded by the scattered papers from his safe. Bessie Bowen, the temp sec, was there too, helping with the sorting. In the outer office the receptionist was saving all his calls or passing them on to Paul's partner.

"Son of a gun, Bessie, what a mess."

"I'm terribly sorry, Mr. Dorys, this is just awful. What did they take?"

"Not a thing, as far as I can tell. Not a damn thing. Whatever it was they were after, it wasn't here." Paul smiled in spite of himself. He had burned his office copy of Martin Moon's files already, but the originals and four other sets were still safe in the bank. His house in Boston had been messed with, he'd been followed all over the place, and now this. Moon was anything but subtle; he must be going crazy wondering where the originals were.

"I wonder how they got in? I certainly take good care of *my* key." Bessie reached into her purse and pulled out an office key proudly. "See?"

"I wouldn't have suspected you, Bessie," Paul said.

"Oh, well." She looked down and started making messy little piles. "No reason you should. I just thought, well, I'm new here and all that. I didn't really think you did." She was horribly embarrassed and it surprised Paul because there was no reason for it unless she had been responsible for the break-in herself. Paul stopped sorting papers for a moment and tried to think. Bessie Bowen. Bessie Bowen. There had been a Bowen in that list of names Martin had. Prostitutes, Paul had thought. Maybe that was it.

"No harm done," Paul said at last. "Just an hour out of

our life when we can least afford it. The clients can wait. Right, Bessie?"

"Right," she gulped.

Jane Hersey had blossomed. In Paris her hair had been cut short and styled around her ears to show her heart-shaped face to advantage. She felt good and took pleasure in feeling the infant within her grow from a dim flutter to an individual doing push-ups. She didn't even object when Sister Cecile asked her to dye her hair brown. In fact, she had been wanting to do that for years. Now, when Jane looked into a mirror she saw a different woman from the scraggly soul who had arrived at the convent last June. The new woman was pretty and confident and supported by a network of kind people. The Zubers had proved to be a good choice for her placement. Jane found the mother she had longed for, and Edith Zuber had a delightful, if temporary, daughter. Jake didn't quite fill the father image, but then Jane already had a father. Still, Jake became a good friend and overloaded her with masculine advice.

Jane walked freely about Dorchester knowing she bore little resemblance to the girl she had been. Martin would never guess she was so near. Meanwhile Sister Cecile had arranged for her to visit Dr. Blish, affiliated with St. Margaret's Hospital, for the duration of the pregnancy. Ferreting out a good obstetrician was a major accomplishment, Cecile discovered, even for a private investigator. Sister Cecile told Jane of her father's part in all this, hinting that he might be ready to be a doting grandfather. But she recommended no contact yet. As for Martin, Cecile was not quite sure what to do, but at some point the file would have to be destroyed. It was that simple. But not until Jane was safe. It was an enigma about which she prayed constantly because she really didn't know what to do. God would figure something out. He had even created Martin, she reminded herself, although Martin certainly seemed to be one of God's more questionable efforts.

* * *

178

Jane's thoughts had been focused on Martin too; being back in Boston had brought his pudgy face back into focus in her mind and she could now see him as he really was. The nuns had helped, explaining over and over that it had not been her fault when Martin hit her. She didn't deserve it. Finally she had believed them. Bertrand had helped too, and no, she didn't love Martin and probably never had. It had all been a mistake and now she knew better. But it wasn't this baby's fault. The baby was a unique person, and Jane already felt love for the tiny, wiggling creature that she carried. But she had fallen for the wrong man.

Next time she would try to do better, but in the meantime she had a terrific urge to see Martin and tell him exactly what she thought of him, that he was a disgusting egotistical monster who didn't deserve to be the father of her baby. Even though he was. She really wanted to tell him off.

She decided to call Sister Cecile.

It took several minutes before Cecile came to the telephone. "Hello?"

"It's me. Jane."

"Jane? Is everything all right?" Cecile didn't know a great deal about having babies but as far as she knew, from this point on anything could happen.

"I'm wonderful."

"The Zubers?"

"Oh, I love them. Edith is like a mother." Jane stopped. The hard part was coming up. "I just wanted to say hello," she said.

Cecile heard the hesitancy over the line. "I'll stop by this afternoon and we can have a chat," Cecile said. "How would that be?"

"Oh, that would be great."

"Why don't we meet somewhere. I'll be free after two, so, say two thirty? Corner of Adams and Ellet? It's not far from you and there's an ice cream shop near there."

"Okay," Jane agreed. "See you there."

Sister Raphael was nearby, as usual. She had begun to hover when she realized it was Jane on the telephone.

"Something's on her mind, Raphael," Cecile said. "I'm worried. It won't be long," she mused. "I think she's nervous."

"I'm worried it's not a girl. I have two pink sweaters done now, one a newborn size and one a six-month size. They're cunning."

"Nobody says 'cunning.' "

"Cunning," Raphael reaffirmed. "Ask her if it's a girl."

"Raphael, I'm afraid she's going to run off and go to Martin. She could be hurt if she tried that."

"Why don't you ask Jane if it's a girl."

"Now, if she says she wants to contact Martin, what should I say?"

"Ask her if it's a girl."

"And then I'll tell her I must speak to Martin first in order to straighten things out about the file. Jane has to realize it's dangerous even though I don't think Martin would dare try anymore."

Sister Raphael's eyes opened wide. "Now that's an idea. Maybe Martin would know. He *is* the father. Ask Martin. My father always knew exactly what my mother was going to have."

"Martin is an evil man, Raphael. I will *not* ask him. I met him, you know. He may be the father, but he doesn't care about that baby at all. Paul suggested he's even killed someone."

Raphael sighed. "Maybe I should do something in blue, just in case. Girls wear blue, anyway."

"How about a yellow blanket," Cecile advised firmly. "Every infant needs one."

Several hours later Sister Cecile set out to meet Jane. It was a classic September day, with the sun beaming down from a bright blue sky. A sea breeze had kicked in at one thirty and sent Boston's heat off to Framingham and brought a taste of the cool Atlantic over Dorchester. Cecile's veil flew straight back and her gold cross danced in the sun. God could even make Dorchester a pleasant place to be.

Jane was there when Sister Cecile strode up the hill. The younger woman was leaning against a tree, staring at Ronan Park, where several ten-year-olds were stripping down a bicycle. Russian tea grew everywhere, sending the sweet scent of chamomile into the air. "Jane, you look wonderful," Cecile called up the street.

Jane turned. She was shaped like a fertility goddess against the breeze, and her arms were open like a statue of Mary. It had been a week since they had seen each other.

"I'm so glad to see you." Jane was hesitant but glad. "I didn't really want to suggest we get together."

"But you don't have a soul you can meet but me and the Zubers. Is that it?" Sister Cecile planted a kiss on a rosy cheek. "You look lovely, Jane." And guilty as hell, Cecile thought.

"And I'm lonesome. You're right. How are things with you?" They began to walk down the incline, Cecile leading them slowly toward an ice cream parlor that she wouldn't feel right patronizing by herself. But Jane needed dairy products and it would be a treat for her, and of course Jane wouldn't want to eat alone. Chocolate almond crunch, or coconut chocolate chip; then Jane would tell what was on her mind.

"I've been busy. The fund-raising isn't quite making it, but I'm sure it will all work out. Now tell me, Jane. You're glad to be back in America, aren't you?"

"Paris was wonderful," Jane said. "I learned how to make beds. A lot of beds. And I saw the Louvre and L'Arc de Triomphe and everything, got a B in my course at the Sorbonne and my French is pretty good now and I met some cool people." She wouldn't mention Bertrand yet.

"And now you're home."

"I'm so glad," Jane sighed. "At first I wanted to stay away forever and never come back. But I got sick of talking in French. The people are nice, though. Did you ever spend any time there?"

181

"Yes," Cecile nodded. Why couldn't Jane come to the point?

It took her all the way to Pringee's Parlor to get there. They were at the critical moment, standing before the list of flavors. Jane had just ordered banana-cream-pie ice cream when it all burst out, leaving Cecile no choice but to make a crash decision and order jubilee cherry crunch, which was Flavor of the Month and at the top of the list.

"I want to see Martin," Jane said. "It's all I can think about. I want to see him."

"Why?"

"Why? Because I have this terrific urge to dump all over him. I mean, I've come to the point where I thoroughly dislike the man, but it's like unfinished business, and then I can forget him. He must have some good points, I suppose, because he's my baby's father, but I can deal with that."

Cecile was relieved at Jane's words, but there were still problems. "He's dangerous, Jane. It isn't safe. We have to settle everything first."

Cecile watched the youth behind the counter thrust Jane's ice cream cone forward. Sister Cecile handed him several dollar bills and received her cone in return. Jubilee crunch. She should have ordered the banana cream pie.

"I know. I know he's no good. But it's just something I have to do. I'm not going after him for child support or anything. It's a moral issue. You should understand that."

Sister Cecile didn't, but she wasn't about to deny knowledge of *any* moral issue. She had her pride, too. The boy handed her some change and she tucked it in her purse and grabbed a handful of napkins. "Let's go outside. I know where there's a bench." They strolled out. Jubilee crunch actually wasn't bad. It had cherries and caramel crunchies in a vanilla base.

"The point is," Jane went on, taking a huge lick to catch the drips, "that I understand him. Talk about a major rat. He was using me, I was dumb and young, but mostly he was just taking advantage of me and the fact that, that . . ." She stopped.

182

"The fact that he was big, powerful, important, and you liked being close to power and importance, and making love wasn't so bad," Cecile finished for her. "Is that a possibility?"

Jane nodded. "You're right. I was trying to blame everything on him again, wasn't I?"

"It's human nature. Of course he deserves most of the blame, but you were there. You took taxis to his place, you agreed to meet him. I'm not saying you were totally culpable, but don't deny yourself free will."

"I know," Jane sighed.

"That part of it is all over," Sister Cecile nodded. They had arrived at the bench, which was under a plastic-lidded bus stop. They sat, Jane very carefully, lowering herself down and thrusting her legs out before her with a small grunt.

Cecile was still talking. "But you are young. Still."

Jane didn't feel a bit young. There were a lot of things she didn't feel, a lot more that she did. "I need to confront him."

"We still have the problem of the red file."

"Damn the red file." Jane spoke venomously, then blushed. "Sorry."

"No. I tend to agree. I'll have to talk to Paul."

"I should just give it back," Jane said, subdued. "Tell him to go back to his crappy life. What do you think?" She licked an array of drips off her cone.

"I don't believe he's ever quit his crappy life. Giving it back might work for him but not for all those people he torments. I did tell you that I gave your father his letter back, didn't I? He was very glad. And we kept you safe. That's what your father wanted for you; that's what he hired me for. He cares for you, Jane."

"Daddy's okay," she admitted.

"I'll tell Paul we should just burn the file, quickly. And tell Martin it's destroyed. That might work. Or he might try to get even. I don't know. I'll speak with Paul about it."

"What's with you and him?" Jane asked suddenly.

"Nothing."

"Come on."

"He's an old friend, Jane."

"What kind of friend?"

There was no escape. "I was expected to marry him, years ago," Cecile said. "Everybody expected it. I loved Paul. I do love Paul. But there was this problem of priorities. I had a vocation."

Jane grinned. "You spent a lot of time with him?"

"Oh, yes."

"Did you have sex?"

"That's none of your business."

Jane shrugged and laughed. "Maybe. Maybe not. But you just didn't love him enough, right? This other thing got there first?"

"Exactly." Sister Cecile bit the top of the cone off and was rewarded with an entire cherry. Angels sang, and she closed her eyes and chewed. The cool ocean air blew Dorchester from her mind and she knew that Jane was going to be all right.

17

When Cecile called Paul to discuss the red file he insisted
that she meet him at Durgan Park for dinner.

"The bribe of your company for discussion of the file,"
he said over his platter of oysters. "You only see me these
days when you have to." He patted the briefcase where it
rested on the floor beside him, implying that the file was
there. He had taken to carrying his leather case with him
everywhere with obvious flourishes of heavy clutching as
he walked through crowds. Moon was still having him followed, and this seemed like a good way to protect his home
and office. Even Cecile was fooled. She half expected to
see the briefcase chained to his wrist.

"I've been busy," she said.

"How's the fund-raising?"

"I need another fifty thousand dollars plus an income of
five thousand a month to get it off the ground." Cecile
squeezed lemon juice on an oyster. They had ordered roast
beef for the entree. Rare.

"Love alone won't suffice," Paul said and watched
Cecile eat. She did it so well. "Too bad you can't save the
poor nuns an oyster. Being a detective is low pay, isn't it."

Cecile sighed. "It's getting desperate, really. We need so
much money, and eight sisters are retiring in the next two
years. Three will need medical care for certain, and there
will be more. A perfect deluge of elderly nuns."

"Even you, someday," Paul said.

"I've raised sixty thousand dollars already, Paul, and

that's a lot to get just from church collections and telephone calls. It hasn't been easy."

"I see." Paul studied her face. It was paler than usual, and her gray eyes showed strain. She really had been busy. "You need a rest, or just a break. Leave the convent, marry me and inherit all your father's millions. Then you could endow them. I could have a lot of fun untying all those trusts he set up. Your order would be set for a century and we could live happily ever after."

"I could marry you for my money," Cecile said.

"Right." Paul sat back, his eyes focused somewhere beyond her and she felt a familiar pang. There had never been a way. There never would be a way. Then he grinned.

"Don't expect me to give up on you, Cecile. When I quit, you'll know I'm dead."

"If you live that long," Cecile said. "I said something like that to Jane not long ago. Or maybe it was something Jane said to me. She's grown up so fast."

The roast beef arrived with minor fanfare and they both began to arrange things to eat. Paul was missing a sharp knife and began hacking with a dull butter knife. "We could use the red file and raise money that way," Cecile said as she cut a rare bite. "It works for Martin."

"Consider ethics, Cecile. Not to mention extortion."

"A bad joke." She sighed. "Jane wants to confront Martin, tell him he's a pig, and get on with her life. I said it wasn't safe and I think she agreed with me, but who can be sure? It frightens me. At least she doesn't love him, and she will be a good mother, I think. Very understanding. But we simply must dispose of the file. I can't see holding it over Martin's head forever. That's just too much like what he was doing to all the people in the file."

Paul shrugged and before he could speak the waitress appeared again, with a proper meat knife for him. "Soup's on," she said. "Dig in, big fella. I'll get you guys some hot buns."

"Why, Paul? Why do you insist on coming to this place?"

186

"It's so genteel. Besides. Look at this beef."

Cecile did.

When she was halfway through she spoke again. "What should we do?"

Paul finished chewing before he answered. "You're right. The file should go. I have this drug business with Lyuba to finish up and then I'll take a trip up to my place on Plum Island and write a few letters to all the people in the file. And have a cookout on the beach with the papers in it. Maybe this coming weekend. Want to come?" He grinned, knowing her answer already.

"Maybe I could bring all the nuns for an outing," Cecile replied. "We all love hot dogs."

"Right," Paul said. "Some other time. It's a tricky legal question, you understand. If any of the stuff in the file could be used in a pending criminal proceeding I don't have the right to destroy it. But I don't believe there are any current lawsuits involving any of these people, so it doesn't really apply. I guess a trip to the safety deposit box is in order. I'll get the stuff, inform all the good folks involved, and have my cookout."

"A blessed relief," Cecile said. The roast beef on Cecile's plate was almost gone. One last perfect bite. "From my point of view, people should all be given a second chance to amend their lives. Perhaps some of these people have already been forgiven. Jane has a second chance. Even Martin has a second chance. Everything must be destroyed."

"You're such a nun, Cecile."

She smiled. "Thank you."

Paul dropped her off at the convent in time for vespers, and when she knelt down in the dim chapel amid the low murmuring prayers of the others, she was still wrapped in the evening. Twenty years ago he had asked her to marry him, and he had never stopped. She wondered if that would have been a better way, and then lowered her eyes to her prayer book. *Despersit, detit pauperibus.* Her life would have been

187

no fun without Paul, she thought as her mind wandered back. But his love was only a beginning.

Barry Rizzo was on the telephone to New York to concretize arrangements for his side of the big drug buy. He hated talking to New York. His contacts there always made him feel like small potatoes, and he found it best to be well prepared for conversation with his superiors. Tonight he'd mixed Gibsons. Three perfect Gibsons.

"I got the order," Barry said to the voice in New York. "Six grand worth of the stuff beyond my usual. Got it?"

He sipped at the first Gibson, listened to a few words, then downed the entire glass.

"Sure, sure, you said I had to take more. Well, I'm wanting more right now. There was no doubt in my mind that I could get the stuff from you people. I got a big deal coming down on Wednesday. I got to have the stuff tomorrow, just like I said." Barry set the first glass down and picked up the second. "Now, here's exactly what I need."

"What! Not till Thursday? No way." He started on the second drink, slow, and put his feet up on the desk beside some insurance forms. "I got the cash coming up front. I got the vendor. I got the buyer. I want the stuff."

He started on the second drink, swirling the pearly onion around, watching its moonish pallor. He poured the onion into his mouth with the last of the drink and blinked. He chewed slowly. Sometimes the onion was the best part. "Before one thirty Wednesday I got to have the stuff in my hand. What's that give us?"

He placed the second empty glass down with an effort. "So we got less than two days to get the stuff together, that's no big thing. I got a man could go down and pick it up, cash and carry. That's six grand to you, Al. And believe me, that's just a start. I got this buyer coming around every week now. You figure it."

Barry stared at the third drink, pale as water. He sipped it as though it might taste different. It didn't.

"Okay, okay. I send my man to New York. He'll be at

your place with money, but it has to be discount. Throw in some extra bags, you know? He gets five hundred for the trip."

Things were dimming for Barry. His hand felt stiff, but his brain felt pleasantly limp.

"Good," Barry nodded. "I understand. Sure. Same address? . . . Yep. Name's Tom Dempsey. New fellow. A Mick looking for big-time. He'll be there."

Barry Rizzo called Tom Dempsey next. "Get the hell over here. I got a job for you."

A half hour later Tom Dempsey was sitting in Barry Rizzo's office. Barry had managed to go next door for a take-out sub and had finished half of it by the time Tom arrived. The white sandwich papers were crumpled on his desk alongside the three empty Gibson glasses. The uneaten half sub sent its odor of onions, pickles, and mortadella into the air.

"How are things?" Barry asked.

It was seven fifteen in the evening and Tom was hungry. He kept his eye on the sandwich. "Smooth. No trouble."

"Want five hundred fast bucks?"

Tom shrugged.

"Go to New York tomorrow. Pick up some stuff. I need it Wednesday, one o'clock."

"I can handle that." Tom looked hard at the sandwich. The pickle had tooth marks and was slipping out onto the desk. Salad dressing made dark puddles beside the pickle. It was a massive sandwich.

"Here's where you go." He handed Tom a paper with an address on it. "Tell them your name, that's all. Give them this." He handed Tom an envelope. "This is money. You mess with this, you're dead meat. Understand?"

"No problem." Tom felt proud with the envelope in his hand. He was moving up, closing in on the big time. He sat straight and took a big breath. "You want I should bring it here, to you?"

"Wednesday noon, right here. Here's three hundred, the rest when you deliver. I'll have my man here to take it in." Barry handed him the cash and nodded his dismissal. He wasn't sure if he could trust Dempsey, but he was short of help. If Tom pulled this off, he would be useful for other things. Tom knew it too. It was the BIG TEST.

Barry noticed Tom's eyes resting on the sub and Barry smiled for the first time ever in Tom's presence. Then he swept the half-eaten sandwich into the wastebasket. "Lousy," he said. "Lousy."

18

Martin Moon's money was about to create vast, undulating waves. It began to move along down the line with each interested party adding or subtracting from it according to his purpose. When Dan O'Neil had approached him for the money, Martin had been more curious than surprised. He'd been collecting from O'Neil every month for three years, ever since he found out about the drug distributorship in East Cambridge. Martin knew better than to ask Dan what the money was really for. A kid needing an operation was not Dan O'Neil's style, and it was a lie worth checking out. When Dan left Martin's Beacon Street office with the money in hand, Martin had him followed by Tracy Green, a reliable employee of his. Tracy owed Martin for covering up a small indiscretion she had committed once, and she paid him back with service. Following people was one of her interesting and varied occupations, and she was good at it. In fact, prior to this new assignment, she had been following Paul Dorys off and on all week, but had been able to tell Martin very little except that Paul Dorys seemed very attached to his briefcase and had recently had dinner with a nun.

Tracy saw Dan O'Neil hail a cab when he left Martin's office. She copied the number of the cab down, checked the Town Taxi office in Charlestown and found that the cabby's name was Vladimir Oskowitz and he lived in Alston. Later that evening, Tracy found Vladimir. Vladimir checked his book and told Tracy, in person, that he had driven the man to an address in the North End. He was happy to give such a beautiful lady the address.

Tracy called Martin and gave him the address she had obtained from Vladimir.

"Barry Rizzo," Martin said out loud when he heard the address and after Tracy had rung off. Tracy had been short on the telephone; she was planning a full evening with Vladimir Oskowitz. She called him Volodya already and had acquired another reason to owe Martin Moon.

"Barry Rizzo," Martin said again. Rizzo was a moderately big drug supplier and everyone knew it. But Martin had never been able to get Rizzo into his file. Martin chuckled. This was a great chance. A big order must be coming in. All he had to do was keep Rizzo under surveillance and maybe get a few good photographs of the transaction. He could start a whole new file. That thought served to remind him that his red file was still out there, probably in that damn lawyer's briefcase.

Martin dialed another number; this time he called a man who had a very small camera and took pictures for a price. Martin chuckled again and Mrs. Parks heard the noise from her outer office and sighed. Martin began to calculate how much Rizzo would be good for. He dreamed about money while the photographer's number rang and he thought how good life was being to him. Except for the file. Finally a male voice answered the call he had put in.

"I got a job for you, Mike," Martin said.

After he told the photographer to get on Rizzo's case for the next few days, he called Tracy Green back at the number she had given him. "Tracy, get on Paul Dorys again. I want full reports, I want to know where he goes, what he does, when he's going to be alone. Got that? And the briefcase. See if you can get what's in it. I want it now."

Tracy grimaced at the telephone. It would have been such a good night, and now she had to stake out that lawyer again. "Okay, Mr. Moon. I'm on my way."

192

* * *

Sister Cecile didn't get to see Lyuba McVey until Tuesday. Lyuba had been out Monday night playing bingo in Watertown with an old friend. It had been a grand night and when Cecile rang the doorbell the next morning, Lyuba was still feeling good. When Lyuba felt good, she sang in a very loud, scratchy voice. Cecile waited at the door, listening to the strange howling, and wondered if the cat with one blue eye and one green eye was in heat and what would happen if a tom with brown eyes should happen by. If there were such a thing as a three-eyed cat, it could be very interesting.

"Good morning," Lyuba burst out, and stood with the door open wide. Her smile was better than ever and Cecile felt her spirits rise.

"What do you want?" Lyuba said, and Cecile wondered if Lyuba remembered who she was.

"I'm Sister Cecile," she said. "Remember?"

"Of course I remember. What do you want?"

"Oh. Well, I did say I'd be by, so I came along. It seemed like a nice day. Should I have called?"

Lyuba squinted out at the sky where a mist of a moon still showed. It was almost full. "You came. Come in. Don't call. I was making soup just now. They sell vegetables at the project." Lyuba went on, more voluble than when she was drinking. Alcohol made her surly. "I got carrots and cauliflower and onions and a piece of meat from the Square. Them farmers come right in with the stuff. Good buys. Ever go to them farm stands?"

"Sister Germaine does," Cecile said and stepped into the dusky interior. It was surprisingly pleasant, dim after the bright daylight; a big change from the starkly black and white shadow patterns of a September sun. The smell of cooking onions filled the room and Cecile sat on the couch. The shades were half drawn, rendering dust and cat hairs almost invisible.

"How is everything?" Cecile asked and delved into her purse to find the small package of *golabki* she had brought with her. Sister Germaine had made them last night for supper, and no one had ever faulted her cabbage rolls. "Sister Germaine insisted I bring these for you," Cecile said. *"Golabki."*

"Mother in heaven! Paulie must have told you." Lyuba sprang forward and took the package, unwrapping a corner of the aluminum foil. She sniffed. "Goddamn good," she pronounced. "I'll put them away."

Cecile relaxed. That was one thing she had done right for the day. She looked around, seeing the room differently from before, when it had been haunted by the specter of Ray McVey. Things had normalized in that short while, and the Siamese cat stared lazily from the bookshelf where it stretched in the single sunbeam that had found its way through the ripped shade. The cat did not appear to be in heat.

Lyuba returned and fell into the green chair. "Tomorrow is the day," she announced. "Paulie's going to be by in the morning with the money for me to buy the drugs. It's set."

"I'd heard," Cecile said. "He won't be by until tomorrow?" She was disappointed. She had thought everything would be finalized today, and her hopes that Paul might be at Lyuba's had absolutely nothing to do with her arrival with stuffed cabbage.

"He's coming tomorrow morning," Lyuba repeated and lit a cigarette. It took her a minute; her pudgy fingers had a hard time with the soft matches. "He was worried about all that money being here overnight. He kids me a lot. Says I might've gone to Bermuda, or might take some friends out to dinner." Lyuba took a tremendous drag on the cigarette, then exhaled, surrounding herself with a blue haze. Her thoughts reached Cecile at about the same time the cloud of smoke did.

"I see," Cecile said.

"So youse guys want to see the action tomorrow?"

"Well . . ." The nun in Cecile paused, but not for long. "Yes. Where?"

"Right in my backyard," Lyuba said triumphantly. "See, I got this idea of making it right for my Ray. So I set it up where they killed him. I know that bastard done it out there, same as he killed my flowers. You could watch me trap that bastard right from the kitchen. Good show. Good seat."

"I could," Cecile said. "Could I see now?"

The view was just as Lyuba had predicted. First the tiny green patch of lawn, then the notorious flower garden that had started it all, then the fence, then the parking lot itself, a desert of beer cans and litter with a few cars parked in clusters near the café. There was only one other thing of interest: a large blue dumpster, a close relative of the one in which Ray McVey's body had first been laid to rest.

"Yes, I'll come," Cecile confirmed. It was safe in the kitchen and she would be invisible. "What time?"

"One thirty. I got to be out in the lot by then for the switch, so get here before then."

"I'll be here."

Cecile looked out over the bleak lot, stark in the sun, summer dead and gone there, Ray the same. A dead place with a few hulks of old cars. She had her first serious qualm. What if it didn't go down? What if someone else died? There were too many downside possibilities.

"I'd better go, Lyuba. Thanks for the invitation. I'll be here at one, or earlier."

"Stay for coffee?"

"No. I've got to . . . to pray," Cecile said. "We need all the help we can get."

Barry Rizzo's usual supply of drugs arrived on Tuesday evening. It had been a good week and he needed every ounce of material for his regular customers, although he had been required to handle an extra allotment of cocaine. His biggest problem was his distribution setup. Some of his boys were doing a hell of a job moving it; some of his other employees needed fires lit under their asses. But with O'Neil's new buyer, things were going to be real good with the New York boys. Barry Rizzo was feeling fine. It was a bull market.

Tom Dempsey was running on a New York high. He wasn't familiar with the city, and he had just discovered how intense it could be. Too many people, too much cement, too many cars. But it was fabulous and he hadn't stopped grinning since he'd arrived in New York City on Amtrak and taken a cab to the address he had been given, and now he was there, in the heart of The Big Apple, ringing the doorbell. This was it. Big time. His heart was pounding hard and one hand was in his pants pocket where he gripped the envelope of money. He stood and waited while the bell echoed hollowly somewhere in the depths of a Centre Street warehouse. It bordered the Soho district; full of artists and would-be artists and those who like the food and ambience of an artistic neighborhood. Nobody answered the bell. His grin finally faded.

It was chilly. New York at six thirty on a September evening was just beginning to rev up for a nasty fall with cold rain thick as dead pigeons. No rain yet, but even the cool weather was getting to Tom, that and the smell. The scent of garbage moved sideways from building walls, it rose from the cement pavement and made waves along the tarred and bumpy streets. This was not Boston. God, he loved Boston. What was he doing here? He sank down to the step and rested his head back against the wooden door and closed his eyes. Half the doorways in New York offered accommodations to men and women who had no other place to rest their heads. Tom didn't realize he looked like one of "Them," fair game for any passing brigand, and it wasn't long before a shaggy creature lurched into him, fell on him and began to reach into the pockets of Tom's pants. But Tom was quick. He kneed his assailant in the stomach; he grasped for the flailing hands, then reached for the creature's throat, yelling instinctively as he rose up, bringing his attacker with him.

Punch! Punch! Blows rained on Tom's face. His nose began to spurt blood, the attacker was smashed to the left, pummeled to the right ear. His head rolled back and forth while he beat Tom.

The passers-by assumed, half-rightly, that it was two winos punching it out, better left alone. Consequently they moved across the street or skirted the battle. A meandering cop finally arrived and stood, taking a pose of dignity. He waited for a few more blows before he bellowed, "Break it up, boys. I'm running you in."

It worked. Both men looked up, filthy and bloody, and saw the officer of the law. Tom felt his front pant pocket and made sure his money was still there. "Have to keep an appointment," he huffed and smiled. It was not a pleasant sight. He backed up, tripped, turned and ran.

His assailant began to whine. "Look what that bastard did to my shirt," he complained, and began to back away.

The policeman shrugged. He didn't want them at the station house, anyway. It smelled bad enough without dumping two more in the tank for the night. They weren't so drunk they couldn't fight. They would be just fine.

The policeman wandered off toward Mott Street and a Chinese fast food stand where he always picked up a snack before he went off duty.

Tom Dempsey was a mess. He didn't know New York well enough to know where to get cleaned up. Nobody knew New York that well. Maybe a park, Tom thought. Maybe a subway station. But he had taken a cab downtown. He spotted a store with a male dress dummy in the window.

MICHAEL WONG'S HABERDASHERY, the sign read. The dress dummy had slanted eyes and straight black hair, but the suit it was wearing was occidental. And the store was open. Tom looked down at his bloody shirt and pants. Why had he worn white pants to New York City in the first place? They were disgusting now, with dark-red smears and soot.

He walked into the store and before the small salesman could open his mouth, Tom spoke. "I want a new shirt and pants. Had an accident. I got cash."

"Yes, yes, sir; yes, sir, right away. Come right here, we fit you."

"You got a sink?"

New Yorkers never allowed customers into the bowels of their stores. Bathrooms were sacrosanct, and Michael Wong didn't want those hands even touching a doorknob in his establishment. But this man had money. Michael Wong always knew.

"Yes sir, come this way. We have sink."

Tom tore his shirt off and used it as a washcloth, crumpled it when he was done, and threw it into the wastebasket. He was clean but not quite respectable because of the welt rising under his eye.

While Tom had been cleaning up, Michael Wong had been busy calling his three cousins who ran the Eternal Tao Martial Arts Institute across the street. They were currently dressed for classes but were happy to hear they might be of assistance. They came at once.

When Tom stepped out of the bathroom, the cousins and Michael Wong were there in a silent group, surveying Tom's bare chest. It was hairy and covered with goose bumps in spite of the heat. Tom gulped audibly and his chest made a convulsive movement, sending the hairs up and down like some undulating swamp.

"I was going to buy some clothes," he said. His lower lip trembled.

Michael Wong came forth between Charlie and Harry Ma and he was smiling in the broad manner that only a true Oriental can manage. "We have very fine suits here, imported from Hong Kong. Finest silk. We also have shirts." He eyed Tom's chest disdainfully. He found Westerners' hairy chests offensive. "Come. I will show you." His English was better with his cousins' support.

When it came time to pay for the silk suit that Michael Wong had pressed on him, and the flower-print tie, the imported shirt and the full set of Mummer's underwear, Tom Dempsey made the appalling discovery that his wallet was missing. The envelope containing the money for the drug buy was still safe in the front of his white pant pocket, but the rear pocket, where his wallet had been, was empty. His own private cash was gone! And his return ticket home!

"Uh, uh, uh . . . I lost it in the fight," Tom mumbled, and the white-robed Orientals began to circle around him.

"You said you would pay cash," Michael Wong said. His smile increased. It was impossibly broad and Tom looked wildly at the Chinese cousins. Their faces were serene and they stood relaxed and ready. Tom could just see past the bill in his face. An outrageous bill.

Tom pulled out the sealed white envelope with bravado. He knew what he had to do. "I will," he said and stood up tall. He puffed up his naked chest so that his back was creased behind his rigid shoulder blades. He counted out the money carefully.

"Twelve hundred and thirty-six dollars and thirty-two cents. That includes state and city taxes, plus two percent for the Howard Fang Development," Michael Wong said and held out the clothes. "You may change in the dressing room."

Tom took his time in the dressing room, carefully counting and sorting the remaining money into two piles. One for the drugs, and one to enable him to have supper and get back to Boston by train. When he finally emerged from the dressing room, there was no question that he looked like a million bucks. He walked directly out, past the tae kwon do experts and past Michael Wong, who bowed as he went by and said: "Very happy to serve you, sir. Please come again."

This time when Tom rang the bell on the Centre Street warehouse door it was opened almost immediately by a short, dark man with curly hair. Tom breathed a sigh of relief. "I'm Tom Dempsey. Rizzo sent me." He looked up the dark stairs behind the man, warily.

"Sure. How much you got?"

"Six grand, but I lost some of it."

The Italian eyed the expensive suit up and down, then

the welt on Tom's face. "I see. Run into a clotheshorse?" He guffawed loudly and slapped his hands together. Tom managed to lift up the corners of his mouth and smile. It hurt.

"Yeah. Something like that. You got the dope? I got to head back. I got a deadline."

"Sure. We always got the stuff. Deadline? Dead? Line?" He laughed again and Tom almost turned back. What a creep. But this was it. He'd made the contact. The die was cast. Tom Dempsey of South Boston was big-time.

And Tom began to follow his contact up the stairs. His future was in sight.

19

Tom followed the man up and into the second-floor loft, leaving the city to recede into dark silence. The man flicked on a dim light and revealed an artist's studio of vast proportions, with a waterbed in the center. Some form of smog hovered in the corners of the huge room, lending it an air of incompleteness. The canvases resembled piles of cracked pottery, mimics of early Julian Schnabels. Everything smelled of library paste.

"Mario's an artist," the dark man said. "I'm Al. Sit down."

Tom sat on the edge of the waterbed and reached for the crushed pack of cigarettes he had salvaged from his clothes.

"Can't smoke here," Al said.

Tom put the cigarettes back in his pocket. He wanted to do business and get out, anyway. "I got $4,703.68. I can't make the six like we planned. What can you give me?" He swayed on the edge of the bed and felt seasick. He had saved sixty bucks to get home. That was more than enough, he figured.

"Oh, we can manage something." Al had a briefcase in his hand that had appeared from somewhere in the gloom. He squatted on his knees, opened it, and began counting out white packets. "Check me. You know how many you're gonna get? Less dough, less snow," he yukked.

Al continued counting until there was a pile of self-sealed white baggies on the bed beside the heap of bagged pills that Lyuba had specified on her list. "Now that's just about right. Four grand, seven hundred and three. Keep the change." He laughed again and Tom cringed. "I'll give you something to carry it in, too. You don't look too set up." Al pushed the empty briefcase toward Tom, keeping back the excess merchandise. He took the money from Tom and stuffed it in his pocket.

That was it. Tom left with a simulated alligator case full of his big buy. Five minutes later he was walking down Centre Street, the briefcase clutched in an iron grip. He looked from left to right every few steps, glancing behind at every corner. His paranoia about New York City had become reality. He knew all those rumors he had heard were God's truth. New York was hell.

It was also expensive. In the steak house he finally settled on for a meal, the tab came to thirty-seven dollars. That meant he would have to take the bus home instead of the train. It also meant he didn't dare take a cab all the way up to the Port Authority bus terminal. So he walked.

It was a long walk, and the propositions came as regularly as the streets. He was sorely tempted to trade one of those little baggies for an hour of pleasure, but common sense prevailed. He made it to the bus stop as pure as he had been the moment of his arrival in Sin City. He found that the next bus for Boston didn't leave until six o'clock the next morning.

Tom Dempsey almost cried. Then he bought his bus ticket and sat down in one of the bus terminal's very small seats with a built-in television. Clutching his bag of drugs, he dropped his first quarter into the slot and settled in to watch his favorite show in fuzzy black and white. Five quarters later he drifted off to sleep amid the gray light and gray faces of predawn New York.

He woke with a start. He'd missed the bus! The case was stolen!

No. He was still clutching the case in a death grip and it was only five o'clock. He felt like hell. His beautiful suit was itchy, and he had to go to the bathroom. The inside of his mouth defied description and he moved his lips slowly around and around to loosen up his face.

* * *

Barry Rizzo had expected to hear from Tom last Tuesday
night. He had sat up watching the "Tonight" Show, and had
gone on to watch a late-night movie, *Dracula*. His wife had
gone to bed early, and the apartment on Commonwealth
Avenue was quiet except for the muffled screams from the
television set. It usually amused Barry to hear low-volume
screams, but tonight nothing amused him. As it grew later,
he slowly gave up hope that he would ever again hear from
Tom Dempsey. His gamble had lost. Dempsey had probably
hightailed it to Pawtucket with six thousand lousy bucks.
The fool. The damn fool. He was dead.

Barry went to bed at two o'clock and didn't stir until ten
the next morning. His wife knew something was very
wrong and was wise enough to be absolutely silent except
for small sounds like "Here's your coffee, darling" and
"The bacon is very good this morning." Tom Dempsey had
never called.

Barry was in his office at twelve thirty, lighting his fifth
cigarette of the day when the telephone rang. It was
Dempsey.

"I just got in," Tom said hoarsely over the wire. "Damn
bus broke down. Damned near everything went wrong
since I left. I only got part of the dope. Most of it, though.
I'll make up the rest. I will. I promise. I'll explain everything. Where do you want me to go?"

Barry bit through the filter on his cigarette. "Fuck and
shit, Tom. Where the hell you been?"

Tom closed his eyes and swayed back into the wall by
the telephone booth. South Station, Boston, was not restful,
and it had been a lousy night. "I been in New York," he
spat. "I got mugged, for Chrissake. What do you want me
to do with the stuff?"

Barry finally started to think. "I need it at a place in
Cambridge in an hour. How much are you short?"

"I got four thousand seven hundred and three dollars'
worth."

"So I make up the difference. What'd you do with it? Smoke it?"

"I'm telling you, I got mugged. I'll make it up to you, I swear."

"Yeah, right. You bet. Lucky I got extra white this week, so I can handle it." Barry looked at his watch. Time was running out. "All right. You take what you got to the parking lot behind the Norfolk Café in Cambridge. Any idea where it is?"

"Sure. I been around."

"So, be there, one thirty. My buddy ain't going to like it, but he's got a deal set up and he don't want to blow it. I'll have to come with the rest of the buy. We'll have a regular party."

"Yeah, sure. A blast. I'll be there." Tom hung up. He couldn't take any more of Rizzo. He only had a couple of bucks to his name and a whole hour to get to Cambridge. That meant subway to Central Square and walk. He could make it in an hour easy and even buy a slice of ABC's pizza in the Square.

Tom smiled for the first time that day. He patted his new suit. It was sharp and it made him look real good even though he needed a shave and he had a hell of a bruise on his cheek. He was one glossy dude.

On the same Tuesday that Tom Dempsey had gone to New York for the biggest deal of his life, Jane Hersey's labor had begun. At first she had thought it was all the prune juice she had been drinking. She had started doing the small stretching exercises that she had been taught, but it hurt. The baby wasn't due for two weeks, she had thought, and had walked into the kitchen to look at the blue cat clock. Eight o'clock at night. Mrs. Zuber watching television, Jake driving the cab. Jane had paced. She found pacing a lot easier than sitting down or stretching, for some reason. When she lay flat she felt like she had to go to the bathroom even though she really didn't. But sometimes she

204

did. Nobody had ever told her what the last weeks of pregnancy would be like.

Suddenly she felt a great lurch inside as the baby shifted wildly. Things were getting tight in there for her, Jane thought. Maybe a cup of peppermint tea would help.

It didn't. It was nine o'clock and Jane had read an entire issue of the *Reader's Digest* in big print and gone to the bathroom two more times. She couldn't stand Mrs. Zuber's taste in television. Game shows, situation comedies, soaps all afternoon. At night Mrs. Zuber flipped from show to show, indiscriminately. The pain was progressing into sharp little spurts. Maybe she should tell Mrs. Zuber. It couldn't be the baby yet, could it?

At nine thirty she told Mrs. Zuber and they left for St. Margaret's ten minutes later. At three o'clock in the morning Danielle Hersey was born. She weighed six pounds, six ounces and had fuzzy red hair. She looked exactly like her mother. It had been blessedly fast. Mother and child were doing just fine.

Jake Zuber called the convent in the morning to tell the news to the good nuns. He felt like a father for the first time and his wife was in heaven. "Jane was just wonderful," he told Sister Cecile. "She was just marvelous! And you should see little Dannie."

"I'll be there this afternoon," Sister Cecile said gleefully. "You tell her not to worry about a thing!"

Sister Cecile called Abe Hersey and told him the good news.

"Grandfather?" he said. "Good Lord. Grandfather. I'll be over there today. I can see her, can't I?"

. "Of course."

Everything was turning out nicely, Cecile thought. She could skip the drug bust. They didn't need her there and nobody would miss her. Babies were much more important. Maybe she should tell Martin. He was the father. Did he have a right to know? He was such a horrible man, truly horrible, but he too was one of God's creations. "God made Martin Moon, too," she said to Sister Raphael, who was wrapping small knit things in white tissue paper, right on Cecile's desk.

"Yes," Raphael admitted. "And God made mosquitoes."

"Mr. Moon probably should know," Cecile said.

"Maybe later?" Raphael questioned.

"It wouldn't hurt to tell him."

"Don't tell him where she is. Promise? He's a mosquito."

"All right, Raphael. I try hard to see good in everybody, but you may be right. I'll just say it's a girl. I promise."

Twelve thirty. He might be in his office, where she had reached him before. She found the number again and dialed carefully. She got a busy signal.

Seconds before Cecile had dialed, Martin had been on the way out, passing by Mrs. Parks's desk when the phone beeped, blocking out Cecile's call. He picked up Mrs. Parks's telephone himself; she was out to lunch. The caller was Tracy. "My contact at the lawyer's office said she thinks Paul Dorys is loose today. He's out of his office and walking. He's got a fat briefcase and he's heading down to Hampshire Street in Cambridge to see some old lady client. From what I know, he's carrying the file. You want to pick it up, get moving. I called his office a couple minutes ago and he's just left, that temp you put there said."

"Where, exactly?" Martin asked. His hammy fist was tight around the telephone, strangling it. He'd get the damn file himself.

"Cambridge, near the Norfolk Café. He was meeting some old lady, she told me. You better get him fast because my contact there says she won't do it no more. She didn't like that break-in stuff. You better get this guy now."

Martin found himself scribbling the words down on Mrs. Parks's notepad. Hampshire Street. Norfolk Café. "What time?"

"One thirty."

"That's soon," Martin muttered and wrote down "1:30," beside the other information. "Good. Thanks."

Martin Moon looked around Mrs. Parks's office hurriedly

206

and thought about his destination and what he should do. Hampshire Street was a minor artery through East Cambridge, and in the afternoon it wasn't terribly busy. He should have no trouble spotting a man walking with a briefcase. Maybe this lawyer was the one he should extinguish. "Kill all the lawyers," he muttered and went back into his office to get the small gun he kept in his lower desk drawer. It was a 9-mm. Beretta M1951 pistol, something of an antique, but Moon's model was light and reliable, made with an aluminum alloy. He put the magazine in carefully, pulled the slide sharply to the rear, then released it. The gun was ready. He pushed the button-type safety from right to left before slipping the gun into his inside sports-coat pocket. The gun made the jacket look bulky, but Moon was a big man and wore his jacket a size too big, just for emergencies like this. He bunched the coat a bit in the front to cover the bulge and patted his chest. "Perfect," he said, and left.

Dan O'Neil had been pacing his living room, waiting for the call from Barry Rizzo; finally it came.

"Barry here," Barry said. "Dan. The stuff's going to be in the parking lot when you are. New York was slow. Special orders cause trouble."

"You got it all?" Dan asked.

"Every blessed ounce. I've got to bring some of it down myself, to make it add up right, so I'll be there too. Your bag lady will meet the whole crew."

"Oh, just great. Thanks, Barry."

This time when Cecile dialed Martin's number, she got through. Mrs. Parks answered in her indolent tone. "Mr. Moon's office. May I help you?"

"This is Sister Cecile. I need to speak to Mr. Moon, please."

"He's not in now."

"It's terribly important. It's about his baby!"

"Oh. The baby! Jane had a baby?" Mrs. Parks had been

aware of Jane's pregnancy. She tuned in to most of her employer's calls, although he certainly wasn't aware of that.

"Yes, a wonderful girl. I think Mr. Moon should know."

"Martin was here a few minutes ago," Mrs. Parks said, almost flustered. "I just got back from lunch. He scribbled something down. Let me see . . ." She read slowly, out loud, the address of the Norfolk Café and its whereabouts. "Now I don't guarantee he's gone there, but I believe that's where he was off to in such a hurry. You could probably catch up with him there. But . . . well, be careful."

"Thank you. I will." Cecile smiled as she hung up. Of course she would be careful. Wasn't she always? The address hadn't rung any bell in her mind. She had never approached the café from the front. Lyuba's house was around the corner, another place entirely. But the directions sounded familiar. It would come to her.

By one o'clock that afternoon, the Cambridge police had taken up positions in the parking lot. Detectives Jones and Adams were in the rear of an old window van decorated with 1960s style flowers and rust. Officer Jiminez was stationed in an abandoned 1978 Oldsmobile that had been in the lot for the past month. Lyuba McVey watched their arrival from the kitchen window.

"Looks good, Lyuba. The cops are cooking," she said to herself. Lyuba was sweating. "We'll pin that Herbie Marshall to the wall. Make him squirm." She moved from the kitchen to the living room and back, fanning herself with a thick hand. "Where the hell is Paulie? He was supposed to be here with the money. He ain't here." She started for the door under the kitchen sink where the good liquor was kept.

The doorbell rang just as Lyuba downed half a glass of straight Scotch. She was looking better already. The glazed look had cleared in her eyes and she was humming as she opened the front door. She saw Paul and almost fell into his arms. "Paulie, darling, I didn't think you was coming."

Paul nodded, speechless.

At one twenty-five, Paul escorted Lyuba out the door and around the block where he let her go, hoping she could make it in a straight line to the assignation. He still carried the briefcase, but it was empty now. Lyuba had the ten thousand dollars in a large manila envelope.

Paul had considered hiding in the dumpster while things were going on, but Jonesy had advised him otherwise, so Paul contented himself with taking a slow walk down Norfolk Street in the direction of Boston. He would turn around and come back as soon as he felt it was safe. Lyuba would need him.

Martin Moon was late and steaming mad that he might miss that lawyer. He was walking up from Inman Square, where he had left his car, and it was much farther than he had thought to where Dorys was supposed to be going. He was out of breath and disheveled by the time he was a block away from the café. He was looking carefully down the street for his quarry and he had been unaware of the fact that Barry Rizzo had driven by in a new pale-blue Cadillac, nor did he know it was Dan O'Neil, city councilman, way down the street turning his wife's three-year-old Thunderbird into the driveway of the Norfolk Café. It wouldn't have meant anything to him if he *had* recognized them.

Suddenly Moon noticed an exceptionally well-dressed gentleman who had to be someone of stature. Moon pulled out the Beretta and slipped the safety off, then stuffed his gun under the left flap of his jacket so that he looked like a very tall Napoleon, walking. The man ahead had to be Paul Dorys because he was dressed great and carried a briefcase. But on second thought the man who was walking confidently ahead of Moon couldn't have been the lawyer after all. Dorys had been described as having prematurely gray hair, and this man had very black fuzz on his head. Moon was just too far away to see that it was his own man, Tom Dempsey, disguised by an expensive suit, who was turning into the Norfolk Café parking lot.

"Damn," Moon muttered. He was really starting to boil,

but then he saw the second man. Paul Dorys, no mistake, and Martin Moon kept right on walking past the Norfolk Café. In the distance he could see the sun striking off the unmistakable light-gray hair of a man who was swinging a brown briefcase. Moon crushed the gun against his chest and started to walk fast. The street was practically deserted at this time of day and he was about to get his file back. One way or another.

20

HOWIE Marshall had big dark patches of sweat under his arms. He had been in the parking lot since shortly after one o'clock and nobody had shown. The biggest drug buy in his life and he didn't even have the dope yet. O'Neil had given his word, though, Howie told himself. Neither of them could afford to screw up. Then he saw the Cadillac cautiously moving in.

Howie patted his pants. Below the paunch, strategically located in the right-hand front pocket, was a gun. It was the same gun he had shot that creep with a while back and he should have junked it then, but Howie was sentimental. Same place, same gun. It had saved his life here once. It was good luck. Besides, now that he was in the fast world of big drugs, he needed a gun. He saw the Caddy pull over and the door begin to open.

Howie kicked an empty Diet Pepsi can into the side of an abandoned Oldsmobile. Inside the Olds, Officer Jiminez winced. Jiminez was down on the wreck's back floor, ready to pounce out. From his hole through the rusty door everything happening outside was slightly distorted, including sounds. He had been watching Howie through the hole and had seen Howie pat his pocket. Gun, Jiminez thought, and felt his own service revolver where it lay ready. He could shoot through the hole in the door if he had to, or be out of the car in five seconds. His heart began to pump adrenaline as the street sounds became hums mixed with September crickets and distant cars and the soft tread of Howie's feet. Then he saw the Caddy and another car coming in behind it.

Dan O'Neil pulled the Thunderbird into the lot directly behind Barry Rizzo's Cadillac. He drove to the side and parked his T-bird next to the dumpster and near the Elm Street entrance, neat and unobtrusive. He got out, his attention riveted on his brother-in-law, who had just emerged, leaving the Caddy engine idling with the car aimed out the Hampshire Street side, gangster-style, ready to move fast.

Tom Dempsey walked briskly in, briefcase swinging. He was nervous and when he was really nervous he giggled. It was hard to keep the giggles in, but the new suit helped. Clothes made the man, he thought and began planning a trip to Filene's men's department for more. His face broke into a huge grin when he saw Barry conversing with O'Neil. He tried to erase the grin, but it wouldn't leave, and an insidious giggle came out. His new image was having a hard time holding up in the face of reality and suddenly he had to go to the bathroom, bad. Then he saw Howie Marshall moving in to one side. An insignificant man dressed like a turd in that yellow shirt. Tom should have thought better of Howie, who was rigidly clutching the gun in his pocket. Howie was scared stiff and dangerous.

Barry Rizzo handed Dan O'Neil a small package. Tom Dempsey, the man in the silk suit, handed a briefcase to Rizzo. Rizzo passed the briefcase over to Howie Marshall. Dan O'Neil handed his package to Howie Marshall. Lyuba McVey appeared, coming in by the entry on Hampshire Street, her cotton house dress swinging with each step. She was gasping for breath, and she held the big manila envelope against her stomach. She saw Howie and smiled happily. He was in the middle of a group, so it must mean everything was working out just fine. Now, if she could only get it right, Ray would be avenged. "Here it is! I got the bucks! I want the stuff." She tugged at the bills so they were almost falling out of the envelope.

Barry Rizzo was anxious to leave. The place was getting crowded, and he turned too fast, bumping into Lyuba. The

212

impact pushed her against the fence and she stumbled and fell. She dropped the envelope, money showing.

Tom Dempsey stood by and watched. He was smug, his giggles just under control, his deal was going through. He looked disdainfully at Howie Marshall in the tight yellow shirt. Howie was still holding all the drugs.

Lyuba declined to get up. Sitting flat, legs outstretched, she bellowed, "You got my money, where's the drugs, Hubert Marshall! Gimme my stuff."

Howie walked over and dropped the briefcase from New York and the package from Barry Rizzo's private stock onto Lyuba's lap. He stuffed one hand into his pocket where his gun was, just for luck. With the other he picked up the envelope full of cash.

That was it. The deed was done. The Cambridge police started to move. "Police! Put up your hands!"

That was when Howie began to shoot. He had been itching to let loose since it all began. He hadn't missed the scorn on Tom Dempsey's face, nor the fact that Dan O'Neil refused to meet his eye. He'd show them just what kind of man he was. He pulled out the Saturday-night special and let off a round at Jiminez, but Jiminez saw it coming and sidestepped fast. Howie shot again, wildly, winging Officer Adams, then Jonesy's well-aimed bullet sent Howie's gun spinning. It was over in seconds.

Down the street, Paul heard the shots and began to run in the direction of the Norfolk Café. His one thought was that Lyuba was in danger and it was all his fault. He made a quick left going into the parking lot just as Martin Moon, surprised at Paul's sudden movement, was about to dash up and grab the briefcase. Moon began to chase Paul into the parking lot, but Paul saw Moon closing in, turned, and threw a left jab at Martin just as Martin pulled out his gun. A shot rang out, and Paul dropped his briefcase and grabbed his arm where the bullet had entered. Moon took a dive for the case and the Cambridge police got into the action. Jonesy let a bullet fly at Moon. Moon shot back, holding Paul's briefcase like a shield. But it didn't stop the next bullet that ripped through the good leather and into Moon's chest. Martin Moon didn't stand a chance.

It took a few minutes for Paul to sort things out. He stood still, looking around, slightly dazed, and saw Lyuba still sitting by the fence, a collection of drugs on her lap. She had opened the simulated leather bag and was staring at the little white baggies and pills. She looked just fine. Then he turned to Jonesy. "You guys call an ambulance?"

"On the way. Shit, Paul, that guy was trying to kill you, who the hell is he?" Jonesy gestured at Martin Moon, sprawled on the ground. Paul shook his head. Paul had been hit cleanly through the arm, but the pain was ripping through him, clouding things. He looked over at the bleeding body of Martin Moon.

"You know who I think that is, Jonesy? It's Moon, Martin Moon. Now what the hell went on here? What did you do with my Lyuba?"

"Over there. You hurt bad?"

Paul shook his head. It was all over. Barry Rizzo, Dan O'Neil, and Tom Dempsey had been cuffed and lined up under the watchful eyes of three plainclothes cops with their guns out. The councilman and his brother-in-law seemed shaken but confident. Any jury would bend to the wind of their high-priced lawyers and benevolent lives. It was all a mistake that they were there. Tom Dempsey stood straight and expressionless in his new suit, hiding the serious doubts he must have had. Howie Marshall was the only one who looked like the criminal he was. He was slouched to one side of the lineup, blood trickling red on his yellow shirt. He had shot a cop with the same gun he had used on Ray McVey. Howie Marshall was finished.

Reinforcements were already audible, and the siren sounds grew louder by the second. An ambulance was the first to arrive, shrieking into the parking lot. While one of the medics kneeled over Moon's body, the other inspected Paul's arm.

"Not too bad," he told Paul. "I'm going to put a dressing

214

on it, but you'd better get to the hospital and get some stitches and a shot."

"Sure," Paul said. "But first things first." He walked over to the fence where Lyuba was still sitting on the ground, humming, rocking back and forth and cradling the drugs in her arms.

"Need a hand, Lulu?"

"No, Paulie. I like it down here."

"How about we head on back and finish up that Scotch," he said. "We owe ourselves a little party, I think, before I head over to the Cambridge Hospital and see about this arm."

"First the Scotch," she agreed, bobbing her head.

"I'll take care of the dope; I'll give it to my old friend Jonesy here. He's a good man. This stuff is evidence."

Light shone in Lyuba's eyes. She lurched to her feet, ignoring Paul's hand. She swayed violently, then righted herself with effort. "Evidence you want!" she bellowed and walked over to Howie Marshall and waved the goods under his nose. "You! You bastard. You killed my baby. You're the one killed Ray McVey. Get that, policemen? This one did it. Check that gun. Whaddya bet it's the one? He done it!"

She stepped back, her head wobbling. She was exhausted. "Take the bags, Paul. I want to go home."

Paul moved quickly. He took the drugs and passed them to Jonesy.

It was time to go. They began walking out of the September world behind the Norfolk Café and back to the street where children were running by and crows were flying overhead. And suddenly there was Sister Cecile, delayed because she couldn't find a cab for twenty minutes. Halfway over to Cambridge she had realized that the Norfolk Café was the place where the drug deal was happening. "Martin must be there," she had said aloud. "Driver, hurry!"

The cabbie gunned it, but it was already too late for anything but a very fast prayer.

Cecile stepped out of the cab at the end of Lyuba's street just as the old woman and Paul came up.

"Paul, you're bleeding! What happened? Are you all right?"

"Merely a flesh wound. Isn't that what they say on TV, Lyuba?" Paul said solemnly. "You're a little late, Cecile. Damn good thing, too. It's all over now, but it didn't look good for a few minutes."

"Martin Moon was coming here," Cecile said, suddenly. "I was going to tell him about the baby. Jane had a little girl! What happened to him?"

There was a moment of silence. They were just walking up to the small green house where Lyuba lived, and they all stopped at the base of her wooden steps. "He's dead," Paul said softly. "He pulled a gun trying to get my briefcase, and he started shooting. He got shot by the cops. Shot through my briefcase."

"But he had just become a father. I wanted to tell him." Cecile was shocked. Her words came out flatly while her mind took in the reality. Tears started running down her cheeks, slowly, one after another as she stood on the sidewalk. "He was a father," she said sadly. "He became a father today."

"How about a drink?" Lyuba said. She didn't care about Martin Moon or fatherhood. Her day was made. Ray was avenged and there was good Scotch waiting under the kitchen sink.

Sister Cecile looked at Paul and he nodded. "For a minute," he said. "You need it. I need it."

They all drank Scotch at Lyuba's house, drinking while the cat watched with one green eye and one blue eye. Cecile had one stiff drink in an almost-clean glass, Paul had several, Lyuba had four and then announced that her soaps were on and they could go.

Paul and Cecile left in a yellow cab, heading straight to Cambridge City Hospital. "You get that bullet wound fixed up," Cecile admonished, "and I'll go right to St. Margaret's in Brighton. I really have to see that baby."

216

Jane had never looked better. She was propped up in the bed with her eyes half closed when Sister Cecile walked into the three-bed ward. Jake and Edith Zuber were standing together beaming, and Abe Hersey was beside them, talking politics, his hands waving, his face relaxed and smiling. "Yes, we're going to go public. To hell with the campaign. Besides, it might be the thing, loving grandfather, beautiful daughter, darling baby. Who can resist? You know what they say: 'Any publicity is good publicity.' Picture Jane on the front page of the *Boston Globe*."

"Of course she's going to nurse the baby herself," Edith was saying, her words beginning before Abe's ended. "It would be perfect for your campaign. Ecological, human interest. I can have the Dorchester La Leche League throw a big rally just before the election. You have no idea about power until you see these women. You've won already. Hands down."

Jake stood there nodding, murmuring "Hands down" a few times. His wife always outtalked him, and Abe Hersey was no stranger to being heard above a crowd. The baby was in a little plastic-sided cart, dreaming of a noisy future, tiny gassy smiles moving magically across her rosebud mouth. Jane's eyes were on the infant now but as Sister Cecile came over to the crib, Jane looked up. "Come see," she whispered above the cacophony. "Come see my baby."

Cecile was there, staring down at Danielle. Her heart ached at the sight of new life, real life, not just some idea, but an entire new human being named Danielle Hersey. "Can I pick her up?"

Jane nodded. "Sure."

The baby smelled sweet, all the clean scents of a hospital, the subtle odor of fresh disposable diapers and her own unique perfume. Cecile touched a fuzz of red curls on the baby's velvet head. "Isn't your mommy the luckiest person," she said softly. She didn't know how to tell Jane that Martin was dead.

But she had to. Maybe it should wait? She looked at Jane, at Abe, at the Zubers.

"What's the matter?" Jane asked.

Cecile lay the baby back into the crib, carefully arranging the tiny pink blanket. "It's Martin," she began and abruptly Abe Hersey was silent. Mrs. Zuber kept talking. "Martin," Cecile said again, knowing she just had to dive in and get this over. "Martin's been shot. He was trying to kill Paul, the police were there, and they shot him. He's dead, Jane. I'm sorry."

Edith Zuber stopped talking. Jane's mouth dropped open, then closed. Abe's eyes opened wide and he raised a hand to his mouth, trying to hide sudden relief. Jake came over to the hospital bed and took Jane's hand and began to pat it with his old, gnarled fingers.

"Martin's dead? He's dead?" Jane asked.

"Yes," Cecile said.

Jane turned her head away from all the people towering around her bed. She looked down at the baby, who had started to hiccup. "What a terrible, terrible shame," she said sadly. "Poor Martin. He missed Danielle. He missed it all."

At that moment the baby woke up and started to cry. Cecile reached into the crib, took up the tiny bundle and handed Danielle to her mother, and for just a moment in time mother and child wept together. The Zubers eyed each other and began to move away from the bed. Abe came over to his daughter's side and patted her gently on the shoulder, his hand hesitant in the unfamiliar motion.

"He was no good, Jane. He would have hurt you."

"I know," his daughter replied. She wiped her eyes and looked up. "I'm all right. I'm fine. He could never have *really* been my baby's father."

Sister Cecile looked on, knowing there was nothing left for her to do. She could go back to the convent now, have Sister Germaine's poached chicken for dinner and actually be on time for vespers.